Mavis Abbott

by

Carl Baxter

Copyright © 2011 Carl Baxter

All rights reserved.

ISBN-13: 978-1468158755
ISBN-10: 1468158759

Dedicated
to
Aidan Cole Baxter

CHAPTER ONE

Independence County, Arkansas—1875

They killed Papa on a Tuesday. I was sitting on the back porch steps corralling night crawlers into an empty pear tin and rigging a cane pole with hook, line and sinker. A shotgun boomed up the road. The echo from the blast rolled down past our cabin and rumbled off the bluff across Cave Creek. I did not understand at first what it meant, but in a few minutes came to realize we were in a mess of trouble.

Mavis walked barefoot through the kitchen door wiping her hands on a dishrag even before the echo quit vibrating off the bluff. I did not look up. I was not supposed to be on the porch and was hoping she would ignore me, but she did not. I felt her eyes boring into the back of my neck, when she walked by to the north end of the porch.

"Chet, who'd thet be? Sounds like hit come from jist up there."

I did not answer Mavis straightway. I chuckled under my breath. The way she said some words reminded me of our late mama. Mavis wasn't exactly dumb and she wasn't exactly smart. She had a year or two of schoolhousing, and a mountain gift for knowing her limitations. She would slap me crosseyed, if she caught me laughing at her. I cannot exactly brag about my intellectual gifts. I graduated fourth grade at the little Cave Creek one room school and church, but spoke little better than Mavis. Anyway, I had no idea who would be shooting a shotgun so close to our cabin. The Osage boys hunted along Cave Creek, homesteaders too, when they were not working their fields. Hunters used heavy rifles for deer and bear, and lighter .22 caliber rifles for squirrel, rabbit, and groundhogs. Most Ozark hill families kept a loaded scattergun within easy reach, but no one hunted game of any kind with a shotgun, day or night.

We Abbotts kept a ten-gauge double barrel Greener model with external hammers loaded with double-ought buckshot hanging on pegs over the kitchen door, our chief instrument for home protection, good for close-up work. Most pioneer family members, including women and girls were acquainted with the shotgun. They could point, cock the double external hammers, pull the double triggers and hit something, even though it meant taking a severe kick on the shoulder and often knocked flat. In those years following the Civil War, and renegades on the prowl, having a shotgun handy saved many a homesteader's life and property.

Mavis wiped her face and neck with the dishrag, as she continued looking up the road.

"Who'd thet be?" she said again, more to herself than to me.

I never did answer. Mavis had made me mad. She had insisted I harness one of our horses to the double shovel and plow her garden plot behind the barn. Plowing the garden did not fit in with my plans. I had planned a short fishing trip.

Papa had driven our mule team and wagon to the Sandtown Trading Post a few hours earlier, a roundtrip of eight miles. I finished a couple of things he left me to do, and thought I would try a little fishing before he got back. Red-eared perch and rock bass were biting in the blue hole below the falls on Cave Creek just down the hill from our cabin. Mavis turned away from looking up the road and turned her spotlight on me.

"Chet, I thought I tole ye to plow up thet danged garden. Hit won't take no time a-tall. Iffen ye don't git busy, ah'm gonna lam the tar outta ye."

Well, I was fourteen and strapping for my age, and was never one for being threatened, but when she laid her hand on Papa's old black razor strop hanging on the back porch by the old blue and white porcelain wash basin, I began to adjust my attitude. The fish were not going anywhere, I was not either, and tomorrow was another day.

Mavis was my sister, or so I thought at the time, and she had been my mama too, for the past fourteen years. I am not sure she liked being either one. Twenty-seven years old, her poor stringbean body, ravaged by hard times, had suffered a lot of abuse and it showed, even on

Sunday. She always looked like she had been rode hard and put away wet. I forgot about the gunshot and fishing and ambled barefoot toward the barn lot.

"Ah'll jist swear Chet yer clothes are a hangin on ye like a skeercrow. Yore a growin too high fer yer britches. Seems like I kin jist get yer britches lags down close to yer feet, and there ye go a growin nother inch or two and there they are agin, halfway to yer knees. You kin jist stretch a garment so fer."

I knew I had not stopped growing. I had passed Papa's near six-foot height by a good three inches and people in the community often remarked about it. They would say things like how did Chet Abbott get so tall. None of his folks ever reached six feet.

I needed one horse to pull the double shovel, so I slipped up on Ned standing sound asleep by the barn lot fence. Ned jumped a little and tossed his head, when I threw the harness across his back, but he did not move out of his tracks. Too much trouble I guess. Ned and Ted were our team of big Scottish Shire horses Papa had acquired in a trade ten years earlier. Why Scottish horses were in Independence County, Arkansas, I never knew, but Papa's papa before him, also, owned a Shire team.

Ned paid little attention to me, when I fastened buckles and snaps on the harness. He did turn his head and with interest, ears up in the alert position, look toward the little Methodist log church across the road.

Brownie, my black and tan hound, crawled out from under the back porch and limped around the cabin on the creek side making short choppy barks. He also looked across the road toward the church. I named him Brownie when he was a pup. In 1875, he was six-years-old and his life had been nothing to write home about. He had lost a right front foot to a bear trap, one eye in a bobcat scrap, one ear in a panther fight, had his tail run over and broken by a steel-rimmed wagon wheel. It hung off him at a rather odd angle. Papa named him Lucky.

No, Brownie was not much to look at, but he was capable, and possessed the truest nose of any trailing dog I ever had. I looked where I thought he looked across the road and could not see anything unusual.

Brownie limped on around the cabin to the split-rail fence that separated our front yard from the Batesville Pike. The fence ran north/south from our northern property boundary, a hundred yards up the pike--marked by a pile of rocks--down past our cabin another fifty yards to Cave Creek flowing near knee-deep across the pike.

I never understood why Papa built that four-rail fence. The fence could not keep any animal, wild or domestic, on or off our property. Our goats often tight-roped down the top rail.

Brownie kept looking toward the church and barking. Ned's ears stayed perked up and slanted forward, he snorted a time or two. I knew he either saw something or smelled something, maybe a bear or wolf. I never felt threatened but something nagged at me.

I put off harnessing Ned, stepped away and looked over the lot fence. I had an unrestricted view past the cabin to the little log church. Nothing moved around the church. I climbed on the heavy corner fencepost bracing timber and decided to sit until I figured it out.

The little log church sat in a flat area across the Batesville Pike from our cabin and about fifty-yards from Cave Creek, a spring-fed watershed creek running east/west emptying into Polk Bayou, a much larger creek, a half-mile west. Behind the church, the terrain sloped upward to the crest of a knoll before sloping down to Polk Bayou. Blooming dogwood trees covered the slope in the full whiteness of spring. A black bear or panther crossing the slope would stand out in the field of white blossoms.

A blue jay scolded something over to my left. The jay was somewhere in the tree line bordering Cave Creek. I looked over there to see what the jay was squawking about. I had a good view over a quarter mile down the tree line where Cave Creek flowed through a narrow flat pasture and junctured with Polk Bayou. Nothing moved. Back to the right, I glimpsed movement in the dogwood grove a couple hundred yards up the slope and realized for the first time Ned and Brownie were not looking at the church at all. They were looking over the church at the slope beyond.

Brownie hammered away in a slow measured cadence, tone flat, unexcited. I remember thinking: not bear nor panther, but something moved through the dogwood grove and more than one.

A small clearing in the dogwood grove caught my attention. Something or someone angled across the hill straight for it. I focused on the clearing. A rider passed through riding a brown horse and leading two mules. I questioned the purpose of anyone riding a horse and leading two mules across that hillside. Why didn't the rider just come down the road? It did not make any sense.

I stood for a moment, trying to understand, and it hit me: those were our mules. I jumped off the fence and ran for the back porch yelling for Mavis. She came to the kitchen door.

"Chet, whut in the world is wrong with ye?"

"Somebody's leadin our mules cross thet slope up yonder behind the church."

Mavis stood stock still staring a hole through me, trying to make sense out of what I had said. Her right hand flew up to her throat like she was choking. "Oh, my gawd, Papa."

A heavy weight fell into the pit of my stomach and rooted me. I stood paralyzed. Mavis ripped off her apron, threw it down, and jumped off the porch. She tore around the cabin barefoot and headed for the road. I got my legs to work and charged around the cabin in time to see Mavis hike her old long gray work dress above her knees and clear the rail fence. She was several yards up the road running hard by the time I jumped the fence and gave chase. She stopped, turned, and yelled, "Go back and brang the horse and a rifle."

I spun around in the road, ran back to the cabin, through the front gate, across the porch, through the front door, and grabbed my Winchester carbine from pegs over the front room window. I charged through the kitchen door, jumped off the back porch, and hit the ground running. Ned, asleep with the harness thrown across his back, tossed his head, and did a little sidestep when I jumped on his back. He acted as if he wanted to buck, but was too tired.

Shire horses barely tolerate being ridden and are not built for speed. I pounded my bare heels into Ned's ribs, but did not spur him to more than a lumbering trot. I maneuvered Ned through the lot gate, around the cabin, through the front gate and turned north. The road curved left a quarter-mile ahead. Mavis was not in sight.

I got Ned to step it up a little. We rounded the bend. Papa's wagon sat in the middle of the narrow rocky track fifty yards father. The wagon tongue lay in the road along with mule collars, singletrees, and trace chains. I did not see a living soul. Riding high on Ned, I was on top of the wagon before discovering Mavis on the ground behind the wagon cradling Papa's head in her lap.

Blood was everywhere, bright red pools in the wagon bed and a broad streak going out the back over the tailgate. Ned smelled the blood, flinched a little, stamped his feet, and snorted. I slid off Ned and went to Mavis.

She rocked back and forth humming something sounding like a hymn, keening the old Irish folks called it. I stood like a fool, trying to think of something to say, to do. I thought I ought to join in with Mavis, so I started humming too, but soon gave it up. I did not feel like singing.

Papa lay stretched out in his long-handle underwear, once bright red, now pink after many lye soap scrubbings, and he still wore his old faded gray wool work shirt. I will never forget the sight of Papa lying stretched out in the road dressed in pink. I know he would have been embarrassed laid out like that.

Where were his clothes? I first thought Mavis had pulled them off for some reason but soon realized the bushwhacker took his clothes, boots, and even his old felt hat, leaving the shirt. The shirt was ruined anyway, shredded with a load of double-ought buckshot. Who would want Papa's old worn homespun wool britches? Both boots had holes in the soles. His old worthless hat had lost its shape long ago. Who would want those old clothes? I was not surprised that Papa's lever-action Winchester

.44 was missing. Guns were valuable commodities. A fifty-pound bag of seed corn was in the wagon. That did not surprise me. A backshooter was not going to start across country lugging a fifty-pound bag of corn.

The killer had taken Papa's life and in the most cowardly way imaginable. Something severe came over me. I was never so mad. My vision blurred, and everything around me turned blood red. I thought I was going crazy. I tried to comprehend what had happened, and became determined I was going to kill somebody over it.

Mavis kept humming her hymn, rocking back and forth and patting Papa's cheek. I did not know what I was supposed to do, so I knelt down beside her and touched her arm. She aroused from her stupor, and slipped out from under Papa's body taking some care in lowering his head on the rock hard road. Mavis's hands and her old gray wool work dress were wet with blood; the dress once belonged to Mama Ida, one of three work dresses Mavis had worn for fourteen years.

"Ah guess mah clothes are ruint," she said.

Mavis and I took hold of Papa, to lift him into the wagon. Papa was not a big man and I doubt weighed more than 130 pounds his whole life, but I held back, I think because of the blood. Mavis saw it.

"Don't be afeered gettin a little blood on ye. Hit'll not be the last."

I caught Papa around the shoulders. Mavis picked up his feet and legs, and we eased him into the wagon. I moved Ned into position and fastened the wagon tongue to his harness. The day was heating up, the air still. The smell haunts me yet. I felt bathed in horse sweat and blood.

A shod hoof striking shale rock rang behind us. Mavis grabbed my rifle lying in the wagon bed and levered a shell in the chamber. I thought the bushwhacker was returning for the wagon. Junior Ulbrick, our German neighbor boy, who rode up on one of the Ulbricks big Percheron farm horses.

"Oh, what has happened here?"

Junior spoke English with a heavy German accent because German was all his family spoke at home and Junior was at home more than anywhere else.

Junior, a year older than me, lived with his mother, father and sister in a cabin on a forty-acre homestead, a mile south of our place, and like our homestead, the Ulbrick homestead bordered the Batesville Pike. The Ulbricks owned a saddle mule, but Junior loved to ride bare back on the big broad-backed Percherons. The Percherons were slower than the mule, but a lot more comfortable, and Junior was never in a hurry to get anywhere.

Mavis put the rifle down when she recognized Junior. "Somebody has kilt Papa," she said. "Did ye see anybody on the road?"

"Nah, ain't seen no one, but Mr. Abbott. We met on the road bout a quarter mile from the trading post. I went on got my stuff and was coming back, when I heard a shot."

"Junior, somebody has to ride to Batesville and tell the sheriff bout this. Kin ye do it?" I asked.

"I can do it, and I will. And I will tell Papa and Mama to come and help you."

Junior clattered on by and kicked the big Percheron up to a trot, not an easy thing to do. I climbed up on the wagon seat and looked back. Mavis stood looking down at Papa's blood splashed across the shale-rocked road. She looked west at a cedar glade bordering the road, the route taken by the bushwhacker, and she screamed a long inhuman howl, with no words in it, starting low, rising to a high pitch and tailing off at the end, like a panther running Cave Creek at midnight. The hair stood up on the back of my neck.

CHAPTER TWO

I wanted to go after Papa's killer. Mavis said no. "You'd probably get ambushed. Buryin Papa'll be hard nough; ah don't need buryin a brother too."

I thought about our two brothers. The oldest, Henry, killed during the War Between the States and buried somewhere over in Tennessee, and the other, Teddy Blue, thought alive somewhere in Texas. Not a sure bet, considering Teddy Blue's legendary temper and general disposition.

I know Mavis thought the killer would be watching his back trail and ambush anyone following, but I did not think so. I thought the killer would be trying hard to get rid of the mules. Our mules liked their corn and oats on a regular basis. Come mealtime, they would be looking for our barn and hard for a stranger to control.

Mavis said the looking would start after we buried Papa.

"We got to git Papa in the ground, weather's warmin. Anyway, they won't kill 'em mules, worth too much alive. We'll find the mules sommeres. Find the mules, the bushwhacker won't be far ah'm thankin."

Emil and Eva Ulbrick and daughter Elsa came up in their wagon, pulled by the Percherons. They arrived an hour before sundown. Junior Ulbrick had switched to the Ulbricks faster saddle mule and rode on to the sheriff's office in Batesville.

The elder Ulbricks were about forty years old. They were short stocky people almost square-shaped. The Germans always dressed in black and gray. Emil Ulbrick wore a black felt hat, with a short brim, and Eva, his wife, tied a black headscarf around her head and in the hottest weather wore a gray bonnet. The German women tended to braid their hair and tie it in a big knot on the back of their head.

Elsa Ulbrick was a big stout girl my age, maybe older; I never inquired. Elsa, like most girls her age and size, had few matrimonial prospects in the hills and early on seemed to have looked in my direction.

I met them at the front gate. Mavis stayed with Papa on the back porch. The Ulbricks were very quiet. I do not believe they said a word getting out of the wagon. Mr. Ulbrick looped the reins over a fence post, opened the gate and walked into the front yard. Mrs. Ulbrick and Elsa followed.

"Papa's on the back porch. Mavis is with 'im."

The Ulbricks followed me around the cabin. Just the clumping of heavy feet and the creaking of shoe leather broke the silence, except I think I heard Elsa sniff once or twice. Mavis sat flat down on the porch close to Papa's head fanning him with an old dishrag, shooing flies. She never turned her head.

"The Ulbricks are here, Mavis."

Mavis never looked up or said anything. I was not sure what to do. Mrs. Ulbrick knew what to do. She went over to our well, a few feet away, and pulled the hemp rope up through the old rusty cast iron pulley and drew out a large galvanized bucket of water. I saw what she was doing. I went up on the porch, got another large empty bucket sitting against the kitchen wall, and carried it out to the well. I poured the well water into the bucket and headed for the kitchen fireplace, Mrs. Ulbrick followed with a second bucket of water.

When we walked up the porch steps to go into the kitchen, Mrs. Ulbrick paused and looked to her right over where Papa lay stretched out along the edge of the porch, Mavis sitting at his head shooing flies and staring out towards the barn. Mr. Ulbrick sat down on the edge of the porch close to Papa and leaned against a porch post. I think he wanted to comfort Mavis but did not know how. He glanced over at Mavis, at the bloody mess she was holding, and looked away. Elsa was in the kitchen. When Mrs. Ulbrick and I entered, we found Elsa sitting at the kitchen table picking apart and nibbling on one of Mavis's cold biscuits she had found in a covered dish on the table.

"Elsa, shame."

"Well, I'm hungry, Mama."

"Could you not wait until we got back home?"

"You know I like Mavis's biscuits."

Mrs. Ulbrick made some kind of grunting sound of disgust. She and I hung the water buckets by the bail on an iron rod in the fireplace. The fire had died down to near embers. She picked up a heavy steel poker lying on the hearth and jiggled the embers into flames. I threw a couple of pine logs onto the fire, watched the flames lick up, and I left.

I was useless. My mind would not work. I thought about saying something to Mrs. Ulbrick about how grateful we were they had come to help us. I embarrassed myself by blurting, "Ah got to go feed the stock."

I walked off the back porch and remembered I had not seen Brownie since we brought Papa in. I turned and looked at Mavis who had stood and turned looking down at Papa.

"Mavis, where's Brownie?"

She nodded and looked down at her feet. I hunkered down and looked under the porch. Brownie was lying on the ground. He had chosen a position under Papa's body. He looked forlorn with his head down on his one good front paw.

I made myself busy in the barn lot feeding the stock. I loaded up the big horse trough with ears of corn for our horses and a smaller, and lower, trough for our goats. Ted, Ned, and my pet goat Billy seemed to know the mules were missing. The horses looked back at the barn a time or two. Billy even went back into the barn, bleated a couple of times, came back out to the horse trough, and jumped right up in the middle of it. The horses nudged him aside had got busy with the corn.

I left the barn lot and wondered up the hill northeast of the barn, to the family graveyard. I sat on a large rock and tried to think things through, while I looked down on the back porch of the cabin. Mavis and the elder Ulbricks washed the blood off Papa, and washed his hair and his beard. Elsa seemed to have a problem tending the dead. She stayed out of sight in the kitchen.

For some reason I took notice of the old swaybacked log cabin. Papa was not one for making improvements on our living quarters. Some of the logs had rotten ends, needing replacement, and the rest needed shoring up. You could tell Papa had built the cabin piecemeal. He started with two-rooms and I guess added on, as his children were born. I doubt he applied reasoning to his method, and I do not think he planned the outcome. The old sway-backed log jumble was a shelter for sleeping and cooking, and even in its best days, never a candidate for an architectural prize.

Elsa walked out on the porch. She took a quick glance at Papa, turned away, walked out in the yard, and looked toward the barn. She was looking for me, but I did not want to talk to her or anyone. She walked toward the barn lot fence, and happened to look up the hill. I think she wanted to come to me, but the steepness of the hill was an impediment to her intentions, and I was glad for it.

After they washed Papa, Mavis and the Ulbricks struggled somewhat trying to dress him in an old moth-eaten black wool suit he had not worn in fifteen years, Mavis had found in an old trunk. She also found a gray shirt, without a collar, made of some course-grained cloth, but she could not find a tie. She later reasoned he did not need a tie; his beard would hide it anyway.

Mavis found a new pair of black linen socks, never worn. Papa owned a pair of old Sunday-go-to-meeting shoes. I did not see a reason, religious or otherwise, to bury good shoes. I could wear them by cutting holes for my big toes. Mavis agreed, so Papa was layed out in brand new black linen socks, no shoes.

Mavis looked up the hill and motioned me to come down. I walked down the hill and helped load Papa's body in the Ulbrick wagon. Mr. Ulbrick drove the wagon across the road to the little log Methodist Church. The rest of us walked behind the wagon. Brownie had come out from under the porch and limped along with me.

The little church did not have windows and was always dark inside. I carried in a coal oil lantern and, with Brownie helping, checked for snakes. Copperhead snakes denned under the church floorboards and with the coming of warm weather had begun stirring. During the year, I often found copperheads inside the church after field mice. The snakes squirmed up through the cracks in the warped floorboards. Every Sunday morning I took Brownie over before the service and made the snake check. We always found one or more big ones.

After I checked the church for copperheads and did not find any, we took Papa inside and stretched him out on two wide pine planks laid across two sawhorses placed in front of the preacher's lectern. Mavis covered Papa with a blanket up to his neck. Most everyone having a funeral preached at them was laid out the same way.

The Ulbricks went outside and left Mavis and me alone with Papa.

"Mavis, how old is Papa? We got to know for the grave marker later on. He sure looks old."

"Dead people generally do. Ah don't know, sixty some odd, ah recken. Ah nary heard said. We use to ave thet kind a stuff in Mama's ole fambly bible, but the cutworms et it."

Mavis had brought over the three coal oil lanterns we kept hanging on the back porch for use around the barn and cabin. She placed one lantern on the lectern, struck a match, and lit it. She lit the other two lanterns, placed one near the door, and hung another on a sidewall. Flickering yellow light played over the dreadful scene. Mavis went to Papa and took his right hand in her right hand.

"They are together now," she said. "Mama and Papa. May God ave mercy on they souls and on us ary one."

Mavis eased Papa's hand down by his side, back under the blanket, turned, and walked out the door; I followed. I wanted to look back at Papa, but could not. I knew Mavis would be back later. She would spend the night sitting in the church with her fiddle, playing those haunting old Celtic ballads Mama Ida sung to her years before. It seemed like Mavis never forgot any kind of musical piece.

We went out and said goodbye to the Ulbricks, as they loaded in their wagon and started for home. Elsa kept her head down. She wiped at a tear.

Mavis and I stood in the road and watched until the Ulbricks started across the creek, where it flowed across the pike. I glanced at Mavis. Her long auburn hair was undone and touched her shoulders. Her fair complexion showed a hint of freckles, which would darken in the summer sun. I wondered how her poor sparse flat-chested Irish body was going to hold up in the days to come. Mavis turned for the cabin.

"Ah'll git us some supper."

The western hills shadowed our little valley in late evening where darkness always came early, but I thought enough light remained to make a quick scout down toward Polk Bayou, the big creek that flowed south twelve miles and emptied into White River at Batesville. I took my rifle from pegs over the front room door and walked in the kitchen to tell Mavis I was going up to the clearing in the dogwoods behind the church and look for tracks. She voiced some objections about my intentions.

"Ah know yer disposed to do somethin, but don't be a goin too fur. Hit's gettin dark."

I took Brownie with me. We were in the clearing in the dogwood grove within ten minutes. The horse and mule tracks were easy to read across the hillside even in near darkness. The tracks cut around the hill and seemed aimed southwest for the juncture of Cave Creek and Polk Bayou at a low-water crossing over a gravel bar. The gravel bar was not far, and I needed to satisfy myself that my thinking was right.

Papa's killer did in fact lead the mules across the gravel bar. Ankle deep water flowed over the bar, but hoof prints were deep and visible in the clear creek water, and I could make out fresh hoof marks where the shod horse and mules climbed the west bank of Polk Bayou. The shriek of a screech owl caused me to flinch. Chill bumps broke out on my arms. A coyote yipped back up the bayou. Whippoorwills, foxes and hoot owls became active and vocal along Cave Creek. Thrashing in the brush across Cave Creek scared the devil out of me, I do not mind saying. I dropped to one knee and cocked the hammer on my rifle. Two white tails flashed at me. Deer. Scared me good though. I turned back to the cabin. I did not want to worry Mavis, or myself.

As I expected, Mavis spent most of the night sitting with her fiddle in a cane bottom chair outside the open door of the little log church. I washed up and went to bed and tried sleeping but could not. I got up, went to the kitchen, and found a can of shredded pipe tobacco on a shelf beside the fireplace. The old blue cast-iron coffeepot hung by a metal hook from a metal bar across a bed of near burned out coals. I looked in the cupboard and found a tin cup with a handle you could hook with a finger. The coffee had been boiling a while and had attained a nice syrupy blackness. Papa was fond of saying he liked coffee that would float a horseshoe. Papa would have liked this coffee. I walked out on the front porch, sat in an old canebottom chair, pushed back on the back legs and pushed a booted foot up against a support post for balance. I could sit for hours pushed back thinking, smoking and drinking coffee.

Yellow lantern light flickered from inside the church through the door, cast a yellow sheen across Mavis sitting with a shawl over her head, and draped across her shoulders. She sat with her fiddle and played those old ballads in a soulful minor key I loved so well. She was not holding the fiddle under her chin as she did, when she was into a serious hoedown, but rather held it in the crook of her left arm and pulled the bow back and forth like a pendulum, and let the notes flow up out of her soul and emerge from her fingertips.

I got up after a spell and went back into the kitchen and got down a heavy clay jug of mountain mist from the cupboard and carried it back to the front porch, pulled the cork and took a few long pulls. Warmed all over, I dozed off sitting in my chair.

Word of Papa's murder spread through the hills. No one knows how something like that happens. Some people called it the Indian telegraph. I don't know why. The Indians in our area did not use drums and sure did not have a telegraph. Mid-morning next day people began arriving at our cabin.

Eagle Carter and his Osage wife, Rachel, who had helped bury a number of men, women and children over the years, arrived with a pine coffin, two berry pies and a quart fruit jar of Dean Johnson's fresh mountain mist. He did not put labels on his jars, but everyone knew his moonshine. He always added iodine for color, and a touch of coal oil in the corn mash for mellowness.

The Ulbricks come up about the same time as the Carters did. Mr. Ulbrick and Eagle lifted Papa's body from its pine board-resting place, on the sawhorses, and placed it in the coffin. Junior Ulbrick and his sister, Elsa, helped Mr. Ulbrick, Eagle Carter and I lift the coffin back onto the sawhorses.

"He ain't weighed much," said Elsa.

Independence County Deputy Sheriff Kel Decker arrived on horseback. He was the Independence County Sheriff Clay Decker's younger brother and chief deputy. He made it known to those assembled in the churchyard that he was representing his brother's office. I guess he saw potential voters in the crowd.

Decker should have brought a posse to search the area and follow the trail of the killer. Everyone in the hills knew we Abbotts were not going to get any help from the sheriff because of my brother Teddy Blue having killed the sheriff's first cousin, John Statin, and three other Batesville men in a dancehall shootout in Sharp County back in 1862.

I pointed out the clearing on the hillside, where the rider and mule team passed through and told him fresh tracks led across Polk Bayou, over a gravel bar, at the juncture of Cave Creek, in a southwest direction. Deputy Decker looked at me and smirked.

The smart bastard said, "I don't want to undertake no long journey for the purpose of seeking redress, which would cost more than the worth of the property taken."

That was a dumb remark to make under the circumstances. I think he came near getting shot over it. Mavis pushed up and said, "Property taken. Somebody kilt our Papa, you squirrel-headed sunavabitch."

Some other people made remarks not normally heard around a church and began pushing up around the deputy.

"Easy Miss Abbott. Must ah remind ye thet ye are talkin to the law and the law takes offense," replied Decker, beads of sweat had popped out on his brow.

Eagle Carter moved up to catch Mavis by the arm. She started shaking and wiping snot and tears. Mad as a hornet I could tell. I remember thinking a good thing she did not have a gun handy.

Decker's countenance underwent a change from one of arrogance to worry as the hostile crowd began pressing up around his horse. He sputtered a bit when he said, "I want you'ens to know thet we a the Independence County Sheriff's Office'll do all in our power to brang Mr. Abbott's killer to justice, even though we are abused by his daughter."

I pushed through the crowd and up close to the deputy's horse and thought about doing something that would land me in jail, but the tall dark half-breed Eagle Carter stepped close in to the left stirrup, looked up and said to Decker, "How old are ye deputy?"

Kel Decker looked down at Eagle for a moment. He was puzzled by the question as I was but replied, "Thirty-two, why?"

"Well, if ye want to live to be thirty-three, I'd ride on outta here and conduct mah investigation somewheres else."

Decker stared at Eagle for a moment. I suspect he was searching his brain for something snotty to say, but abandoned the search, when he recalled he was twelve miles north of Batesville, and one hell of a long way from home, when you were up in the hills on horseback alone and wore a badge meaning nothing to hill people. Decker was not a smart man, but smart enough to know to keep his mouth shut. He eased his horse around, walked it out to the road and turned north. To get in the last word, he called out, "Ah'll start mah investigation up at the tradin post. Thet was the last place the deceased was seen alive."

"Decker ain't foolin a soul with thet announcement," said Eagle Carter. "We left Rachel's brother, Hershel Three-Toes, holdin down the store till we git back. We jist got in a fresh supply a mountain mist from Dean Johnson's still. Decker'll be in the moonshine first thang, Hershel too. I spect they'll both be drunk afore long."

About three o'clock, when we thought no one else was coming; we held a funeral service for Papa in the little log Methodist Church. A Methodist preacher by the name of Whistler Lewis conducted the service. Whistler was a local homesteader and part-time Methodist preacher. Some people called him Preacher Lewis.

Lamont Lewis, a tall gaunt man with a slim face and prominent chin, had piercing black eyes cocked out of alignment. When he was in the pulpit, one of his eyes always focused on you, regardless of where you sat, sometimes the right one, sometimes the left. He seemed to look at the whole congregation at the same time, which bothered me somewhat. I never liked a preacher staring at me, but with Whistler, you couldn't get out of his sight.

He acquired the nickname, "Whistler," because of two missing upper-front teeth. When the spirit overtook him, and it overtook him often, he got into his sermon chant pretty heavy and whistled through the gap in his teeth. Hell and damnation admonishments accompanied by bird-like chirps made his sermons different if not remarkable.

After a service that went far too long, most everyone climbed the hill with Mavis and me to the little Abbott graveyard that looked down on our cabin and outbuildings. Earlier, several men with picks and shovels had dug Papa's grave next to Mama Ida's grave.

The Abbott family graveyard started when they buried Papa's brother, Lester, and his wife, Eunice (Mama Ida's twin sister) on the hill under an old black mulberry tree. Uncle Lester and Aunt Eunice Abbott died young some said from consumption, a charitable thing to say because, truth be known, they were poisoned by drinking green moonshine whiskey.

In 1868, Papa and I took a stack of pine boards we got from the sawmill located northeast of the Sandtown Trading Post and built a little picket fence around the site. Papa bought five gallons of whitewash at the trading post and a big horsehair brush and made me whitewash the whole thing. Every spring, thereafter, I had to whitewash that fence. I did that every spring for twenty straight years. When I became a man of some substantial means, I hired it done.

Eagle Carter carried Papa's coffin in his springboard buggy up the hill to the graveyard. A small procession of men and women followed. Whistler Lewis made his "dust-to-dust" and "ashes-to-ashes" speech at the gravesite. Everyone came around, shook hands with me, and hugged Mavis. The people straggled back down the hill and went home, leaving Mavis, Junior Ulbrick and me. I never did ask Junior why he stayed. I don't know if Mr. Ulbrick told him to or not, but Junior was always my friend. I guess that was reason enough.

Mavis sat on a large round flat rock, her fiddle in the crook of her left arm. She was deft with the bow creating a sad minor key refrain. She played for a while, stopped and sat dried eyed, as Junior and I closed the grave.

We filled the grave, took our shovels and tamped down the loose dirt. I didn't know what else we were supposed to do, so we leaned on our shovels and looked at Mavis, but Mavis did not seem to notice. Junior gave me an inquiring look.

I think we were both wondering if I should say something, since I was the only son present. Mavis stood as if she was going to speak. She straightened her shoulders dropping her arms down to her sides, holding the fiddle in one hand and the bow in the other. I wondered what she was going to say. I expected something charitable about Papa, but it wasn't.

"I aim to kill somebody o'er this."

She took one last look at Papa's grave and turned down the hill toward the cabin. Junior and I picked up our shovels and followed. There was not anything else to say.

CHAPTER THREE

When Junior and I reached the back yard, Mavis stood on the south end of the back porch, one arm looped around a post, looking down and out. She stared at the falls in the creek, her mind off somewhere. I stepped up on the porch and walked over beside her. Junior, head down, passed in front of us on his way around the cabin to his saddle-mule tied to the front rail fence.

"Hit was nice a ye to stay and hep us Junior," said Mavis.

If Junior heard, it did not show. If he said anything, I did not hear it. He kept looking down as if he had something on his shoes. I did not have enough sense to say anything nice to Junior. I came to regret it later.

Mavis and I stood side-by-side looking at the creek, neither of us in a talkative mood. The water whispered over the falls like murmurings of a thousand ghosts. I think we were reflecting on our troubles, and how we had arrived at our sorry state. Deep down, we knew trouble lay ahead.

Junior stepped upon the top fence rail, held his balance for a moment, stepped across his mule and into the saddle. He tugged at the reins, turned the mule south and walked the mule down where Cave Creek flowed knee-deep across the road. The mule stopped of its own volition in the water and lowered its head to drink. Junior slumped on its neck, as if he was tired. A black buggy pulled by a prancing solid black Tennessee Walker appeared from out of the cut through the timber on the far side of the creek. That Tennessee Walker was the prettiest horse with the prettiest running-walk gait I ever saw in my life. Both Junior and the mule perked up when they saw the buggy coming. I wondered what that mule thought when he saw the horse with bowed neck prancing down to the creek. Mules have their place in the world, but mules are not pretty and I think that mule knew it.

A second rider sitting a big roan gelding followed the buggy. The big thick-chested dark-red horse was no slouch either in the looks department. One day soon, I would own that horse, but I had no inkling of it at the time.

The buggy driver and the other horseman pulled up in midstream, both horses lowered their heads to water. Junior spoke to the men, turned and motioned toward Mavis and me. Junior slapped the reins along the mule's neck, nudged him in the ribs with his heels and headed for home. The buggy driver flicked the reins and the Tennessee Walker pranced up the hill, as if he was not pulling anything. The man on the roan followed. I glanced at Mavis. Her eyes narrowed, brow furrowed.

"Mavis, we got company."

"Yep, and ah know who it tis and ah'm not surprised. He didn't wait long."

We stepped down off the porch and walked around the cabin to the front gate, a whitewashed five-foot-high swinging oak-board gate hinged inside a rectangle-shaped eight-feet-high by six-foot-wide cedar-log frame. That gate was the most formal looking thing on our place. The sheetmetal hinges were store bought. Scrap pieces of old leather harness usually served as gate hinges in that country.

I was proud of that gate and whitewashed it every spring at the same time I whitewashed the picket fence around our family graveyard. Most people coming into our yard from the road passed through the gate even though they could step over the rail fence anywhere without difficulty.

I reached inside the front door frame and took hold of Mavis's Henry rifle, stepped out onto the front porch and sat down in one of the old cane-bottom chairs. I laid the rifle across my lap. Mavis never looked at me, but she caught my move out of the corner of her eye and made no objection to what was a clear breech of hospitality on my part. Papa shot dead and buried on the hill left us both feeling considerably less than hospitable.

Mavis could handle the conversation. I did not feel like talking anyway. The old man in the buggy pulled his horse up to the gate. A bearded man, middle-aged, dressed in black, wearing an Abraham Lincoln stovepipe top hat, a hat not often seen in the hills. He looked at Mavis, at me, and back to Mavis. He gave no indication of stepping down, and Mavis gave no indication she cared.

"I'm Lazarus Statin."

"Ah know ye are."

"Ye must be Mavis. Ah'm sorry bout yer daddy."

The man on the roan stayed back in the road. He had dark sun-weathered skin, wore faded jeans, a long sleeved faded blue shirt, short crowned-short-brimmed black hat, and square-toed high-heeled black leather boots. Strange dress for the hills, but strangest of all, the bright red handkerchief around his neck. Hill people did not tie handkerchiefs around their necks like that. He slumped forward in the saddle stiff-armed, thin yellow calfskin gloved hands on the pommel. A walnut rifle stock glistened in the saddle scabbard. He wore a gunbelt, and a big pistol in a holster not tied down. The roan switched his tail at big green horseflies that always swarmed when the weather warmed in spring.

I caught bits of the conversation between Mr. Statin and Mavis, but the man on the roan drew my attention. He looked like he could get dangerous in a hurry. I tried not to stare. I played the fingers of my right hand on the brass breech of the Henry lying across my lap. I remembered I had failed to check if a cartridge was in the chamber. Should the situation change, and it could change, when a Statin confronted an Abbott, I would have to find out quick. How long it would take me to do it?--a question I wish I had left unattended.

I remember thinking old man Statin must have forgotten his manners, because he never introduced the man with him, or removed his hat, a serious breach of courtesy in the presence of a lady. I suspect old man Statin did not consider Mavis much of a lady.

"Miss Abbott, ah know our famblies ain't got along since thet thang in '62, but ah'm sorry bout yer daddy. We come into this country close to the same time. Ah knowed Austin Abbott to be an honest man. Can't be said fer a lot a men out here."

Well, I knew about that thing in '62', to which Statin referred. That thing was when my brother, Teddy Blue Abbott, seventeen-years-old at the time, killed the old man's oldest son, John Statin, along with three other men in what the locals referred to as The Pine Hill Shootout, a dancehall gun-battle on the old Smith Brothers sawmill grounds across the Sharp County line.

"Whut do ye want Mr. Statin?" asked Mavis.

"Ah did come to pay my respects. Ah would've come fer the buryin, but ah jist got word late this mornin and couldn't git here in time."

Sitting at an off angle behind Mavis, I checked her reaction. Her jaw twitched. I thought she was measuring her response. Mavis could not carry on a formal conversation. She did not know how, never practiced much. She talked in bits and pieces, mostly pieces.

"Pardon me, iffen ah find hit hard to beleve a man like yerself would ride all this a way jist to pay respects to a fambly thet yer fambly give a lot a grief to o'er the years. Yore boys ridin by here in the middle a the night shootin up this cabin. And yer oldest needed killing in '62, fer whut he done to the Stroud boy." Mavis's long speech amazed me. It did not have one cuss word in it.

The shooting in '62' had become a local legend. It started over John Statin stabbing my brother Teddy Blue's friend, Merle Stroud, in the top of the head with a butcher knife, twice, killing him graveyard dead, after Merle tried to act the pacifist in a squabble between Statin and a female dancehall patron. Merle had stumbled dazed around the dance hall floor, blood pouring out of his scalp, and fell dead at Teddy Blue's feet. Teddy sat at a table, where just moments before Merle and he had sat sipping out of a quart jar of mountain mist.

According to legend, Teddy Blue stood and walked to the front and single door in or out of the dancehall, barred it from the inside, turned in front of the door, pulled the old .36 caliber Navy Colt he had carried since age ten and from twenty feet shot John Statin between the eyes. Three armed friends of Statin jumped up from a table, kicking chairs over and yelling and made their play. Two got shots off and missed. Teddy Blue, in little more than bat of an eye, killed all three with single shots to the head.

Lazarus Statin looked hard at Mavis for a moment with little beady black rat eyes. He glanced over Mavis's shoulder; his eyes settled on me. I do not think he knew me. He looked back at Mavis.

"Well, ah don't blame ye fer bein upset bout 'em boys ridin by here and doin a little shootin. Ye put a stop to it, as ah recall. Thet was ye, I hear, put buckshot in Billy's leg. Ye ruint a good horse. Had to put 'im down. Gutshot."

"Ah shot low. Guess the shot glanced offen a shale slab outten the road. Sorry to hear bout the horse. Ah'll shoot higher next time--with mah rifle."

A faint smile tugged at the corner of Statin's mouth. "Ah bleve ye are a dangerous woman, Miss Abbott."

"Ah might be--to varmits. Whut are ye here fur anyway?"

"Ah'll git right to the point Miss Abbott. Ah want to buy this here place. Ah made the offer to yer daddy several times."

"Well, he turned ye down."

"He did thet."

"Well, ah'm turnin ye down."

The old man took a long beady-eyed look at Mavis, and again looked over her shoulder at me. "Are jist the two a ye gonna try farmin this here place?"

"We are. We are gonna do more'n try. We are gonna do hit."

"It's gonna take more'n a girl and a skinny ole boy to make this place pay."

The man on the horse behind Statin eased up straight in the saddle and stared at me. He was measuring me, wondering if I was capable. I was wondering the same thing. He reached up with his right hand and played the brim of his hat through his fingers. I expect he wanted to make sure to keep his hand away from the gun on his hip. He was not fooling anyone. We had our eyes on him and he knew it. I heard Mavis say, "Ah quit bein a girl a long time ago, and ah recken the boy can carry his weight. Has fur a long time."

"Well, ah guess our business is finished Miss Abbott. Ah wish ye'd take mah offer. Ah spect ye two won't be able to raise nough crops to pay the taxes on this place. Ah'll be a watchin the courthouse records and spect ah'll end up gettin this place on a tax sale. Remember mah offer Miss Abbott and a good day to ye."

Mavis did not reply, but the back of her neck blushed crimson when Statin mentioned the tax sale. Statin pulled the Tennessee Walker around and started back toward the creek. The other man turned to follow, taking one long passing look at Mavis and me. Mavis stepped off the porch and walked toward the front gate. I stood up with the Henry in my right hand. I stepped off the porch and walked up to stand beside Mavis. She put her arm around my shoulders, displaying rare affection toward me. I felt as close to her at that time, as I ever did. I slid my left arm around her slender waist. She was nothing but skin and bones.

Statin and the rider stopped in the middle of the creek, they looked upstream and took some time studying the area around the falls. Lazarus Statin turned and said something to the man on the roan. They proceeded south toward Batesville.

"Chet, evah see the man on the roan?"

"Nah--ain't."

"Well, watch yerself, he's a danger, iffen ah ever seed one. Don't nary go outten this cabin agin, to the barn, garden, even to the outhouse thout a gun on ye. Member how Cal Tucker was kilt squattin in his barn during his mornin absolution."

We stepped up on the front porch. Clinking iron-shod hooves on shale rock caught our attention. Around the bend up the road, a man on horseback appeared; the horse walking easy, head bobbing, the rider slumped over to the right, head down, not looking left or right: Deputy Sheriff Kel Decker--drunk as a skunk. I turned around and sat on the porch steps. Mavis walked back out to the front gate. We watched horse and rider plod by. Decker had puked his guts out and was down to gagging dry heaves. Mavis or I never said a word when he passed. We watched him as the horse ambled on down the hill and splashed across the creek and continued watching until horse and rider passed out of sight into in the timber beyond. Mavis stood at the gate for a moment, as if she were thinking. She turned toward the cabin and looked at me. "Whut a sorry sunuvabitch thet is."

She stepped up on the porch and went inside.

Dusk settled over Cave Creek valley. Restlessness agitated me. Brownie was down by the barn pestering a groundhog. I called him. Carbine in hand, I crossed the road, Brownie heeling. We walked around the church, up the slope and entered the dogwood grove carpeted with dogwood blossoms, some fresh bright white, some fading to gray. I went straight to the clearing, where Papa's killer had passed through with our mule team.

The steel shod hooves had cut a nice trail into the soft hillside. I followed the trail down to the gravel bar crossing at Polk Bayou. Even in dusk of late evening, the hoof marks were clear, where horse and mules climbed the west bank of the big creek. Any law officer worth his spit, and that wanted to, could have followed the tracks.

I waded through the ankle deep water over the gravel bar and followed the hoof prints southwest until the trail faded on a rocky hillside. Near dark, I turned back. Hoot owls, whippoorwills, foxes and coyotes began their sundown serenade. Mavis joined in--calling me--giving me a long whoop. She had warned me about trying to do too much on my own. Mavis was busy with supper, when I walked into the kitchen.

"The trail points to the Osage camp on White River."

Mavis did not say anything for a minute. She looked at me. "The killer took Papa's clothes and crossed the crick tord the Osage camp. Seems to me he tried awful hard to make hit look like a injun kilt Papa, but ah got my doubts bout thet."

"No, warn't no injuns," I replied. "Ah'll tend the stock."

"Don't take too long. Supper'll be ready dreckly."

I lit a lantern and went out to the barn with carbine in hand. After Papa's murder, I would have to remember to carry a weapon with me every time I left the cabin for any reason, even to go down to the creek to take a bath or wash my feet.

Four in the morning, still dark outside and would be for another hour, I stumbled half asleep into the kitchen to the smell of sizzling fatback, baked biscuits and steaming black coffee. Mavis and I sat for a while not speaking eating our breakfast, but I knew she had made up her mind about something.

"Chet, we're a-goin to the Osage camp."

She paused, waiting for a reaction. I was laying into a big cathead biscuit smeared with goat butter and honey and did not answer right away.

One Osage Indian family remained in the county. The family's permanent campsite was several miles southwest of our cabin near the White River. The old patriarch was Chief George--I never knew his last name--George's several wives were Indian and white.

Chief George had fathered twenty sons, one daughter, and counting. His daughter, Rachel, married the half-breed Eagle Carter, proprietor of the Sandtown Trading Post. Old George was a civil old soul, but some of his boys were scamps, and they loved their beer and mountain mist.

In years past, several Osage boys hi-jacked two beer wagons enroute from the White River docks at Batesville, to the Smith Brother's sawmill northeast of Cushman. The Osage boys put the wagon drivers afoot, and drove the two wagonloads of St. Louis brewery beer to their camp on White River. The boys went on a month-long drinking binge and three drowned.

"Ah figured as much. The last time ah heerd, the camp was ten, twelve miles o'er tord White River."

"Heerd thet too," replied Mavis.

I doubted Osages murdered Papa. Papa was a good friend of Chief George. He traded with him over the years. Chief George visited our cabin several times and shared meals. He liked Mavis's cooking and, on several occasions, offered Papa hogs for her. Papa declined. He liked Mavis's cooking too.

Papa traded George potatoes, dried apples, corn, and sorghum molasses for beaver and raccoon pelts. Papa was good at tanning the pelts and selling them to peddlers at Batesville, peddlers who came down White River on paddle wheelers from Memphis and St. Louis. Papa also made our coats out of animal pelts. We sometimes went hungry in the winter, but we were warm doing it.

"We got to start sommers," said Mavis, "and the Osage camp is good a place as any. Iffen the injuns hain't got our mules, maybe they seen 'em passin through."

Crossing hill country through woods, canebrakes and creeks with a team and wagon was out of the question. I thought we could get a wagon through on the old Osage trail that ran southwest from the Sandtown Trading Post to White River. The Osage still used the trail when they came up to the trading post; although, they seldom drove wagons; most walked or rode mules.

I thought we might intersect with the old trail a mile or so west of Polk Bayou. I thought the trail would be overgrown with brush and close in places, but I figured a wagon could squeeze through with a little help from a double-edged chopping axe.

I got up from the breakfast table, took a lantern to the barn and harnessed Ned and Ted. At first light, we loaded in the wagon. Brownie intended to go with us, so much so that I had to lock him in the corncrib. He set up a howl. We could still hear him raising a ruckus all the way down to the gravel-bar-crossing on Polk Bayou.

Mavis handled the reins. I rode shotgun with our old 10-gauge Greener. We also carried my .44 caliber Winchester carbine and a box of shells for both guns. Soon after crossing Polk Bayou, we jumped a deer out of a brushpile. It crashed off into the brush.

"Whooee, scared hell outta me," said Mavis.

I had the same reaction. I flinched and cocked both hammers on the Greener. Chuckling at Mavis's exclamation, I eased the hammers down.

In heavy timber near the Osage trail, a pair of red wolves smelled the horses and came in close. Ned and Ted pranced, snorted and flared their nostrils. Mavis struggled to hold them. The wolves closed to within thirty yards, heads low, ears laid back. They were so intent on the horses I do not think they knew Mavis and I were in the wagon. I killed one with my carbine, and the other disappeared. We did not spot another game animal suitable for the cooking pot, except a few red squirrels.

"The injuns have bout kilt everthin," said Mavis.

Three hundred yards from the spot where I killed the wolf we cut the Osage trail and received a pleasant surprise. The trail showed recent activity. Fresh axe or hatchet marks were visible on cut saplings piled along the route. I suspect the Indians decided the trail needed clearing for wagon traffic from White River to the Sandtown Trading Post. Neither Mavis nor I anticipated such an easy trail.

We made good time and pulled into the Indian camp at high noon. The camp, a warren of a dozen or so rough-hewn single-room log cabins and lean-to's, nestled in a small clearing. Two spavined broken down sway-backed horses grazed on scrub oak bushes. There was not a mule in sight.

A single outdoor fire, inside a ring of stones, sizzled and smoked in front of one of the cabins. Two tattered grubby women, who did not look Indian, were cleaning fish and a small animal close to the fire. They stopped their work and watched us come in. The women stood stooped seeming unable or unwilling to stand straight. They stared at us as a blind person might--vacant stares--nothing behind the eyes.

Dirty ragged children, of various ages, sizes and genders, played around the camp. The children stopped their play. Some came running. A young girl, maybe twelve, in rags, came over and stood by the wagon, looking up at me. She never said anything, but her eyes were hungry. I became uneasy. Three younger children approached the wagon. An Indian boy took hold of one of the rear iron-rimmed wagon wheels, placed a foot on the hub and began to pull up into the wagon. Mavis turned on him with hard eyes.

"Git down offen here."

The boy eased down, but held his ground, a hard look in his eyes too.

I looked for the Indian men. I did not think we needed to fear them, but I levered a shell in the chamber of the carbine and cradled it in the crook of my left arm, right hand over the trigger guard, and thumb on the hammer.

Mavis addressed the nearest woman. "Mam, ah'm lookin fer Chief George. "

The woman, working on a bloodstained flat rock, scraped scales from a big yellow carp with a large butcher knife. When Mavis spoke to her, she dropped her right hand holding the knife to her side. She had an aged and harried look, forty-years-old looking sixty, hands blackened by blood and wood smoke. A tobacco chaw bulged her right cheek. Tobacco stains yellowed her fingernails, teeth and chin. Stringy reddish hair streaked with gray did not look real, more like a poor grade of moss. Her bare feet were calloused, dirty and black. She wore a tattered dress, once black, made from some unidentifiable material faded to gray.

"George hain't here, ah reckon. Gone off huntin a new camp."

"Are ye a white woman?" Mavis asked.

"Ah was. Injun now."

"Whut in tarnation does thet mean?"

"It means missy, mah man nary come back after the war and me and mah kids, whut hain't died, come o'er here to these people to keep from starvin to death, when they warn't no people of our own kind whut would hep us. When the war come, mah man left me and the four little'uns to fend fer ourselfs. Hit warn't right, but hit appened. Many a time at night, when ah laid me down, ah couldn't sleep on account a my pore condition and bein forced to see my kids suffer from cold and hunger thout power or prospect a hepin 'em. Chief George come by one day and said ah ought to go with him. He said he'd feed us, so ah bundled up my kids and went."

"Who are ye?" Mavis asked.

"Agnes Whitehead."

"Ah know ye. Ah member ye barely. Yore fambly use to come to church at Cave Creek."

The woman studied Mavis hard for a bit. "Whut's yer name?"

"Mavis Abbott."

"Ida Abbott's girl. Ida died a long time back, as ah recall. Died too young. We all die too young out here. The girl leanin on the wagon is all thet's left a mah bunch."

"Whut's wrong with her?" asked Mavis.

"She hain't right in the head. She hain't been fer some time. She's been used up. Me and her are two a George's wives. We're a-gettin ready to move o'er to the calico rock on White River. We're allus movin sommers else," replied Agnes. "Whose boy ye got with ye?"

"My brother Chet."

Agnes Whitehead took a long hard look at me. I could not look her in the eye. I turned away and studied the camp, but I listened.

"Hain't thet Eunice Abbott's boy?" Agnes asked.

I was puzzled by the question, but I knew Eunice Abbott was Mama Ida's twin sister. Ida and Eunice Berry married my Papa and his brother, Lester. I looked around in time to catch Mavis giving the woman a hard look, as if she wanted Miss Whitehead to drop the subject.

"Nah, this is my baby brother, Mama's last," Mavis replied, firm, hard like.

Agnes started to say something more on the subject but a look from Mavis, and a quick headshake, cut her short. I had quit trying, a long time past, to get Papa or Mavis to talk about Uncle Lester and Aunt Eunice.

"Ain't no use dwelling on the past," is all I could ever get out of either.

Mavis lowered the strain out of her voice. "Why don't ye git yer possibles together and ye and the girl git in the wagon and come away with us. We'll find some way a takin care a ye."

Agnes did not take any time at all to reply. "Nah, we made our bed and we'll sleep in it, I recken. Ole George don't bother us much no more, and he keeps the young bucks away from the girl."

I did not understand what Agnes was saying, but sometime later came to realize what she meant. It embarrasses me today, to think of it. Mavis made another try.

"Ye can come. You'ens got folks sommeres."

"Nah, recken not," said Agnes. "Ah may ave folks sommeres, ah don't know. But ah don't want none knowin bout this. We git worked hard, but we git fed purty good, thet is iffen ye like fish, squirrel and possum. Ye ever been hongry, missy?"

"Some."

"Ye ever et tree bark?" Agnes asked.

"Nah," replied Mavis, "I hain't never et no tree bark."

"Well, ye hain't never been real hongry," said Agnes.

Starvation stories circulated through the hills and told as true that some homesteaders once resorted, during the war years, to eating tree bark boiled in salt water.

In the lean drought years of 1870, 71, I often hunted along the creeks and found cottonwood trees with the bark stripped up as high as I could reach. Those were the years, when I learned how to find edible wild greens, in the spring and summer. Hill people thought a cow would not eat anything poisonous. We did not own a cow, but some ran wild around us. They could be dangerous if they had a calf. If I came across a cow in the woods, while out hunting, I watched what she ate. I followed her around and found wild lettuce, burdock, poke salet, sheep sorrel, lamb's quarter, tongue grass and deer's tongue, all edible, when boiled and tenderized in salt water. Not anything to brag about, but anything was better than nothing.

Spring fed Cave Creek never dried up. I discovered how to construct rock and earth dams and divert creek water onto our garden and around our apple tree, so our family did not suffer as much as others did during drought seasons.

Those were the years when we Abbotts ate a lot of corn mush and hominy grits, Mormon Johnny-Cake, corn pone and rabbit, deer and salt pork. We ate the same meal for breakfast, dinner and supper and was glad to get it. We drank something pioneers called acorn coffee, made from crushed acorns, awful tasting stuff. One time Papa came back from Batesville with a cloth sack full of chicory. He said people in Louisiana drank ground chicory as a coffee substitute. I do not want to disparage people from Louisiana. But after trying chicory a couple of times we went back to acorns, and fed the chicory to the goats. They did not like it either.

Mavis decided the conversation ought to go in a different direction.

"How many white women are o'er here? And where are the injun women?"

"All gone to the big calico rock o'er on the river. We stayed behind to clean out the rest a the camp and carry it o'er there. Eight, ten white women and some kids come here at first, after the war, but jist two a us white women are left: me and Sarah Evans. Thet's Sarah o'er yonder by the stump cleanin a possum. One other white woman passed a few days past: Eulis Murcer."

"I member Eulis. What'd ye do with her?" asked Mavis.

"Drug her outten the woods yonder. Throwed some rocks o'er her, keep the wolves and hogs off. What year is it anyhow?"

"Eighteen-seventy-five," I blurted out and startled myself.

Agnes stared at me for a moment. Maybe I should not have butted into the conversation. She turned away, as if looking for something, but remembering she was doing.

"Ah been here twelve, thirteen years now. Seems like mah whole life. What'd ye all want anyway?"

"We're lookin fer a gray mule team thet was stole, when our Papa was kilt. Bushwhacker taken the mules, left the wagon," replied Mavis.

"Well, hain't seen no mules sich as thet," replied Agnes. You'ens got a lot of gall runnin round out here, a white woman and jist a boy. I recken you'ens hain't much used to travelin in the woods."

"Me and the boy here ave spent our share a time in the woods, I recken," said Mavis, in a hard voice. "Somebody kilt our Papa and stole his mules. I recken we find the mules, we find the one kilt 'im."

"Whut ye gonna do, ye find 'im?" asked Agnes.

"We aim to kill'im, iffen we got time," replied Mavis.

She said it in such a hard voice it caught my attention. I sat straight up on the wagon seat, but stayed quiet. Agnes involuntary took a step backward, like she was afraid something was going to happen. She didn't have anything to fear, but you never knew with Mavis's temper and a gun handy.

"We heerd bout thet," said Agnes.

"What'd ye hear?" asked Mavis.

"Well, we heerd a white man got kilt up near the tradin post, but it warn't none of these here people did it. You'd best be lookin o'er to Batesville, is whut ah heerd," Agnes replied.

"Whut ye mean? Say hit plain out," said Mavis. She spat out the words like tobacco juice.

"Nah, hain't sayin no more," replied Agnes, cowed a bit, head down. "Don't know no more, no way. But we knowed somebody be wantin to blame the injuns, but you'ens is the first ones come lookin." She snapped her head up, looking Mavis straight in the eye. "Thet ought to tell ye somethin."

Mavis stared hard into Agnes's eyes. "Yeah, hit tells me the law hain't carin, or they'd a been here. The law, sich as it is, knows who done it."

Mavis picked up the reins and pulled the horses into a slow turn. The Whitehead girl took one step back from the wagon but kept staring at me. What, if anything, was going through her mind? Agnes Whitehead returned to her fish-cleaning task and the children to running and playing in the trees.

The trip home was uneventful, boring even. Woodlands are always quiet in the evening. I kept nodding off, lulled by the wagon's rolling motion. Mavis stayed quiet, but did relay our next day's schedule.

"After sundown tomorry, we're gonna git our mules back. Them mules is at Batesville, and ah know whar."

She surprised me. "Whar?"

"Theys in the livery barn, and thet's whar we're gonna be come midnight tomorry night. We need to git our rest tonight, cause tomorra is gonna be a long day."

CHAPTER FOUR

The next day, Mavis and I dropped water-soaked seed corn over five acres of plowed ground. I had soaked the big yellow grains overnight in a tub of lye water. The soaking puffed them like hominy grits causing better germination, or so the old folks thought. Since the corn always came up, must have been some truth to it.

We each took a shovel, made little dirt mounds, in rows that were not very straight. Planting seed by hand in a straight row across a plowed field was an art neither Mavis nor I ever mastered. I swear those rows were so crooked it made me dizzy trying to plow them.

We punched three of the big golden kernels down in each mound one-finger length and patted the ground down with our shovels. If the seeds were good--and they usually were--all three would sprout.

After the corn stalks reached a height of four inches, we had to thin the corn and chop the weeds out. I hated hoeing corn with about the same degree of passion, I felt toward tending a tobacco crop.

We worked from sunup to sundown, took a short break at noon, and finished the corn planting at dusk. We walked out of the field dead on our feet and still with a long night ahead.

I tended the animals, while Mavis fixed supper. I kept listening for Papa's voice among the barn sounds admonishing me to do something better. If you do something boy, do it right. But there was no Papa, just shadows, stable sounds and memories.

Mavis seldom mentioned Papa, but his absence showed in her actions. She often stared into space, jaw set, the smallest tear trickling down her cheek. I felt the need to say something at times like that, but her manner put me off.

Mavis fried fatback in a Dutch oven that hung by the bail on a rod in the kitchen fireplace. She took time to make Mormon Johnny Cake, a mixture of cornmeal, flour, baking soda, butter, salt and molasses, also baked in a Dutch oven.

After supper, I stretched out on the oak-planked back porch and watched a half moon rising over the barn. I drifted off to sleep thinking about what the rest of the night might have in store. We planned taking our horse team and wagon. Mavis wanted to enter Batesville at midnight or after, when most everyone was off the streets. She shook me awake at seven o'clock.

I took a lantern off the back porch, walked to the barn and harnessed the horses to the wagon. I do not believe Ned and Ted were happy to have been included in our plans. Horses are used to working daylight hours. Harnessing them at night confuses them.

Brownie wanted to go. He was a natural hunting dog and anytime we went outside at night with a light of any kind, he thought we were going to the woods. He bounced around the wagon, whimpered and showed his willingness to run even though he was missing a front foot. I locked him in the corncrib. I hated to, but we could not have a noisy dog messing up the works. But we did take my pet goat, Billy, and for a good reason. I reasoned the mules, if found, would follow the wagon and Billy home with little coaxing. Mavis liked my idea and approved. I had plowed the fields with the mules for over five years and often rode them to and from the field. The mules and the goat followed me around the barn lot like pets, while I did my chores. Billy spent considerable time with the mules. He followed them everywhere even sleeping in their stalls at night. For one thing, the mules got good things to eat, which Billy also enjoyed. He even followed the mules to the field and frolicked, while the mules labored. The mules seemed to like him, and hard to tell if the goat thought he was a smaller version of a mule, or the mules thought they were larger versions of the goat.

I tied Billy to the wagon tailgate with a ten-foot length of rope and threw several ears of corn in the back of the wagon bed. Dropping the tailgate allowed Billy easy access. I hoped an abundance of corn would keep him pacified for the twenty-four mile roundtrip.

Billy was a year old. His mother was one of the nannies we kept for milking. I fooled with him a lot, and he always looked for me, when I was outside around the cabin or the barn. Mavis didn't cotton to Billy. She and Billy butted heads on several occasions, in a manner of speaking, because of the goat's natural bad habits, where humans were concerned. Billy looked at an open door as a personal invitation, and sometimes he looked for me inside the cabin. The little gray goat, object of several broom attacks and a few swift kicks, once lowered his head and charged Mavis in her own kitchen. She caught him by the horns and slung him through an open kitchen window.

We had taken to raising goats, because milk cows were hard to find. We had owned two milk cows over the years, both killed. One killed by the sheriff, when he burned the barn looking for Teddy Blue in 1862, after the shootout at Pine Hill, and later another good milk cow was shot and left dead in the woods across the creek next to the bluff. Papa suspected the Statins shot her from atop the bluff, because of an entry wound from a heavy caliber rifle between her shoulder blades. Papa could never prove anything, and he could not gain anything by trying.

I was a baby and doing poorly sucking on a twisted rag soaked in sugar water, called a "sugar tit." There were no women around to breast-feed me. They were all too undernourished and flat chested. I turned so yellow daffodils were envious. Mavis said I got poor as a snake. A homesteader's wife told Papa he needed to get a milk goat for me or I was going to die, so he did. He bought two billy goats and two nanny goats from the Wilson family at Wilson Springs over on Polk Bayou.

I thrived on goat's milk, and Mavis found it good for her cooking. Mavis said the goat milk made me hardheaded, and mean as the devil. Later on when I was old enough to understand things, she said I was going to sprout goat horns. I did not know she was putting me on and for a long time, I would slip into Mavis's bedroom and look into the old cracked mirror she kept hanging on the wall and I would feel my head for bony nubbins.

Mavis handled the reins. I sipped my third tin cup of hot coffee, as we started south down the Batesville Pike. A loaded .10-gauge Greener shotgun and Winchester carbine leaned against the wagon seat.

"Mavis, whut iffen we find the mules and somebody tries to stop us?"

"'Em mules is a comin back one way or tother."

I checked the loads in my rifle.

We passed the Ulbrick homestead a mile south of our place. Their cabin, fifty yards off the road, was in a clearing cut out of a pine thicket. Unlike us Abbotts, the Ulbricks did not have a creek near their cabin. However, they did have a good spring back of their cabin that never ran dry.

We did not want to draw attention to our passing, but ringing shod hooves and iron-rimmed wagon wheels clanging on shale rock could not be muffled. The Ulbrick's two hounds came up to the road and, from behind a rail fence, raised a ruckus. A thud and a rustle in the back of the wagon alerted us that Billy now stood amidst the loose corn ears eyeing the Ulbrick hounds. Billy's horns were gaining prominence, but were no match for big dogs, a fact not lost on Billy.

Mavis slapped the reins on Ted and Ned and kicked them up a little. Lamplight coming through the front window silhouetted Junior Ulbrick on the porch with rifle in hand looking in our direction and yelling at his dogs. Things settled a bit after we got a quarter mile down the road, except for the clatter of hooves, wagon wheels and Billy's munching on a corn ear.

Mavis concentrated on the rocky track and said little. She never made the trip to Batesville more than once a year and never at night. The old buffalo trail now called the Batesville Pike slashed through heavy timber and was difficult even in daytime. We had to rely on the horses' instinct to keep us out of trouble in the moon's half-light.

Billy's munching got me to thinking about Elsa Ulbrick, who, I thought, must have eaten her share of corn. I would have rather thought of something else, but it is strange how at times you cannot control what you think. My mind wandered across Elsa's ampleness, wandered off, wandered back and settled.

Elsa was marrying age. She was somewhat attractive in my view. I suppose not having a lot of selection in the hills might be cause for my charitable observation. When Elsa cleaned up and put on a calico dress, I thought her pretty, but her nose was large enough to cast its own shadow.

Before Papa's murder, Elsa made regular trips to our place--to visit Mavis, or so she said. She always arrived late in the day about the time I came in from the field. I did not understand it at first. She always waded the creek and walked up to the cabin barefoot, shoes in hand. She often brought us three or four eggs, because we did not have chickens. Mavis used eggs and goat milk for baking, and all us Abbotts liked an egg now and again with our cornbread, so I welcomed the sight of Elsa crossing the creek.

We could not keep chickens or ducks because of foxes, wildcats and coyotes sneaking around our barn and along the creek. We could not keep house cats either for the same reason. A fox would not bother an old house cat, but a coyote would get one every time the cat got out anywhere near the barn. I heard some awful screams and fights during the night out back of the barn. "Nother cat gone," Mavis would say.

Elsa's coming and going got so regular Brownie did not even bark to announce her arrival, but she always knocked on the front door.

"Elsa, agin," Mavis would announce, smiling, looking at me sideways.

Elsa always left her shoes on the porch. She puttered barefoot around the kitchen exchanging pleasantries with Mavis, but I did take some notice that she looked my way a lot. It took some time before I realized Elsa was coming to see me. Papa and Mavis, knew it all along. Papa never said anything though, but he cut some glances at Elsa when she was around and a slight crease showed at the corner of his mouth.

After supper, weather permitting, Papa pursued his ritual of taking a cup of coffee and a corncob pipe full of tobacco down to the creek, where he sat for an hour on a cane-bottomed chair on the big flat rock hanging over the blue hole. In the darkness, the flickering fire in his pipe always betrayed his presence. I guessed he was thinking about Mama Ida. Often, Mavis would take her fiddle down to the creek, sit down on the rock close to Papa and play those old sorrowful Irish ballads. I guess she was thinking about her mama too.

"Why don't you and Elsa go out on the front porch and visit, while ah clean up the kitchen," Mavis would say.

I always offered Elsa coffee. She always declined. We would go out on the front porch, sit in the cane-bottomed chairs and try to talk. Talking to Elsa was difficult for me. All she wanted to talk about was cooking and babies. All I knew was mules and farming.

The week before Papa's murder, Elsa came one day, and as usual, we ended up on the front porch alone. She brought her chair over real close; our hands touched. I thought at first accidental, but it wasn't. She looked straight ahead showing me her profile, which was significant.

"Chet, do you ever think about getting married?" she whispered, as if she did not want anyone else to hear.

I was startled by the way she came out with it, considering the implications. I knew some hill girls got married when they were eleven or twelve, and I heard of one girl marrying at ten. So for girls to marry at a very young age was not unusual, but I found difficult the thought of getting married and having to raise children, crops and animals. I could not imagine how I could marry and work a hardscrabble farm like Papa, and I said as much to Elsa. She said she thought it possible, if two people cared for one another. I agreed there was a smidgen of truth in what she said. She became encouraged. I could have bitten my tongue off.

The Ulbrick place was eleven road miles from Batesville. Two other homesteader cabins were close enough to the road to cause us concern. We knew it would be difficult to get by them without attracting attention because of dogs, and people would think it strange that a wagon passed in the night toward Batesville.

People were interested and wary of night travelers. Homesteaders going to Batesville at night in a wagon often meant a doctor's visit, but it was plain neither of us was sick or injured, and no stores were open at midnight.

It was against Mavis's Christian upbringing to lie about why we were on the road at night. In this case, if questioned, we would have to shade the truth a bit, Christian upbringing or not. She brought up several things we could say, if someone met us on the road. None made sense. Mavis settled on a plan. She said, if we happened to meet someone on the road let her do the talking, maybe something would come to her from on high. I did not say anything, but I wondered if the Good Lord had the time or inclination to provide his humble servant with answers regarding a little gray mule team.

We passed two more darkened cabins setting back several yards off the road. I did not know who those people were, Germans I think. As expected, dogs noted our passing, but we did not see anyone. I felt sure someone holding a rifle or shotgun watched us from the shadows.

We kept conversation to a minimum, voices low. Calls of owls, foxes, coyotes, and a wolf mixed in with ringing hooves, creaking jingling harness and clatter of wagon wheels. Ted and Ned lumbered on toward Batesville. Mavis handed me the reins, stepped over the seatboard and kicked Billy out of the wagon.

"Thet danged munchin is a-gettin on mah nerves."

Billy nimble-footed along behind the wagon, his exuberance limited by the length of his tether. A wolf howled yards away. A thump in the back of the wagon announced Billy's return. He stood rigid among ears of corn and stared into the dark woods. Considering the danger passed, he lay down on top of the corn and rode quietly the rest of the way to Batesville.

A freight train rumbled past a couple of miles east. The St. Louis and Pocahontas Great Northern Line arrived twice each week in Batesville at 10:00 p.m. Another train whistle from the south signaled the arrival of the Great Southern Line, also arriving in Batesville at 10:00 p.m., coming in on another track from San Antonio, Texas. Both engineers parked their trains in Batesville overnight and left in opposite directions the next morning at 8:00 a.m. We knew we were getting close and would be in town by midnight.

In 1875, Batesville, a bustling town of fourteen thousand, had a number of businesses, churches and the Soulesbury College. Mavis and I were interested in the livery stable on the southwest edge of town close to the juncture of Polk Bayou and White River.

Mavis thought Papa's killer took our mules toward the Indian camp to throw suspicion on the Osage, but turned to Batesville and hid them in the livery barn until sold and transported out on one of the river steamers. Mules were valuable, people said more than humans. Bushwhackers often killed travelers, but would not kill horses or mules, if they could help it.

If the mules were in the livery barn, I was sure I could slip them out even in the dark. The mules knew me by sight and smell, and of course, they knew the big horse team and Billy.

We arrived in the north edge of town, as the big clock on a Main Street bank struck twelve-midnight. On a quiet night, I bet you could have heard it gonging for five miles. We did not continue on Main Street though. Mavis pulled the horses into a turn west toward Polk Bayou, to the road paralleling the bayou and dead-ending on the riverbank. The livery barn and corral were in a flat area less than a hundred yards from the river.

The bayou road passed behind the Decker and Statin-owned saloon and billiard hall. Light shone through rear windows of the billiard hall. Voices and the clanking of cue balls, cue sticks and racks filtered out to the road. Miners from Cushman frequented the establishment. They drank St. Louis brewery beer, gambled on billiard games, and threw dice on the tables.

A half-moon overhead bathed the area a golden hue. Mavis pulled the team over to the side of the road behind the barn, in the nightshade of a large oak tree. I jumped down rifle in hand. Billy hit the ground and scampered around. I caught him and removed what remained of the rope from around his neck. Billy had chewed through the rope and had eaten most of it, which Mavis noted.

"Thet danged goat'll eat anythin."

Billy followed me through the corral gate and dashed past me heading for the barn. I do not believe I have ever known a more confident goat. Mavis climbed down out of the wagon and stood outside the fence gate with the double-barreled Greener.

She had thought to bring a coal-oil lantern and some matches, so we could find our way around inside the barn. I did not intend lighting the lantern until I was through the big swinging double doors. Billy scooted past me and on ahead to the rear stalls. I stood in the dark for a moment, listening. We did not think there would be a guard at the barn, but you could never tell who might be in there. A hobo off the train or passenger off the riverboat unable to afford boarding house prices might find the hayloft a cheap place to spend the night.

Movement of animals, heavy breathing, and snorts caught my ear, but I listened for something human, like snoring and coughing. Billy began bleating. I struck a match and lit the lantern, and had the fool scared out of me. Several bats flushed from the rafters and rushed through the hole in the loft with a loud rustle. I flinched. Hair stood up on the back of my neck. I dropped to one knee and cocked my rifle.

Recovering my wits, I held the lantern high. Billy bounced around in front of one of the back stalls. I had found the mules. When I opened the stall gate, the mules walked right out and nuzzled up to Billy. I whispered to them and scratched behind their ears, and like a couple of dogs, they followed me right out of the barn and through the corral gate Mavis held open. Not ten minutes passed from the time we pulled up to the livery barn, until we were heading back out of town up the Batesville Pike, mules and goat tagging along behind the wagon.

The trip home was uneventful. The mules stayed close to the wagon. Billy leaped in and out of the wagon bed like a kangaroo. He would jump up amidst the corn and munch on an ear for a while, jump down and run around the wagon and sometimes out in the woods. The mules would come up to the rear of the wagon, select an ear of corn and eat it along the way. Sometimes one or both of the mules would walk up beside the horse team. Ted and Ned seemed indifferent to the drama playing out around them and plodded on. I am not sure they cared that much for mules.

Daylight broke through a light cloud cover, as we passed the Ulbrick cabin. Lamplight shone through a window. A lantern bobbed toward the barn; Junior Ulbrick heading out to do his chores. Chores awaited me at our place, and I was too tired to think straight.

While crossing the creek, we spotted a horse tied to our front gate.

"I thank thet's Eagle Carter's chestnut," said Mavis.

Sunlight streaked the treetops, the cabin still in morning shade. Eagle sat in a chair on the front porch smoking a pipe. Venturing a salutation, I said, "Yore out awful early, Eagle."

"Yep. See ye got yer mules back. Whar they be?"

Mavis answered, "Batesville livery stables."

"How'd ye know thet?"

"Didn't know zactly, but hit ware a good guess."

"I wist I was a fly on the wall onct whoever put 'em there finds 'em gone. I bet that'd be somethin to hear."

"I spect it'd be somethin all right. What'r ye doin down this a way so early?"

"Got somethin I thank you'ens need to know." I got out of the wagon and pulled open the gate through the split rail fence. Mavis drove the wagon through, mules and goat followed.

"We got to ave some coffee, Eagle. We'll be in soon's we turn these animals loose. Go on in. Stoke up the fire in the kitchen. They's some kindling wood on the back porch. We'll be in dreckly and ye can tell us what ye know."

From the barn lot, Mavis and I went straight to the kitchen. Eagle had stoked the cinders in the fireplace and had thrown in some kindling. It had blazed up nicely. I carried in a few heavier sticks of wood I had cut for the fireplace and placed them on the blaze. The fire felt good in the chill of the early morning. Mavis filled the big black coffee pot with well water, threw in a cup of ground coffee beans, and hung the pot over the fire.

Eagle entered the kitchen. He and I sat down at the kitchen table. I was ready to pass out. All I wanted was a cup of strong coffee. Eagle stayed quiet about the purpose of his visit, while Mavis went about frying slabs of fatback in a Dutch oven. A cedar cupboard stood against the wall beside the fireplace, but unlike Old Mother Hubbard's cupboard, this one was not bare. Mavis took out half a leftover dried apple pie and a covered pan of biscuits. "What is hit, Eagle? Ye hain't nary been here this early a the mornin."

"Mavis ah'm on mah way to Batesville. Ah thought ah'd better stop by. Ah thank ye and Chet may be in mortal danger. Chet probly more'n you."

Mavis poured coffee into three tin cups. I was ready to take my first sip, when Eagle's statement stopped me cold.

"Why Chet, more'n me?" asked Mavis.

"Cause they's people wantin this place. They kilt yer pa and they'll kill agin, but not likely a woman."

"So ye don't thank it were injuns?" asked Mavis.

"Why hell no, it warn't no injuns."

"Well, ah didn't thank so neither, but me and Chet did ride o'er to the injun camp, to satisfy ourselfs bout thet."

Eagle said, "Man or boy gits hisself kilt up here, don't raise much of a fuss, but a woman gits kilt attracts notice of maybe a United States Marshal from Little Rock. Member that time when thet ole boy from Cushman killed Hazel Bush with a rock. Word ain't been out no time with that, when a U.S. Marshall showed up."

"What'd they ever do bout thet?" asked Mavis.

"Hazel's daddy kilt thet boy afore the Marshall ever got to 'im. Anyway, they's a faction in Batesville don't want a U.S. Marshal up here messin round."

"Eagle, ye know more'n yer sayin," said Mavis.

"Well, ah try mindin my own bizness and a killing up here ain't all thet unnatural, but yer daddy was mah friend and ah beleve he were kilt by somebody hired to do it. Ah don't thank it were a chance selection by a bushwhacker. And whoever done it, won't stop there. Somebody wants this place, and ah ain't sure who, but ah kin tell ye this: They was one of them engineers from the Cushman mines up at the tradin post yestiddy, one a 'em thet knows rocks, educated man. He's been walkin round this area. Tells me he's been down the crick behind yer barn. He looked at thet bluff runnin down the other side of the crick."

"Whut's thet got to do with us? Thet's Statin land startin with the bluff," said Mavis.

"Did ye ever notice them streaks of black rock thet runs along the face of thet bluff?

"Yep, seen hit all mah life, so whut?

"Mavis, thet's manganese ore deposits. Thet minin engineer said thet's one of the richest veins he's ever saw, and he's saw a lot. Thet bluff is worth a ton of money. They's minin manganese ore o'er at Cushman and sendin it off on railroad cars to steel mills up north. They make iron and steel out a thet ore and this county is rich with hit."

I was listening, sipping my coffee, my mind still on the statement Eagle made about me being in mortal danger. I recognized the word "mortal" from the Bible. I was not sure what it meant, but thought it had serious implications, and I did not want to be found on the wrong end of it.

Mavis pulled the fatback off the fire, poured the grease drippings into a white ceramic bowl, and set it on the table. She put a tablespoon of coffee grounds into the hot grease and stirred it up to make red eye gravy that we poured over our biscuits. Busy as she was, I could see she was trying to absorb Eagle's comments.

In 1835, Papa acquired a forty-acre homestead, paralleling Cave Creek east to west and parallel to the fifty-foot high bluff across the creek. After acquiring a second forty-acre grant, Papa owned the land on both sides of the Batesville Pike, including the hundred-yard strip of timber, between Cave Creek and the bluff. Locals speculated at one time whether Papa could legally close the Batesville Pike and charge a toll. Some people in the hills did set up tollgates on trails across their property. Hard feelings resulted in a few fights and at least one killing, but Papa never did it.

I did not think Mavis cared about the bluff or its potential riches. She faced too many problems to consider anything but surviving on a hardscrabble farm. I knew what Eagle was getting at and said so. "Thet bluff ain't worth a plug nickel, if they can't git their machines in here to mine it, and they can't git to it unless they come cross our land. Thet's it, ain't it Eagle?"

"Thet's bout hit. They's a deep ravine on the other side a the bluff, as you'ens well know, and thet ravine keeps 'em from comin in from the south. They got to cross yer land, to git to the ore. And, ah'll tell ye fer sartain, ah thank they's bout to come o'er ye."

"O'er me dead body," said Mavis.

"Thet's whut ah mean."

He got up from the table and drained his cup.

"Ah got to be goin. Thanks fer the coffee and biscuit. Ah try to mind my own bizness, but ah'll try to hep iffen I kin. You'ens be keerful."

Eagle left through the front door. In a bit, I heard his horse clicking the shale rock toward the creek. Mavis and I walked out on the south end of the back porch, coffee cups in hand, and watched until Eagle crossed the creek. "Mavis, whut are we gonna do?"

"Chet, ah don't rightly know. Mah mind is muddled right now. Ah'd pray iffen ah thought it'd do any good. Ah tried prayer once or twict like the preacher cautions bout, but it hain't nary did no good. Ah warn't never shore whut ah was supposed to be prayin fer. Ah ast Whistler bout hit, and he said probly the Good Lord didn't ave an ear fer hardscrabble farmers. Anyway, ah'm plumb tuckered out. Ah gotta lay me down a spell. Ye need yer rest too. We'll thank clearer, when we've rested some."

Mavis returned to the kitchen and took a cork-plugged stone jar of mountain mist out of the cupboard. She popped the cork, and we each took a hefty pull. It jarred my innards when it hit bottom but soon produced a soothing result. I got sleepy real quick. Mavis went into her room, did not remove anything but her shoes, and threw herself across her bed rattling the old corn-shuck mattress. I stretched out on the back porch.

Brownie's hammering woke me from a sound sleep. Blinking in the brightness of an overhead sun, I rolled over and looked down the road. Two men on horses crossed the creek. I recognized Deputy Sheriff Kel Decker, and thought I recognized the other horse. As they came up, I realized the other man was the same that had come up with Lazarus Statin. I did not like the way things were playing out.

I went into Mavis's bedroom, shook her awake. I collected my carbine and walked on out to stand in the front door. I leaned my carbine, on full cock, inside the doorframe. After Eagle Carter said what he did about me being in danger, I did not know what to expect and I was not taking any chances.

The two men walked their horses up from the creek crossing to the front gate. The dark man on the roan led the way, as if he was in charge. In mid-to-late thirties, he looked different this day: more dangerous.

On the previous visit, I did not notice his unusual saddle. The pommel was thicker and studier than our local saddles.

The fenders were wide and the wooden stirrups were wide and one piece. He was not wearing a pistol belt when he came up with Mr. Statin, but this time he carried a big blue-steel black-handled revolver on his right hip. The pistol looked shiny new. I could not make out the model, but thought it one of the new Colt .45 caliber Peacemakers. Eagle Carter had a new Peacemaker in a glass case at the trading post. I wanted it bad, but I did not have the thirty-five dollars. I did not have thirty-five cents. I did not even have two pennies to rub together.

Reining up in front of the gate, the dark man pulled his short-crowned black hat from his head and slapped at the dust on his jeans. His hair cut close to his temples was long and black on the crown, giving the appearance of a scalp lock. He had cut his own hair or his barber was drunk. Big ears flattened against his head. A long face culminated with a long round chin. He sported a small thick black moustache cut past the corner of thin lips, and I noted for the first time it covered a harelip. He had round black eyes under a high forehead. The left eye turned in toward the base of a narrow nose. On his last visit, he had sat his horse farther out in the road and let Mr. Statin do the talking and I did not pay attention to his appearance. This time he looked mean as hell up close.

Both riders sat side-by-side looking over the gate at me. Decker wiped sweat from his eyes, and it was not a hot day.

"Is thet yer mules out there in the lot thet ye said got stole?" asked Decker. The words came thick, slurred, tempered by strong drink.

"Thet's them."

Decker seemed a little put out. He twisted in the saddle and looked at the other rider, who continued to stare at me. Decker turned back to me.

"How'd they git here?"

"They walked up to the gate last night, out a the woods. Mules'll do thet. Come home, I mean, on they own."

The two men glanced at one another, not direct, but on the sly, as if they knew what I said was not so. They knew the mules were in the livery barn at Batesville, but did not know how they got out.

My suspicion about the stranger raised questions: What was his interest in the mules? Did he kill Papa and rustle them? Why was he riding with Decker?

My stomach began to knot. I stood in the open doorway and ciphered how quick I could get back inside, if either of the two men made a sudden move for a gun. I should have known better than to go out naked like that, but I still thought a lawman ought to be on our side. I should have known better.

A rustle behind and inside the door caused me to take notice. Mavis stood to the side of a front window with the double-barreled Greener. Deputy Decker must have seen her through the window. He looked away from me and stared into the window.

"Where's yer sister at?"

Mavis stepped by me onto the porch holding the shotgun in her right hand, finger inside the trigger guard, barrels pointing down, external hammers in the cocked position. Both riders saw it. They looked at Mavis and the shotgun, and their eyes indicated an acquisition of mental reservations about committing mischief.

"Spectin trouble, Miss Abbott?" asked Decker.

The other man sat still leaning forward in the saddle, both hands on the pommel. Mavis appraised both riders and took a moment before replying.

"Ah allus spect trouble out here. We hain't got no damn law in this county."

"Oh, ah wouldn't say thet," said the deputy.

"Well, ah damn shore would. Ye find who kilt Papa and stole our mules?"

"Well, yer mules seemed to ave come home."

"Thet they did, but no thanks to you."

I eased back by Mavis and stood inside the door. I reached over with my left hand and picked up my rifle by the barrel, but kept it out of sight behind the door facing.

"Well, we're up here tryin to git a lead on Mr. Abbott's killer. We thank it were injuns. Some of 'em Osage boys'll kill a man o'er a good pair a shoes or a biddle of whiskey."

"Well, Papa's boots were wore out, not good enough to get kilt over. Nary carried no whiskey."

"Are ye and the boy gonna stay here?" asked Decker.

"Tend to, yes," replied Mavis, "but whut bizness is it a yourn?"

"Well, Mr. Neil Crow here," said Decker, nodding toward the other rider, "is lookin fer some land to buy. Thought ye might be interested in sellin, seein's how they ain't nobody left, but you and the boy to farm this here place."

"Well, we aim to stay. Farm's not fer sale," Mavis replied. "And Mr. Crow ought to know thet, cause he was up here two days ago, when I told Lazarus Statin the same thang."

The conversation--what there was of it--pretty much ended on that note. Mavis set her mouth and looked at the two men. The two men looked at Mavis searching for answers to questions not yet asked. Crow broke the silence. "Come on," he said, and sawed the reins backing his horse away from the gate out into the road, keeping his eyes on Mavis. He squinted and stared at Mavis like he did not see well, like he needed glasses, and I hoped he did.

Crow knew he was without protection sitting in the open road, and he did not know Mavis. Maybe he saw what I saw: the knuckles on her right hand had turned white from gripping the shotgun stock. She raised the tip of the barrel.

"We'll go on up to the tradin post, and see if Mr. Carter might have any idears bout anythin," said Decker.

Decker pulled his horse around and followed Crow up the road. I stepped out on the porch with Mavis, not saying anything, watching the two men until they passed from sight around the bend in the road, near the spot where Papa was bushwhacked. Mavis broke a small silence. "Crow hain't no land buyer, and he's bout the ugliest sunavabitch ah ave ever saw. More'n likely the one thet kilt Papa. If ah could've been Christian shore, I'd a shot his ass offen thet horse. And Decker, the lyin' bastard, comin up here, had to ave passed Eagle Carter on the road. He knowed damn well he hain't up at no tradin post."

Mavis lowered the hammers on the shotgun, set it down butt first on the porch and leaned it against the wall. She walked to one of the porch posts, hooked her arm around it and stood looking up the road, not saying anything. I stood back behind her wondering what was going through her mind. Mavis and I were in trouble, but I did not know what to do about it. I hoped she did.

"Nobody's takin this land from us, but they're gonna try. Probly try to kill us. Thet'll take some doin, ah'm thankin. We might not ave a pot to piss in, but by gawd we own eighty acres of prime crick bottomland and thet makes us somebody to deal with."

CHAPTER FIVE

A worried Mavis faced spring planting, and of course she was concerned about my welfare, particularly after Papa's murder, the recent activity around our homestead, and Eagle Carter's statement that I might be in danger. I thought I was old enough to look after myself. It is a tendency of the young and foolish to think such.

She knew Papa kept a running bill at the trading post that he paid on once and awhile, but she did not know where he kept his money. Sooner rather than later, Mavis would have to ask Eagle Carter about our bill, but she was afraid to at the moment, hoping he would not mention it.

Mavis and I finished our late evening chores and sat down to a supper of cornbread and black-eyed peas with a little fatback mixed in--one of my favorite meals. After supper, we went out on the back porch to smoke our corncob pipes and drink the rest of the coffee Mavis had made for supper.

"Chet, Papa must ave stashed a little money sommeres. We've lived here a long time and he sold stuff. Ah know he sold barrels a tobakker and sacks a corn ever year and sometimes other thangs, so whut did he do with the money? He didn't go into Batesville, but once or twict a year, and as fer as ah know, he trusted nary a bank. And sometimes he come up with money, when no one else had any."

I did not answer right away, but I put my mind to work thinking. Thinking was something I did not do on a regular basis, was not much need for it on a hardscrabble farm. Eventually, something came to me.

"Mavis, ye know whut Papa allus said bout the fireplaces. He said when a cabin or house burns usually the fireplace is left standing. Iffen there's money in this cabin, ah bet it's in 'em fireplaces sommeres, but he ought to ave tolt ye whar it's hid."

"Papa allus kept money matters pretty close to the vest. Ah recken he didn't plan on gettin kilt."

We went back into the kitchen, sat down at the kitchen table and faced the fireplace. Papa had built two fireplaces in our cabin. They were a mismatch of stacked slabs of flat shale rock, mortared with a clay-gravel mix, one in the front room and another in the kitchen. The fireplace in the kitchen was a big wide affair. Mavis hung her Dutch ovens on a heavy steel rod that ran across the fireplace and was fastened into the fireplace wall on either side.

Mavis and I sat quiet for a spell thinking. Mavis stood, walked over to the fireplace and pulled at the stones. I caught on right away, and started looking on the other side. I pulled at the shale slabs looking for a loose one. I discovered one, where the side of the fireplace went through the cabin wall. I worked with the stone a bit and pulled it free, revealing a hollowed out space behind it.

"Mavis, look at this."

Mavis brought the coal oil lamp from the kitchen table and held it up to the hollow place. Jammed back aways, a brown leather pouch looked like a dead rat. Our fireplace poker had a hook on the end. I used the poker to fish out the bag. The seamed two-piece rawhide bag sewn with a thin leather string had the top tied with a knotted rawhide tie. I loosened the ties on the bag and dumped several silver coins and a few twenty-dollar gold pieces onto the kitchen table. Mavis whimpered like a small animal. Her hands shook. I thought she was going to drop the lamp. She handed me the lamp, and sat down heavy at the table as if all the air had left her body. I thought she might faint.

"Mavis, ye all right?"

She nodded. I wondered. Tears ran down her cheeks. I looked back into the hole, and pulled out two more leather pouches like the first, chock full of coins of different denominations. I took my time examining the rest of the fireplace, but never found another loose stone. Mavis managed to stand and accompanied me to the fireplace in the front room. In the exact location, as in the kitchen fireplace, next to the wall, another loose stone and behind the stone three more rawhide pouches full of gold and silver coins. In a matter of minutes, we went from abject poverty to a level of moderate wealth.

"Chet, they might be more sommeres, but ah got no idee whar to look. Ah spect most a whut Papa stashed is in these six bags."

"Mavis, ah kin cipher purty good, ye want me to try to count hit?"

"Nah, not right now. Put hit back like we found hit. Hit's sich a blessin knowin we hain't busted. Chet, don't nary say nothin to nobody bout this money."

"Mavis, do ye take me fer a dang fool?"

Mavis put her arm around me and kissed me on the cheek. I was not used to affection from any quarter and was somewhat embarrassed.

"Nah hon, ye hain't no fool, danged or otherwise, ah know thet."

Mavis sat back down at the kitchen table and began to shake like she was chilled. Tears dropped off her nose and splattered on the tabletop. I did not know what to do or say. I put my arm around her, hugged her, and patted her on the shoulder. I often did the same thing with the horses and mules when they were upset and nervous about something. It seemed to work on them. I thought it ought to work on Mavis.

"Whut's wrong Mavis?"

"Ah'm thankin bout them little sacks a coins. Thet's all there is to show fer all these years on this danged place, and Papa and Mama dead on the hill."

Mavis kind of squalled out and jumped up from the table.

"Chet, ah'm gonna make a fresh pot of coffee and a dried apple pie. Ah thank we need to celebrate."

"Whut are we celebratin?"

"Chet, we got nough money to pay off our debt at the trading post and start buildin a grindin mill out there in the creek, and thet's what we'll do."

I was never too keen about staying on the farm, and I always thought I would leave one day and go to St. Louis, or maybe out west somewhere. I knew I wanted out of the hills.

"Mavis, with this money, and whut we could git from sellin this place to the minin people, or even ole man Statin, maybe it's time to thank bout leavin."

"Chet, I can't give up this farm. Hit's all ah know. Hit has kilt my Mama and Papa. I can't jist go off and leave 'em up on thet hill. Ah jist can't."

"Mavis, how we gonna stay? Iffen the Statin bunch wants this place bad enough to kill Papa o'er it, they'll kill us too. Ah don't thank they're gonna let us run a mill up here, specially with the bluff along the creek full of thet iron ore."

"Ah don't rightly know how we'll stay, but ah hain't leavin', and thet's fer damn shore.

I was not ready to concede the debate. I was ready to go somewhere, anywhere, and here was a chance to do it.

"Mavis, they'll pay us good money fer this farm. Maybe we could go off sommeres and start fresh. Maybe St. Louis or maybe we could go find Teddy Blue down in Texas. Ah ain't nary been further than jist a crost the Missouri border, and you hain't been further than Batesville yer whole life. Maybe hit's time to go sommeres and see somethin sides these same damned old hills ever day."

"Chet, don't blackguard. Lookit me. Whut's a woman, run down like me gonna do in St. Louis, or any town fer thet matter? Mah life has allus been here. Hit's all ah know. What am ah gonna do in some town? How am ah gonna git on a train, iffen ah was to have to? Ah hain't nary rid a train."

"Mavis, ah ain't got no answers, but ah know we are gonna ave a rough time stayin here lessen somebody heps us, and ah don't see no prospects a thet."

"I wisht to God, Teddy Blue was here," said Mavis. Ah writ letters to 'im o'er the years and he hain't nary answered even one. Now Papa's dead and ah don't know how to tell 'im. He probly don't even know Henry's dead fer thet matter."

Mavis mentioning our oldest brother, Henry, and next oldest brother, Teddy Blue, in the same breath, to my recollection, seldom occurred. Henry, killed in 1864 over in Tennessee at the battle of Franklin, was fighting on the Rebel side. Teddy Blue ran off to join the Union Army at Little Rock, after the 1862 Pine Hill shootout. A rumor floated around the Cave Creek Community after the war that Teddy Blue had left the Army in Texas and joined the Texas Rangers.

"Maybe Teddy Blue's dead or--"

"Nah, he hain't dead. Ah beleve we'd a knowed hit, iffen he was. Hit's somethin else."

"He can't come back, ah recken. The sheriff'd hang 'im."

"Nah Chet. The sheriff might want to well nough, but ah talked to Eagle Carter, and Eagle said there's a thang called a statue of limits, or some sich thang, a seven years, on a crime. Eagle said they couldn't arrest Teddy fer a crime, which he didn't commit no way. He was jist watchin out fer his friend. The Statin boy started the whole thang, when he stabbed Merle Stroud in the head fer no reason. Hit's pretty common knowledge bout thet."

"Do ye thank he'd let'em arrest 'im, iffen he comes back?"

"Nah. Teddy Blue's different'n the rest a us. He was tempered lack our Grandpappy Abbott. I nary knowed Grandpap Abbott, but Mama said he was mean and evil-tempered. Teddy Blue was allus a little unsettlin. He scart me sometimes. Mama said he was dangerous, and he loved thet old pistol and could outshoot anybody, even Papa, when he was twelve. Ah doubt he's changed much. Nah, nobody'll arrest Teddy Blue. They might kill 'im, but they won't arrest 'im."

Mavis wanted to continue the spring planting. But, truth be known, our newfound wealth allowed us the luxury of surviving a long time without working the fields. Mavis didn't think we should sit idle. She knew if we slacked off, people would get suspicious, and so for appearance sake we had to continue with our normal routine, as if we did not have a dime.

"We'll be sparse with our money and take some time to settle our bill at the tradin post. We'll pay a little a long cause we got to keep tradin with Eagle Carter."

Mavis and I were not about to forget Papa's murder, but sometimes justice calls for patience. Mavis said we would go about making our living. Someone, sooner or later, would let something slip, and we would find who did it. Mavis showed every intention of killing that person if she found him. She was consistent when she set her mind to a task, and it gave us something to look forward to.

Our luck held and took another turn for the better, when a circuit-riding preacher rode into the Cave Creek community on a big blue mule, with a big bible in his saddlebags. The Methodist Church Board sponsored the preacher. He traveled the hills preaching at every church he could find. If he could not find a church, he mounted a stump or a wagon bed and preached the gospel, and it mattered not how many were present, and it did not have to be on a Sunday.

The preacher stopped at our cabin late on a Saturday night intending to preach Sunday morning at the little log church across the road. He asked if he could put his mule in the barn for the night and if he could sleep in the barn loft. Mavis, who leaned toward Christian principles in theory, although not in practice, was accommodating.

"We got a spare room in the cabin, if ye don't mind sleepin in a dead man's bed."

"I've slept in a lot of beds. I suppose people have died in some of 'em."

The preacher, about forty, claimed he did not have one living family member. He and his mule lived on donations of money and food, mostly food, and they slept where they could. I thought being a circuit-riding preacher an admirable occupation and considered it myself. It did not look hard and seemed to beat the devil out of hardscrabble farming or running a gristmill.

The considerable bible study required and the ability to stand before a congregation and lecture impacted my thinking in a negative way. I was never keen on reading anything, and I could not stand before a congregation and lecture on something I knew little or nothing about; although, Whistler Lewis did it all the time. After giving it some serious thought, I discarded the idea.

The preacher took supper with us. Mavis asked him to say the blessing. He did and took so long about it I came very near getting up from the table. I thought if the length of the blessing was any indication, I could not see myself sitting through one of his sermons.

After supper, we went out on the back porch with our coffee and smokes and took to discussing a variety of subjects. The rushing waterfall down at the creek drew the preacher's attention.

"What a good place for a grist mill."

Mavis said, "I been thankin long them lines, but hain't knowed how to begin buildin one, and don't have no idee how to git the mill parts."

"Well," the preacher said, "You remember the '67 flood that washed away five mills on Polk Bayou leaving the single Statin mill a mile north of Batesville"

"I member," replied Mavis. "Christine Pierce and her baby got drownded somehow. Nobody knows. Their bodies ware found two, three miles downstream after the water went down."

"Well, do you know the Wilson family fished out their mill parts? They've got the grinding gears in the barn."

"I knowed the Wilson family lost their mill, yes. Nary thought further on hit."

"I stayed over in the Wilson barn last night. Mr. Wilson said he'd give the parts to anybody who'ed haul 'em off. They's two, three big wagonloads."

I became uncomfortable, when Mavis showed an interest in this revelation.

Mavis and I were acquainted with the Wilson family. Later, I found Mavis knew the Wilson family a lot better than I thought. At one time, the Wilson family attended the little Methodist Church across the road from our cabin. Ludi, the boy, was a little older than Mavis. His sister, Lois, and Mavis were the same age. Lois was once sweet on Teddy Blue, but after the '62 Pine Hill shootout, Teddy Blue left the country, and when it seemed he wouldn't return, or couldn't, she married a fellow living near Cushman on Christmas Day, 1864. A coalmine cave-in killed her husband a year later. She never remarried and people said her mind became detached from reason. In a crowded room, she always seemed to be off somewhere else.

When Mavis was twelve or fourteen, she was sweet on Ludi Wilson for a while. He courted her at dances and church suppers. I heard Mavis say once Ludi danced like a mule among chickens--everybody had better watch their toes.

But Mama Ida died forcing Mavis to take on the responsibility of being the woman of the house and raising me, leaving her little time for courting. Ludi visited her a few times at our cabin, but Mavis never encouraged him, so he sought companionship in another direction.

The Wilson home place, consisting of a four-room log cabin and outbuildings, similar to ours, sat on the west side of Polk Bayou on a knoll fifty yards from the creek. Mavis and I crossed Polk Bayou with team and wagon at a gravel bar. Our Shires were big strong horses and the crossing was not difficult. We made the sixteen-mile roundtrip three days in a row, before hauling away all of the mill machinery.

I enjoyed visiting the Wilson family in their home, especially taking dinner with them. Mrs. Wilson was good about inviting people to her table, and she was an expert in the art of bread baking. Mr. Wilson said if you did not like the smell of fresh bread, you should quit the bakery.

It had been years since I had last seen Lois Wilson, and that was a chance meeting at the Sandtown Trading Post. If I had met her on the road or on the streets of Batesville, I would not have recognized her. Once a little plump, she was now a thin comely girl, not bad to look at, with long brown hair knotted in a bun. She had a pleasant disposition and smelled of lye soap and baking powder. I being shy around people, Lois being detached in mind and spirit severely limited conversation between us.

I thought it must have been lonely for Lois spending most of her waking hours with her parents. I know Mavis was lonely. The two people Mavis talked to most of the time was Papa and me and after Papa's murder, only me. She did talk to the farm animals, especially the mules. She was nice to the mules, but she was bad to cuss the goats, particularly Billy.

Of interest to me, was how Mavis related to Ludi Wilson. They often huddled in a corner and talked in low voices like it was a secret, and Mavis's gray-blue eyes gathered light, and her face flushed.

For the three days we visited the Wilsons, Ludi, a tall rough-handed fellow, wore overalls over a faded blue cotton shirt and an old felt hat that did not do much toward keeping his unkempt blonde hair covered. I mentioned Ludi's penchant for wearing the same clothes every day. Mavis said she thought Ludi, once finding favor in a garment, did not like to give up on it.

Ludi seemed to like me. He talked to me about farming, hunting and such. He always seemed glad to see me and took such an interest in me that I wondered if it was because he did not have anyone to talk to most of the time other than his papa and mama. He sure was not going to get much out of Lois.

The Wilson family liked their tobacco and corn liquor. Mr. Wilson kept his still in the barn. He colored his moonshine with a few drops of iodine and added a little coal oil for flavor. He aged the moonshine in oak casks, giving it a rich mellow flavor. Mavis said it was the smoothest corn whiskey she ever tasted, and I, though inexperienced in the matters of good whiskey, imbibed freely, for the warming effect against the cool late afternoons on the ride back to Cave Creek. Mavis did a lot of singing on the way back home, and sometimes laughed out loud for no apparent reason.

We stored the mill parts in the barn out of the weather and coated all of the metal with wagon wheel grease. Mavis did not know how to begin constructing a mill and stated as much in Mrs. Wilson's presence. Mrs. Wilson had secured the blueprint for their mill in the bottom of an old trunk, and did a good job of it. It took her two days to find it.

Ludi Wilson told us he would help on the mill. He usually worked in the mines at Cushman during the winter, but said he did not care for working a hole in the ground; he would rather be a carpenter outside, even in the dead of winter. Mavis later told me she thought Ludi would work cheap. I did not know how cheap until I came to realize she and Ludi knew something I didn't.

Mavis wanted to keep our intentions quiet.

"Chet, don't say nary a word bout us thankin bout no mill. Ah don't want the Statin bunch or anybody else knowin our plans. Iffen word gits out, ah thank we'd be invitin trouble shore nough."

I got around to ciphering the monetary amount of the gold and silver coins found in the fireplaces and came up with a total of eleven hundred and fifty-one dollars. Mavis took a few coins, and with rifle lying across her lap, rode one of the mules to the Sandtown Trading Post to pay on our bill. She took Eagle and Rachel Carter into her confidence regarding her intention to build a gristmill. Eagle said he had good relations with the owners of the sawmill that was located a mile northeast of the trading post, and he would make sure Mavis obtained the necessary lumber at a reasonable price.

Mavis returned home in good spirits and said we had to get our planting done. She said if we made a good crop of tobacco and corn and sold some of it, we would have more than enough money to begin the mill in the late fall, after the crops were out and stored in the barn. I did not like what I heard. We had always hunted and fished some after harvest, made sorghum molasses and apple cider. What Mavis proposed did not lend itself toward rest and recreation.

Considerable activity had taken place within ten days of Papa's murder and even having found Papa's money, pressure still lay heavily on Mavis. At times, her strong will appeared near the breaking point.

"There's too much goin on. I hain't use to thankin so much."

The pressure never let up. We knew Lazarus Statin wanted our homestead, and we suspected the Statin and Decker clans were behind Papa's killing, and they would not hesitate to kill again to get what they wanted. We needed help, somebody good with a gun.

CHAPTER SIX

Mavis and I were sitting in the kitchen drinking coffee, when Brownie's barking aroused us. Mavis walked into the front room, to one of the front windows. I looked through the other.

"Now whut? said Mavis. "Is thet nother one a them missionary people?"

He was well dressed in dark clothes showing some trail dust on his britches legs and boots. Could be a preacher I thought, except for all the armor, a rifle in the saddle scabbard and two pistols in belt holsters.

Mavis went to the front door, opened it, looked out, and whispered to me. "He hain't a preacher, with all 'em guns. Ah'll go out. Ye stay in here and take holt a the rifle. We are gettin way too much travel up and down this road to suit me."

The rider pulled his horse up in front of the gate, but did not dismount. Mavis stepped out on the front porch. I stood in the doorway behind her. I held my carbine in my right hand, finger on the trigger, thumb on the hammer, muzzle pointing toward the floor. The man called out, "Have you seen several riders pass this way?"

"Nah, nobody but Mr. Ulbrick goin up to the tradin post a little while ago," said Mavis.

"Trading post?"

Mavis pointed. "Sandtown Tradin Post, up Batesville Pike four miles yonder."

"This rocky trail is a pike?"

"Thet's whut they call hit. I didn't name hit. Runs from up in Missouri, through here to Batesville, crost White River all the way to Little Rock, so ah'm tolt. I hain't nary rid hit."

The rider stretched his arms out and placed both hands on the pommel. He arched his back and shoulders.

"A bunch of men robbed a train down in Texas. They're supposed to be coming this way with a couple of Texas Rangers in pursuit. They crossed the Arkansas River at Dardanelle. Thought they might cross the White and move on up into Missouri."

Mavis was not being friendly, I could tell. She did not ask the man to step down off his horse and have a cup of coffee, or even a dipper of water. She was being suspicious.

"You the law?"

"In a manner of speaking," he said, and did not say more, and Mavis did not push it.

His manner of speaking was unusual. Yankee, I thought. His words were clipped, but understandable. He was an educated man, past the fourth grade anyway.

He asked, "You know where the Springfield Road is?"

"No," Mavis replied, because she did not, and I did not either.

I had heard about a road above the Missouri border splitting in two branches, one branch led to St. Louis, the other to Springfield, but I did not know how to get on it.

"You hill people don't know much, do you?" he said, unsmiling.

I was standing behind Mavis. The top of her ears turned red, which meant she was about to give the man a little tempered response. "Ah know one thang mister."

"What's that?"

"Ah hain't the sunuvabitch thet's lost."

The man did not reply for a while. He stared at Mavis; I think he was trying to think of something to say. A hint of a smile creased his face, and he said, "There ain't much between you and fool is there?"

"Nossir," said Mavis, "jist thet fence."

He turned his horse north toward the trading post and called over his shoulder, "Be careful." I guess he wanted to get in the last word.

I walked out on the porch beside Mavis and we watched the rider until he rounded the curve.

"What'n hell do ye thank thet was about?" said Mavis.

Thunderstorms marched in during the night to the beat of thundering drums and chain lightning. Rain followed driven sideways by a hard southwest wind. Next morning, I stood on the back porch looking out on a muddy yard, water standing in puddles, running in rivulets down to the creek. It was too wet to plow, and I was glad.

Midmorning, I was still drinking coffee at the kitchen table and dozing off from time to time. Mavis tried to keep me awake by rattling dishes, pots and pans in a number-three sheetmetal tub half-full of hot water she had heated over the fireplace.

"Chet, hit wouldn't hurt ye a damn bit to grab thet dishrag over there and dry some of these thangs."

I hated housework of any kind, but I got up and picked up an old mangy rag Mavis kept for drying. Jingling, squeaking sounds like harness leather makes on moving horses caught my ear. Mavis heard it too. She walked into the front room wiping her hands on her apron and looked through the window. I could see her through the doorway of the kitchen. She stood wiping her face with the tail of her apron. Her left jaw muscle twitched. "Oh, hell."

"What is it Mavis?"

"Eight riders."

"Eight?"

"Shore as the devil."

I walked up behind Mavis and looked over her shoulder. Eight men on good horses, the men wore yellow slickers and sat side-by-side armed to the teeth. Pistol butts glittered up and down the line. Each of the men wore at least one pistol, most wore two. The stock of a heavy rifle showed from a saddle scabbard riding under the right leg of every rider.

I made a move backward toward the kitchen where our shotgun hung on a deer horn rack over the backdoor.

"No use Chet. They'll kill us fer shore, iffen we try anythin. They got nough guns out there to shoot this cabin all to pieces. Ah don't beleve they mean us no harm. Iffen they did, they wouldn't be settin out there like thet."

"Miss Abbott!"

"They know ye Mavis."

"Seems so. Ah'm goin out. Ye stay put."

Mavis went to the front door, pushed it open and stepped out onto the porch. I moved to stand in the doorway, but I was ready to bolt for the shotgun, if anyone made a suspicious move, but I thought: what good would that do? I tingled all over; my arms rashed up with chill bumps.

"Ah'm Mavis Abbott."

Mavis spoke in a strong voice and it calmed me.

A tall man center of the line spoke up. "We heard you make good biscuits. We wondered if you would make us some. We got all the fixins and would be willing to pay for your trouble."

That voice was not from the hills, not even southern. Yankees, most likely, but the war ended ten years past. What would a bunch of Yankees be doing here? Jay Hawkers? Cattle buyers?

"Whar did ye hear ah make biscuits?"

I thought I noted a hint of pride in her voice, pride of recognition. Mavis never was recognized for much.

"People back down the road a piece. We bought some fresh ham and eggs off them," the tall man replied.

"The Ulbrick family, I guess," said Mavis.

"A big girl came out on the porch, kind of pretty, big nose though," said the tall man.

"Elsa Ulbrick, German family," said Mavis.

"I guess," replied the tall man, "talked funny, not like most people around here."

"The Ulbricks allus liked mah biscuits. Allus et 'em all up at church suppers. Whut ave you'ens got fer fixins?"

The tall man motioned to his right. The man next to him held a burlap bag.

"We got flour, salt. Even got baking powder. Got a big ham and some fresh hen eggs. Don't have any cow's milk though."

The man holding the burlap bag spoke up. "Got some coffee too, Jess."

"Got some coffee too," the tall man echoed.

"Hit'll take a little spell. Ah got goat's milk and butter," said Mavis. She showed no fear, but the palms of my hands were sweating.

"Ye men take yer horses and go round to the barn. Mah brother'll git some corn and oats fer yer animals. Ye kin water yer horses at the crick. If crick water don't suit ye men there's a well round behind. You'ens need to warsh yer hands and clean the mud offen yer boots fore comin in mah kitchen. Ye kin do thet down at the crick. They's a big bar of lye soap or two down there on thet big rock. Hep yerself to hit."

Mavis was always partial to her kitchen over the other parts of the cabin, and she could get right bossy about it.

"Yes mam," said Jess. A sly smile creased his mouth. He turned and looked at the older man to his left. The older man looking down smiled, but did not say anything. Jess turned back to the man holding the burlap bag. "Give her the bag, Bob, and be careful of them hen eggs. Where's the ham?"

A rider, to the left of the line, dismounted and came forward with another burlap bag, holding the ham.

"Come on in," Mavis said, to the man with the ham. She took the bag with the eggs. The man carrying the ham followed her through the front door and looked at me, as he went by. He never said anything, but he took a good look at the shotgun hanging over the kitchen door. He looked back at me and nodded toward the shotgun.

"Greener model?"

"Yep."

"That's a goodun."

The riders passed through the barbed wire gap in the rail fence and filed around the right of the cabin, back to the barn lot. I left the kitchen, as Mavis and the man began laying out the supplies on the table, being very careful with the eggs.

I was out the back door and a few steps toward the barn, when I glanced back over my shoulder. The riders followed in single file. A tingle ran up and down my spine. I was thinking, are you scared? And the same answer kept coming back, damn right, I'm scared.

I opened the lot gate wide. The riders rode their horses through to the long wooden trough in the center of the barnyard. From the grain bin inside the barn, I scooped dried oats into two five-gallon metal buckets. I carried a bucket of oats in each hand and emptied the buckets in the feed trough, and returned to the barn for more.

The men dismounted, not saying much. They hobbled around stiff-legged like they were saddle sore, stretching their backs and massaging the seat of their pants. They removed saddles, but not bridles, and set the saddles on top of the lot fence. One man examined the back of his horse and muttered, "Sores."

I returned to the barn and brought out a can of ointment used for such things and handed it to him. He took the can, smiled, never said a word and started rubbing the ointment into the saddle sores. Another said, "Bob, I need some of thet stuff when yer through."

"For you or the horse?"

"Both."

The man called Jess, said to the older man, "Frank, this looks a lot like our barn, don't it?" "Yeah, it does. I wonder where the idea first come from. Most of these old barns are built the same, Missouri, Kansas, same as here, like they were based on the same pattern: hayloft over stables."

A big heavy-set man walked up to Frank and Jess. He, too, studied the barn. "The idea must have come from the old country, Germans probably. I don't think the Scots and Irish even had barns. Kept their animals in the house with 'em. What mama said."

Ted and Ned smelled company and clopped around the corner of the barn.

"Good Lord, what are them things?" said Jess.

"They're Shires, Scottish horses," I said.

"God Almighty," said Frank. "They look like they could pull trees up by the roots."

Several of the men came up, circled the big horses, patting them. I heard one say, "A team of these were at the fairgrounds in Kansas City some years back."

Jess stepped away, where he could see the road in both directions. He turned back to the group milling around the Shires.

"Cole, get a couple of men out on the road, one about fifty-yards up the road and another down where the creek crosses. I don't want no surprises."

Cole turned toward the men over by the lot fence. He pointed the way he wanted them to go and said, "Jim, take a rifle and go down to the creek. Clell, you go up yonder a-ways. "

The two men turned to their saddles hanging on the fence, pulled rifles from the scabbards and walked around the cabin toward the road. Cole called out to them, "We'll take care of your horses and get you fed, when Miss Abbott gets it done."

I filled a couple of large metal buckets with ears of corn from the corncrib and dumped them in the feed trough with the oats. Jess looked at the corn, walked over and picked up an ear with large yellow square kernels. He studied it for a moment.

"You folks grow some good looking corn here."

For some reason, I became more cautious of my manners.
"Yessir, in the crick bottom," I said, pointing east up the creek.

The men's horses were in good shape, but showed signs of hard riding. They were all colors: bays, buckskins and blacks, no two alike, all heavy built with thick chests, looked like they could travel long distances. They were hungry and pushed up to the feed trough. I made several more trips to the barn and corncrib.

Most of the men stood around or leaned against the lot fence smoking cigars. One took a small silver snuff can out of a saddlebag and sniffed some of the powdered tobacco up his nose. He stifled a sneeze and put a pinch of snuff inside his lip. I had never seen anyone sniff tobacco up his nose. He caught me staring and smiled.

"Bub, you want to try a snort?"

"Nossir, don't beleve ah do."

He laughed. "Clear your head, I bet."

Conversation was sparse. I would liked to have heard more. The men seemed content to sit and rest against the fence. After letting the horses feed a spell, they caught up the reins and led them through the lot gate, and down to the creek.

Each man held his horse's reins; some held two. The horses seemed to enjoy the sweet water. All the horse-holders sat down on the rocky creek bank, beside their horses, removed boots and socks and dangled their bare feet in the cold, spring-fed, creek. I watched as they massaged their feet and splashed water on their faces.

None removed side arms. I was curious about what they were packing and eased around trying to see if I could identify the pistols. The man called Bob looked a lot like the one called Cole and carried two Walker .44s. Jess packed a Navy Colt .36, as did Frank. The other men favored the Navy Colt .36, an older model pistol, but reliable. The one called Charley carried what I thought was a new model silver-plated, ivory handled, .45 caliber Colt Peacemaker in a black leather holster. I had to know.

"Colt Forty-five?"

"You got it."

I guess he recognized the hunger in my eyes.

"Wanna see it?"

"Well, I--"

He was sitting flat on the ground with his feet in the creek. I did not see his hand move, but the pistol came out as if by magic, flipped in the air. He caught it by the barrel and held it out to me butt first. That pistol was a work of art, the most beautiful thing I had ever seen.

"I'd let ye shoot it, but I don't think we ought to make a lot of noise, do you?"

"Nossir, ah guess not." But I wanted to shoot that pistol awful bad.

I picked up bits and pieces of conversation, but could not figure out who they were or their business, and I was not about to ask. I kept thinking about the man who rode by the day before, and I thought these men must be the Texas train-robbing bunch the man was looking for. I wondered what a man by himself planned to do, once he caught up to this bunch. Probably like old Brownie, when he was a pup, always wanting to catch a skunk, until he did and ended up with stink all over him. He smelled bad a long time, but he was the wiser for it.

Mavis came out on the back porch and called for everyone to come in. We had a wooden bench in the kitchen and enough chairs to seat everyone around our large oak-planked kitchen table. Jess sat down and studied the burn marks and scars on the tabletop. The surface boards, snug fitting when new, over time, had dried out from the kitchen heat. The boards warped and shrunk leaving gaps big enough for knives and forks to fall through. Mavis set the table with solid-white ceramic plates, and actual silverware, which surprised me, because we never used it. Even when the preacher visited, we always ate off tin ware or pewter.

"Lots of history on this old table, Miss Abbott."

"Yep, mah papa made the table afore ah was borned, and the plates, cups and silverware belonged to mah Grandma Abbott and was left to me when she passed."

"Your folks living?"

"No, both buried up yonder on the hill," said Mavis, and nodded toward the hill northeast of the cabin.

"Pass natural?"

"Mama died a somethin--we hain't shore whut--and Papa was kilt jist up the road couple weeks past."

"Killed? How?"

"Bushwhacked."

"Who killed 'im?" asked Frank.

"Don't know yit, but ah got my suspects," replied Mavis.

"Damn shame. They got a law here?"

"They got a law sich as it is, but they don't favor us none."

"Any particular reason?" asked Jess.

"The sheriff is related to a family thet wants our land, and mah older brother kilt the sheriff's cousin many years ago, when the war started up."

"Where's your brother at?" asked Frank.

"Gone to Texas fer as ah know. We hain't seen nor heerd a him in o'er ten years now," replied Mavis.

Mavis tended four Dutch ovens hanging in the fireplace. She opened the lid to one, and the smell of fresh baked biscuits rolled out across the kitchen.

"That smell is something I've been missing, Miss Abbott. It's enough to bring tears to my tired old eyes," said Jess.

The men made exclamations of approval, as Mavis dumped out a large pan of biscuits onto a cooling pan and set the pan in the middle of the table following that with bowls of goat butter, muscadine jelly and blackberry jam.

"Ye men go ahead and start. Ah'll git the rest out dreckly," said Mavis.

I stood by the window near the stove and watched the men, as they passed around the butter bowl. Each forked a biscuit out of the pan, knifed it open, and layered in slabs of goat butter.

"My God, this is good," said Jess. "Goat butter huh. I've eaten it, but don't remember it being this good."

No one else spoke for a while. The clatter of silverware striking ceramic, the sight and smell of butter, fruit jams and a jelly applied to hot smoking biscuits by a large number of armed men sitting around our kitchen table is unforgettable.

Mavis opened a shallow Dutch oven and dumped fried eggs and ham onto a large white ceramic platter. She scrambled a dozen eggs and set them out on another platter. Next came a large bowl of fried potatoes and two water buckets of boiling strong black coffee. She walked around the table pouring coffee into thick white ceramic mugs. The men murmured among themselves, marveling at the feast before them. After pouring the coffee, Mavis walked over and looked out the window.

"How bout them fellers in the road?"

"We'll relieve 'em once we've eaten, and let 'em come in," said Frank.

"You folks seem to be kind of out of the way," said Jess. "Did you have any problems doing the war?"

"Not too much," said Mavis. "One night a party of armed men rode up to where the Crislers lived, a mile or so back up the crick. They kilt Mr. Crisler in his dooryard. Me and Papa heerd the shooting and was still out on the back porch thankin we might need to go up there and see bout it, when we saw Miss Rose Ness, sister to Mrs. Crisler, come runnin round the barn. She was cryin and yellin all at the same time, like to have scart me to death. 'He's shot all to pieces Austin.' I remember her saying."

"She ast Papa to go hep take keer a the body. Ah went with Papa. The body was tore up purty bad. Mrs. Crisler was fainted in the floor. Ah first thought she was shot too. We got her up, but she warn't much help and went to bed. Papa, Miss Ness and me carried Mr. Crisler into the cabin and dressed 'im the best we could."

"Those times must have been hard for you," said Bob.

"Yeh," Mavis replied, "Ye couldn't trust nobody. People ye knowed all yer life come to church meetins, and made ye thank they was angels, but after the war broke out, they'd be changed into robbers and would steal and take anythin they could git holt of. Papa's own cousin and his cousin's black freedman walked five miles down here in the middle a the night and stole taters outta our barn. Papa discovered the taters missin and found tracks. He knew who twas and tracked 'em home. Meant to kill his cousin, and ah guess the freedman too. When he walked up the lane to his cousin's cabin, he got attacked by his cousin's bear dog. He kilt the dog, turned round and come home, said he had lost the element a surprise. We nary had no more taters stole after thet."

I thought Mavis enjoyed being the center of attention, and her talkative mood concerned me.

"Nother time, four men rid up on both sides a this cabin whilst we set right at this table takin supper, and they started shootin through the kitchen winders. They proved to be bad shots. The damage bein one ball hit a water pitcher and a piece of the pitcher hit Papa in the chest. He first thought a bullet hit 'im, but he jumped up and run to the door there and took down thet old double-barrel .10 gauge loaded with buckshot.

He emptied one barrel through each side winder. Two men went down. The other two rid off in a hurry. Ah run and took holt a the rifle we kep hangin o'er the front door, but there warn't no need to use hit. Both men was shot dead. We buried 'em out behind the barn. Cept fer a few run-ins with the Statin family o'er hogs runnin wild and gettin in our corn patch, they hain't been much trouble lately, til somebody shot Papa."

"God Almighty," said Bob.

"Some story, Miss Abbott," said Jess, "Sounds like you've known your share of trouble."

I was fascinated with Mavis's stories. I had heard them before of course, but awhile past, and I liked the way she told them. I began to think Mavis might be capable of most anything.

"You'ens afeered a somethin? Puttin men out in the road like thet." Mavis asked straight out. She knew who those men were, but she played innocent. I was standing next to the stove sipping a cup of coffee and looked for a reaction, but everyone remained noncommittal and kept eating, except Jess.

"We're strangers in a strange land, Miss Abbott. It pays to be careful."

"Ah suppose yer right bout thet. You'ens come up thru Batesville."

"Nah," replied Bob. "We waded the river west a here at a sand bar."

"Ah hain't nary been crost White River."

"You ain't?" said Bob, surprised at Mavis's statement.

"Nope. I hain't been much a nowhere."

"We been down to Texas," said Jess, though bites of hot ham and eggs. "Been buying Texas cattle, and now we're on our way home to Missouri."

"Whar's the cattle?"

I cut her a hard look, not liking her asking so many questions, but Mavis was enjoying herself.

"The cattle are on a train, or was. Probably in the Kansas City stockyards by now," said Frank.

"You'ens live in Kansas City?"

I kept thinking, God will she just shut up.

"Nah," replied Frank, "We're farmers mostly. We have farms like this one between Kansas City and Springfield. The farms don't make us a living, so sometimes we have to find some way to supplement our income. Cattle-buying is one way to do it."

I picked up a biscuit and knifed in a slab of goat butter, ate my buttered biscuit and sipped my coffee, while looking through the window at the man in the road north of the cabin. The man paced back and forth his rifle ready. I got to thinking about the smart-assed fellow from the day before, and how I would like to have seen him come riding up in his fine suit of clothes. I wondered what he would do. I chuckled to myself, when I thought he would probably have a strong urge to jump up on a stump and start preaching.

The table conversation slacked for a moment. The clink of cookware and utensils seemed louder than usual. Mavis broke the silence," Ah hain't nary rid no train."

Jess eased back from the table.

"Miss Abbott, I've been in some fine hotels in Kansas City and Chicago, but I don't reckon I've ever had a better meal than this."

Mavis looked a bit embarrassed at the compliment. She dropped her head and caught up her apron and wiped her hands. "Well, hit was the best ah could do on sich short notice."

Frank stood and pushed back his chair.

"Well," he said, "It's the best anybody could do."

Frank motioned to one of the men sitting at the table. I judged him a bit older than I.

"Jim, come on with me. We'll go relieve them boys in the road."

As Frank started away from the table, he paused, reached in his pocket, pulled out a shiny new twenty-dollar gold piece, and laid it in the middle of the table, right next to the ham and egg platter.

"Boys," said Frank, as he passed through the kitchen door, "It's always proper to tip the waitress after such a meal as this."

The clatter of hooves striking shale rock faded up the Batesville Pike. I watched from the kitchen window until the riders passed from sight around the curve.

"Well, they gone."

Mavis sat staring at the kitchen table. I thought she was in a trance. Soiled ceramic plates, eating utensils and ceramic coffee mugs covered the table. A small mound of coins glistened in the center. I moved over to take a look.

"That's quite a bit a money Mavis. I see three gold pieces and the rest looks like silver dollars."

"Chet, ah don't know whut business them fellers is in, but ah don't beleve they's cattle buyers."

"Nope."

"Well, all ah know is, we got nough money here along with whut we got out a the fireplaces, to give us a good start on buildin a grindin mill. Maybe my prayers worked after all, but the results ware jist slow comin in."

CHAPTER SEVEN

    Sunday evening I sat on our front porch mending harness. I enjoyed working with my hands and I liked the smell of oiled leather. Brownie limped around the corner of the cabin, hammered a time or two and went to the front gate. Billy danced around the cabin and joined Brownie to see what was going on. A rider on a big bay stallion crossed the creek. As a matter of habit, I picked up the carbine lying next to my chair and laid it across my lap. I kept working the harness but never took my eyes off the rider.

    He sat the saddle different than most. Homesteaders tended to slump humpbacked in the saddle, but this man rode sitting straight up. He rode easy, like sitting in a rocking chair. The bay came up, head bobbing, shod hooves clicking shale rock. The horse did not pay attention to me on the porch or Brownie at the front gate, but his head went up, ears slanted forward, and he turned his head toward the barn, when he saw our horses. I heard a nicker from the barn lot.

    The rider reined in at the front gate and sat tall and terrible in the saddle. Black hair close-cropped with light sideburns. He had a sunburned complexion, a square face with strong chin featuring a wisp of black whiskers. Dark eyes squinted in the sun.

    His dress was unlike anything I had ever seen in the hill country. A black leather vest over a long-sleeved faded blue shirt with the cuffs unbuttoned and rolled up, hands encased in light tan calfskin gloves. A black felt hat with short brim and a short round crown sat square on his head; the crown featured a single black star on the left side, the black band tied on the left side with a shiny black bow--a Texas hat. He had tucked the cuffs of his black denim trousers into calf-high, black, round-toed boots with a medium heel, and no spurs.

    He held the reins in his left hand. His right hand hung loose near a .44 Remington pistol with blue-black finish and walnut grips, holster hanging from a black gun belt inlaid with silver Mexican Conchos the size of silver dollars. A narrow black leather belt, no more than an inch wide, that had a tiny silver buckle, fastened the holster to his right leg. The holster, cut low in front, exposed the hammer, making it easy to pull and cock--a fast draw holster--a gunfighter's rig.

A second cartridge belt, looped over his left shoulder with a holster hanging under his left arm, held another Remington .44 revolver, silver-plated with pearl handles. A heavy caliber lever-action rifle, in a tooled leather scabbard, rode tight under his right leg. I had never seen such a magnificent apparition and will never forget it.

Brownie continued to hammer away. The bay tossed its head, snorted and pranced a little. Billy stood up on back legs with front feet on top of the rail fence and looked at horse and rider and bleated a couple of times. The stranger looked at the goat and smiled. His piercing black eyes measured me.

"Chester, ah don't beleve ah evah saw a watch goat afore."

The stranger knew my name, but nobody ever called me Chester.

"Chet. Don't keer much fer Chester."

"Never keered much fer Chester neither. Wondered why they named ye thet. Like Chet though."

I sat dumbfounded, tongue-tied. The stranger looked like someone I ought to know, and it hit me: He was an Abbott. I was face-to-face with a legend, a man-killer at seventeen, who left the county running from the law and went on to fight in the war, mustering out somewhere in Texas. I was looking at my brother, Teddy Blue.

I sat for a moment trying to regain my wits. I jumped up and knocked my chair over with a clatter. I stepped back through the front door, choked with emotion, calling for Mavis. Papa returning from the dead would not have had a greater result. Mavis came to the door, paused a moment, stepped out on the porch, holding a dishrag in her left hand. She stood staring, not saying a word. Her right hand felt for her face and two fingers touched the corner of her mouth.

"Mavis, ye've turned into a handsome woman."

Mavis's right hand shook. She dropped it from her mouth, caught the end of the dishrag she held in her left hand and began twisting it like she was wringing something out.

"Thet's a cold comfort to me now. Ye shore taken yer sweet time a comin home. How come ye nary answered even one a mah letters?"

"Mavis, I didn't git any letters from ye."

Mavis started to break. Tears showed in the corners of her eyes. She blinked tears down her cheeks. She walked over and sat down in one of the two old cane-bottom chairs we always kept out on the porch. She looked across the fence at Teddy Blue.

"Ah don't know how the mail works. Ah give letters o'er the years to Eagle. He said he'd mail 'em, but ah heerd nary more bout hit. Ah didn't know whut else to do. Ah'm dumb as a fence post bout sich thangs."

She dropped her head in her hands that lay open on her bony knees. Her shoulders heaved a little, and she cried for a spell. I could not tell if she was glad, sad or mad. Mavis was hard to read that way.

She recovered quickly, stood and wiped at her eyes. Teddy Blue sat not saying anything. His eyes wandered over the cabin. He turned and studied the falls at the creek for a moment, twisted in the saddle and looked at the little log church across the road. He removed the cartridge belt with holstered pistol looped over his left shoulder and hung it over the saddle horn, dismounted and walked through the gate, across the yard, stepped up on the porch and hugged Mavis close. She laid her head on his shoulder. I could see her face contorted like she was in pain. Teddy Blue caressed her hair still did not say anything. His eyes moistened a bit, and mine did too, truth be known. Mavis seemed to come out of a trance. She pushed away.

"Hit's time to git supper."

Teddy Blue turned and looked up at me. "Damn Chet. Yer tall as a Kansas sunflower. They ain't no Abbotts ah ever knowed was tall as you. Ye must be a throwback."

We went into the front room, where Teddy Blue and I lingered, while Mavis passed on back to the kitchen. Teddy Blue went over to a table by the front window and picked up a coal oil lamp. He removed the globe, turned the wick up, struck a match on his belt buckle and lit the lamp.

"Is this Mama's lamp? Seems like ah member it."

"Hain't the same one, but one like hit," Mavis replied, from the kitchen door. "Mama's lamp got busted, but ah found one like hit up at the tradin post."

"Tradin post. Eagle Carter still up there?"

I was staring at Teddy Blue, awestruck and speechless, but did manage to squeeze a word out. "Yep," I offered.

"Still married to thet purty squaw?"

"Yep. Fat now."

"Happens."

Teddy Blue looked around the cabin. He had been gone thirteen years, but the cabin and its contents had changed little. Mama Ida's old spinning wheel stood off in one corner of the front room seldom used. Mavis would try, on occasion, to card some wool, but she did not have enough patience, or time, to use a spinning wheel. Mama Ida's old rocking chair was still in use, except it showed some repair work, where Papa had tied it together with baling wire. An old cedar chifforobe, over a hundred-years old, stood in one corner. You could still detect the musty cedar odor. Most all our best clothes hung in it. Else, they hung on nails, backs of chairs and bedposts. There was an old tintype in a round frame of Mama and Papa. The tintype hung on the front wall near the window, the tintype made inside a hardware store in Batesville in 1860. A fellow came down from St. Louis on a river steamer and set up shop in the store. Word got up country a man in Batesville was making pictures of people. Papa talked Mama Ida into riding to town in a wagon and sitting for the now yellowed black and white portrait. The photographer sat Papa in a chair and had

Mama stand beside him with her hand on his shoulder. I thought it should have been the opposite. I do not know what Papa paid for it. I hope it wasn't much.

Teddy Blue took the tintype down, held it in the light coming through the window and studied it for a moment. Years of toil and sickness showed in Mama Ida's face. She died within six months of having that photograph made.

Teddy Blue raised his voice so Mavis could hear from the kitchen.

"Mavis I know bout Pa's murder. Word come in a telegram from Cushman. Not clear who sent it, but somebody knew or suspected ah was with the Rangers in Texas, Eagle most likely. Ah spect people in Batesville ave been stoppin yer letters gettin to me. Papa's murder is part of the reason ah'm here."

"Do ye know bout Henry dyin in the war?" asked Mavis.

"Yeah, I know bout Henry. I seen his gravestone in a Confederate graveyard o'er at Franklin, Tennessee. John Bell Hood got mad at his boys cause they had General Schofield trapped south of Nashville and let him git away. Hood punished 'em by makin 'em charge crost an open field ginst fixed breastworks backed up ginst a little river south a Franklin. They ort to ave hung the sunuvabitch."

"Franklin, Tennessee," I said. "Ah allus thought he was kilt at a place they called Shiloh Church."

"Nah. He was wounded there, but went on to fight some more. Was kilt at Franklin."

While Mavis fixed supper, Teddy Blue and I went outside. He walked his horse around back, removed the saddle and put it on the back porch, took the bay down to the barn and turned him loose in the lot. I scooped oats and corn into the horse trough. The little gray mule team and the Shires came out of their stalls and joined the big bay. The bay seemed to get along with the rest of the stock. When Billy jumped up in the middle of the horse trough, it seemed to unsettle the bay a bit, but he nudged Billy aside and kept after the corn and oats.

Teddy looked around at the sagging weather-beaten log buildings, the cabin, barn, corncrib and outhouse. He looked up the hill, northeast of the barn at the little family graveyard, the white picket fence sparkled in the late afternoon sun, but he didn't say anything about it. He looked all around.

"Ah missed these hills, the smell a cedar and pine in the cool a the day, all the greenery. They ain't nothin like this in Texas."

"Ain't they got hills in Texas?" I asked

"Not in places ah was. It's all flat, sunburned and dead. Many a time, ah thought a thet waterfall o'er there in the crick."

Mavis came out on the back porch and called us to supper. Mavis had made Mormon Johnny Cake, a pan of biscuits, fried some fatback, scrambled some eggs and made a big pot of coffee.

"Mavis this is the first time I've et Johnny Cake since ah left here. Ye make it like Mama did. I plumb fergot how good it tis."

After supper, Teddy Blue went out on the back porch, to where he had stashed his saddle against the back wall of the kitchen. He took a box of little cigars out of one saddlebag. He called them cigarillos. He came back in the kitchen and passed the cigarillo box to Mavis and me. We sat around the kitchen table drinking coffee spiked with mountain mist and smoked cigarillos. Mavis took a pull or two on her cigar.

"This is strong tobakker. Whar do they grow hit?"

"South Texas--Mexico."

"Ah guess hit takes some gettin use to. Ourn is milder."

"Well, Papa allus did make fine cigars," said Teddy Blue, "They ain't got any near as good in Texas."

Papa always made good flavorful cigars and blocks of chewing tobacco from each year's tobacco crop. Papa made cigars. He cut and rolled tobacco leaves into a six-inch-long roll, after he smeared the leaves with a mixture of sorghum molasses, cinnamon and cloves. Many in the community favored his cigars and chewing tobacco.

I felt good sitting with my brother and sister, smoking and drinking coffee. Mavis ruined it. "Teddy, I thank ye could do with a haircut and a bath. Ye too, Chet."

"Well, ye got a tub?" asked Teddy Blue.

"Ah was thankin more'n in line with the crick as the best place. Ah can cut yer hair with my scissors. Lord knows ah practiced nough on Papa and Chet."

"Ain't thet crick water awful cold. Ah ain't used to no cold water. They ain't got cold water in Texas."

"Teddy, hit ain't so bad," I said. "Jump in the blue hole with a bar a lye soap. A few scrubs and yer done."

"Well, maybe. But, ah'm thankin more long the lines a tub a hot water on the back porch."

Teddy Blue got around to why he was in Independence County.

"You'ens seen a bunch of men pass by?"

"Yep, they was here, eight a 'em," I replied.

"Here?"

"Right here at this table. Mavis made biscuits fer em."

"When?"

"Day afore yestiddy. They was on they way to Missouri. Said they was cattle buyers."

"Cattle buyers mah granny's ass, thet was Jesse James and his brother, Frank, and the Younger brothers. I don't know who else. They robbed a train down in Texas and kilt a guard. Well actually, ah don't thank they laid a hand on 'im. Ah thank he died a fright. Another Ranger and myself ave been after 'em fer the past month. Mah partner come down with a fever, left him in Fort Smith. Afore I left Fort Smith, I telegraphed the Pinkerton Detective Agency in Springfield. They was supposed to try to block 'em. Ah guess they didn't."

"Some fancy dressed feller was here the day afore they showed up," I said. "We thought he was a preacher at first. He didn't say exactly whut he was, but somethin like the law. He didn't know where they was, and he didn't know where he was. Last time we saw him he was goin up the road toward the tradin post."

"One man?"

"At's all."

"One man ain't nough to stop thet bunch. They'd kill 'im. They already kilt several of the Pinkertons."

"Teddy, ye hain't but one," said Mavis.

"Yeah, but ah cover all the ground ah stand on."

Teddy Blue stayed the night in Papa's room and left early the next morning.

"Ah'm gonna ride o'er to the Cushman minin camp, and use their telegraph to send word to the Pinkerton Agency in Springfield. Tell 'em the James bunch is in their territory sommeres. Ah'll be back soon's ah kin. Ah'll stay a spell and hep on this place. Ah'm tard a Texas and tard a fightin injuns. Ah'd like to be a farmer a spell. And by the way, don't tell nobody ah'm here. Word'll git round soon nough. They won't be no legal trouble with Decker. The Sharp County Sheriff nary brought charges agin me. He nary did like none a 'em Deckers nor Statins no way. Oh, the Statins might try somethin onct they know ah'm here, but they's a cowardly bunch."

At noon, the day Teddy Blue rode north up the Batesville Pike, I was in from the field for my dinner and was sitting at the kitchen table, when Brownie announced the arrival of visitors. Mavis looked out the kitchen window. I turned around and looked at Mavis. From the way her jaw twitched, I decided to take a look for myself. Lazarus Statin was back again, Neil Crow with him.

"Whut the hell are they doin back up here?"

"Don't know Chet, but ah expect Statin's gonna keep after us about this place. You stay in here. Get the shotgun and watch out the winder. If thet Crow so much as touches a gun, ye got my permission to shred 'im."

She walked through the front room and out onto the front porch. I took the ten gauge down from the antler rack over the kitchen door, checked the buckshot loads and eased up beside the open front window. I stayed out of sight, but peeped around the sash and watched Crow.

Crow, armed like the day he came up with Deputy Kel Decker, no longer made any pretense of being a land buyer. He was nothing but a hired killer pure and simple. He sat his roan in front of the gate. Mr. Statin pulled up parallel to the rail fence and talked across the fence without getting out of his buggy.

"This old cabin looks like it's bout to fall down."

"Well, hit's been here a while, ah guess. Hit's gettin a little swaybacked, and hit's been patched and boogered up, but hit'll do."

"How'd ye like a new whitewashed clapboard house in town, rather'n this ole broken down log contraption?"

"Wouldn't. What'd ye want up, Mr. Statin? Ye ain't come all the way from Batesville fer nothin."

"Ah want to buy this place, Miss Abbott. Make ye a fair offer."

"I told ye last time ye was here this place hain't fer sale. Hit warn't fer sale yestiddy. Hit's not fer sale today, and it hain't gonna be fer sale tomorra."

Statin stared at Mavis for a moment collecting his argument.

"Ye and yer brother could move into town. Ah'd git ye in a nice house and you'ens could git jobs."

"Now what in hell would ah do in town?"

"Well, ye could cook in one of them cafes or take in laundry, ironing, thet sort of thang. The boy could work at the blacksmith or livery barn. You'ens'ud do all right."

Mavis was an impertinent woman, when she wanted to be. "Shoot, we already doin all thet right here. Don't need to move into town to cook, wash and iron and take keer a bunch a damn animals."

The old man smiled. "Yore a sassy woman, Miss Abbott. Ah admire tough sassy women. My wife ain't. She wants to go back to Illinois, whar she was borned. Ah got tard a her naggin and showed her a road map a the way home. Told her to shut up or hit the road. Ain't heerd much outta her since."

A breeze ruffled through the tops of the pines down at the creek. A mockingbird shashayed around the house from some unknown outpost and landed on the gate. It said something to Crow's roan. The roan nodded.

Statin was thinking of another angle. I knew Mavis wasn't going to budge from her position, but I was hoping she would. I liked the idea of moving off that farm into town. I liked the thought of working in a livery barn.

"How ye gonna keep this rundown place up, jist ye and the boy, and ye jist a wisp of a girl?"

"Mr. Statin, ah quit bein a girl a long time ago, and mah brother makes a good hand. Anyway, ah'm makin rangements fer a hired hand."

There, she threw it out, but she needed to be careful. She did not want to reveal Teddy Blue was home. Old man Statin did not know. He would find out soon enough.

"Who'd come up here and work on this place?"

Mavis did not hesitate. "One a Chief George's boys said he would."

"A injun, workin on a farm?"

Neil Crow stared through the window to Mavis's left. I was not showing myself, and I think he was uncomfortable sitting in the open and not knowing where I was or my mindset, and my mindset was not good. Mavis and I were being crowded, and I did not like it. Crow tugged at the reins and started backing his horse out in the road. The horse bowed his neck, pranced a little and danced around facing south.

"We might as well go. They's nother day," said Crow, low like.

Statin did not answer Crow or look his way. He was used to getting his way and did not like taking no for an answer. He kept looking at Mavis as if he was having a hard time accepting the fact she would be able to hire someone to help work our farm.

"Ye can't make expenses on this farm, let alone pay taxes and hard hep, specially iffen ye ave one bad crop. Ah'll end up gettin this farm fer the tax bill."

"Well, hit looks like ah'd better pray fer fair weather," said Mavis.

Statin stared at Mavis for a moment. A smile creased his lips enough to expose yellowed coffee and tobacco-stained teeth. He picked up the reins, pulled to the left and flicked them over the horse's back, putting the Tennessee Walker into a turn. Crow was half way to the creek. Statin looked back at Mavis. "Ye'd better pray fer somethin more'n fair weather, Miss Abbott, somethin more."

Crow pulled his horse up in the middle of the creek, where it crossed the road, and let Statin catch up. Statin pulled the buggy up beside Crow's horse. They dropped the reins and let the horses drink in the knee-deep water, talked in low tones not loud enough to carry up the hill. Statin pointed up stream toward the falls high up along the bluff on the other side of the creek, looking at the black veins of manganese ore. Mavis and I went inside and watched them through the kitchen window until they passed on across the creek and from view in the timber beyond.

"Chet, thet Crow is a killer iffen ever ah saw one, and he's the back-shootin kind. We got to watch ourselves."

Teddy Blue did not return from Cushman that night. It concerned me, and I believe Mavis was worried. We tried not to make much of it next morning at breakfast. Cushman was fourteen miles west over a rough wagon road. There were creeks to cross, including Polk Bayou. We did not know what he was going to do in Cushman. Something could have happened.

After breakfast, I took our big horses to the field and plowed bottomland along the creek. The moon was right for planting tobacco. Mavis and I had already agreed to plant our customary acre. An acre does not sound like much, but tobacco takes a lot of care, and one acre was all two people could handle along with everything else.

Our most important crops were corn and wheat and those crops would take up most of our cleared land. We needed the grain for the stock for one thing, but this year would be different since Mavis planned building a grinding mill after harvest. We would not have to load our grain on the wagon and haul it to the Statin mill at Batesville, or Cave City. Cave City was twelve or so miles northeast, about the same distance as Batesville, but the road to Cave City was difficult at best, in late fall and winter. This year we could store grain in the barn and grind it during the winter months in our own mill.

We planned to continue Papa's practice of making sorghum molasses. Sugar cane did well in the sandy soil along the creek at the east end of our homestead. Papa developed a reputation for making fine clear molasses. I knew the secret was in the cooking of the cane juice and I wanted to continue making the clear light syrup we sold to Eagle Carter and a few of the local homesteaders. Abbott molasses was so popular Eagle could not keep it on hand at the trading post.

When I drove Ned and Ted in from the field at noon, I unharnessed them in the lot and shoveled corn and oats in their feed trough. I always fed and watered my animals before I fed myself. After the horses ate and began to show signs of restlessness, I knew they wanted water. I drove them out of the lot and down to the creek. Mavis called from the back porch, "Chet, whut's wrong with thet goat?"

I followed her gaze. On the far side of the creek, Billy charged out of the woods like hornets were after him. He splashed across the creek, right between the two horses, and made for the cabin. I walked over to intercept him. The little goat danced up bleating at me and flicking his tail. "Billy, ave ye gone crazy?"

I hugged Billy around the neck and pulled him against my legs. Tremors coursed across his rib cage. Mavis came down off the porch. She did not care much for the goat, but this time she showed concern.

"He acts like he's scart pert near to death. Thet looks like blood on his lag. Wonder iffen he's been snake bit."

I got down on my knees and examined Billy. He struggled and bucked, but I wrestled him to the ground and sat on him. Mavis and I looked him over and could not detect any wounds. I turned him loose. He bleated, made for the creek, jumped in, bucked across, and ran back into the woods. "Maybe a painter," said Mavis.

I understood her concern, because the same thing crossed my mind. I had mentioned earlier finding fresh tracks of a big cat along the sandy banks of the creek, a quarter-mile behind the barn.

Panthers passed down the creek through our homestead on occasion. I had heard stories at the trading post about a panther traveling Polk Bayou late at night and screaming like a woman. The big cats occasionally killed deer and cattle, particularly young calves, and they liked goat best of all. "Ah don't thank hit's a painter," I said. "Billy wouldn't be a goin back out there."

"Well, ah guess yore right, but he's shore actin strange. Whar's Brownie? Ah hain't seen nor heerd 'im since early mornin."

Brownie missing at dinner time was unusual. His location at mealtime was at the kitchen door waiting for a biscuit.

"Ah heerd 'im trailin crost the crick middle a the mornin. And thet's nother reason ah don't thank hit's a painter. Brownie wouldn't be in 'em woods, after gettin tore up so bad last time."

One morning, a few months past, we found Brownie torn and bleeding, an ear missing, lying in the back yard almost disemboweled, near death. He was too weak to offer resistance, when Mavis packed his entrails back into his belly, took a large needle and heavy thread and sewed together a gaping wound ripped open by heavy claws, the classic work of a panther. Brownie recovered after hovering near death for a week. If a panther was on the wind, Brownie stayed under the back porch. Brownie was no coward, but he was no fool, either.

Mavis walked down to the barn lot fence and angled over toward the creek. She cupped her hands to her mouth. "Here Brownie, Brownie here."

She stopped, listened, and called again. She turned back to the cabin. You could not tell about dogs. Brownie might be over the hill somewhere trailing a deer. As Mavis walked back to the Cabin, Billy bleated from across the creek. He ran out of the woods and upon the creek bank did a little dance and dashed back into the woods.

"Well, whut in the world. Chet, take yer gun over there and see whut thet goat is tryin to tell us."

My Remington carbine leaned against a barn lot gatepost. I had begun carrying the carbine, while working the field, in a leather rifle scabbard tied to a plow handle. I picked up the rifle, checked my loads, rolled up my britches legs, and waded barefoot across the creek.

I followed Billy into the woods on a well-worn game trail. The rest of the goatherd browsed along the edge of the woods indifferent to what was taking place around them. I looked the herd over. Two old billies, two nanny milk goats and a motley assortment of others were eating through a briarpatch.

Billy usually stayed close to Brownie and shunned the other goats. I questioned if Billy thought his status as honorary dog, which Brownie seemed to have conferred on him, justified an importance above his more common stable mates, or if he was confused as to what breed of animal he belonged. Some days he thought he was a dog, some days a mule.

The heavy arboreal canopy shut out the noonday sun making it difficult spotting Billy in the deep shade. I called his name. A bleat answered from near the bluff. Billy stood near the base of the bluff looking at something on the ground. I walked along a path and almost stepped on Brownie's head. It scared me so my legs gave way and I fell to my knees.

Brownie's head lay in the middle of the path, eyes wide open. Billy came over and nuzzled up to me. I gathered myself, got to my feet and investigated the scene. Buzzing green flies alerted me to Brownie's body lying a few feet away on top of a log. Bloody chop marks on top of the log indicated Brownie's killer used an axe or hatchet.

I examined the crisscrossing game trails looking for sign. The large swarm of green flies indicated Brownie had been killed several hours earlier. Mavis called. I did not answer, but I knew I was not going to accomplish anything worthwhile. I was not going to find a clue in that brush. I left Brownie where he lay and walked back through the woods, waded the creek with tears in my eyes and on toward the back porch, where Mavis waited.

"Whut's wrong Chet?"

"Brownie's dead."

"Dead. How?"

"Head cut off."

"Whut in hell."

"Somebody's taken a choppin axe to 'im."

I began to get mad. I blinked back tears of rage. My hands shook. My voice broke. Mavis did not say another word. She turned away and entered the kitchen. I stepped upon the porch and went over to the washbasin sitting on a shelf attached to the back wall. I splashed cold water on my hot tears and dried my face with a ratty old hand towel. I entered the kitchen.

"Set down Chet and eat. Ye'll feel better."

Hell of a thing to say. Eating does not make you feel better about somebody killing your dog.

"Ah ain't nary gonna feel better bout somebody killin old Brownie."

We sat at the table, neither speaking for some time. I drank some coffee and picked at my food. Mavis picked at her food and stared at the wall. She remained quiet considering her temperament and what had happened.

"Chet, we got to thank this out. Brownie was kilt fer a reason. He was a good watchdog and somebody don't want 'im watchin this place. Ah beleve somebody is gonna be coming fer us. We gonna ave to watch ourselves. Don't dare go outside thout a gun on ye, and keep yer eyes on them woods crost the crick."

"Mavis, hit ain't Christian to say sich, but iffen ah find who kilt Brownie, ah aim to make him pay and ah don't rightly know how nor to whut length."

"Well, a dog's a dog and a killin's a killin, and hit don't rightly matter animal or sich, but ye hain't gonna ave to worry none bout hit, iffen ah git to 'im first."

"Before ah go back to the field, ah'm gonna take a shovel and go bury Brownie. Flies already after 'im."

"Well yes, thet's the proper thang to do and tonight, iffen Teddy Blue don't git back, we are gonna sleep on pallets on the front and back porches with our guns. Ah hain't takin no chanct a us gettin slipped up on in the dark."

After I buried Brownie in the woods, I returned to the field. I stumbled along behind the plow, crying some, blowing snot, not thinking straight, not thinking at all. I should have been alert.

Sundown caught me five-hundred yards east of the barn and near the creek. I looked into the setting sun yet again. Laminear bands of color bled out under hammered clouds. A violet color hooded the earth. I unhitched the trace chains from the single trees. The thirsty Shires didn't waste any time heading for the creek.

I took my time and let the horses walk on ahead, while I loosened the leather ties securing my rifle scabbard to the plow handle. That done, I turned to look at the woods across the creek, already darkened by late evening shadows. Dog tired and sick in spirit, I stood a minute and listened for Brownie running in the woods across the creek, but I knew I had heard him for the last time. Standing there, a feeling came over me that I had known all my life. Trouble was close at hand. Not that I was going to get into it. Just that it was there.

The horses snorted, stopped in their tracks, threw their heads up ears forward. They saved my life. Without thinking, I dropped flat behind the heavy doubled-winged plow. A heavy rifle boomed in the woods. The slug notched the left wooden plow handle a foot above my head, zinging past like an angry bee.

The doubleshovel plows a deep furrow and throws dirt in opposite directions. When I unhitched the horses, I had pulled the plow out of the furrow and left it sitting upright. The top curved edges of the steel wings were two feet above ground providing adequate protection from a head-on shot. The plowed furrow behind the plow allowed some protection but not much. I knew if the shooter moved laterally left or right, he could hit me in the body or legs. I knotted up behind the plow.

I had never been a target for someone trying to kill me, and I do not know why, but I was cool as a cucumber. Another bullet pinged off the plow. He had the range. I am sure he thought I had a gun, but I thought I had better give him a reminder, in case he thought to charge me across the creek. I stuck my rifle over the plow and fired twice into the woods.

The smell of the shooter's horse had warned the Shires and had caused them to stop before getting to the creek. They stood side-by-side, as if still in harness, and looked into the woods. They seemed oblivious to the bullets zinging by. They halted in a position that blocked my view of the shooter's position. I figured the shooter sitting his saddle had a height advantage and could see me, but I could not see him. It was just a matter of time, before he made a lateral move for a better shot.

When Mavis entered the fray, relief spread over me like a warm blanket. She opened, from the barn lot, with her Henry, firing five times, in as many heartbeats. She could not see the shooter, but she followed the Shire's line of vision and knew the shooter's approximate location. Bullets zinged through the timber. I peeked up over the plow in time to see one of her shots cut a good-sized limb off a pine tree. I expect the shooter and his horse got a little nervous when that limb crashed down.

I looked toward the barn. Here came Mavis, barefoot, across the plowed ground, firing on the run, hair flying, that old gray dress flapping. Following another shot from the woods, I heard an awful groan. I raised my head over the plow and saw Ned go to his knees. The son-of-a-bitch was killing the horses. Another shot and Ted dropped without a sound. I stood up mad as hell and started shooting over the fallen horses into the woods. I did not give a damn about myself anymore. My vision turned dark red. I got a glimpse of a horse moving through the timber and I opened on it. I wanted that horse down and the shooter afoot. My bullets cut limbs and zinged ricochets, but if I hit that horse, I could not tell it.

Mavis and I got to those big beautiful horses at the same time, Mavis cussing and crying. I was crying and cussing. I picked out a place in the timber where I thought the horse and rider might be, if he went east down the creek. I fired three times, as fast as I could lever a shell.

"Chet don't waste yer shells. He's gone. He's done his damn sorry bizness."

Mavis was down on her knees with her hand on Ned's poor head. Ned had a bullet hole above the right eye, and Ted had taken a bullet in the forehead. Those big black horses lay like mounds of coal, dead on a plowed field. The sight haunts me yet.

I was so choked up I could not speak. Mavis gained control of her emotions after a spell, and I heard her say, "We'll find the sunavabitch thet did this, and when we do ah intend killin 'im slow."

Darkness had settled over the land by the time Mavis and I walked to the barn. I looked for Teddy Blue's horse, but it was not there. I saw Mavis look too, but she did not say a word, as we walked around the barn lot into the back yard. She stepped upon the back porch and went into the kitchen.

I went over to the wash rack on the back porch, where we kept a bucket of water. I dippered water into an old tin washpan. My hands shook so badly I could hardly wash them. I toweled off and walked in the kitchen. Mavis was working with something in a Dutch oven. I noticed she was wiping tears. We did not pass a word between us. I picked up my corncob pipe and a small cloth sack of shredded tobacco off the kitchen fireplace mantel and went out to sit on the front porch steps, have a smoke and settle my nerves.

Whippoorwills called from across the road over near the creek. A fox yipped back in the woods. An owl hooted off in the distance. Crickets and cicadas chirped. I caught movement out of the corner of my eye. A doe and twin fawns crossed the road on the other side of the creek. The deer trotted past the waterfall and disappeared into the woods. Billy appeared around the corner of the cabin. He ambled over to the front gate and in a poor imitation of a dog, bleated a couple of times. The little gray goat looked up and down the road and looked at me. Looking a little lost, he flicked his tail, and headed for the barn. Billy could not understand the loss of Brownie, his friend and mentor. I was as bad off as the goat. I wondered what Billy was going to think, when he did not find the big horses in the lot.

Shod hooves ringing on shale rock jarred me out of my thoughts. I would be lying, if I said I was not happy to see Teddy Blue bringing the big bay in at a walk.

"Give up on me?" Teddy Blue asked, as he came up to the front gate. "Ah got a late start outta Cushman."

"Well, ah was beginnin to wonder," I said, trying to keep the relief out of my voice.

Mavis came out on the porch. I thought she might say something about Brownie and the dead horses, but she put it off. Anyway, Teddy Blue could not have done anything about it. She never asked Teddy Blue where he had been or anything, but I could tell by her actions that she was relieved to have him home. Neither of us wanted to lose him anytime soon.

"Teddy, supper's bout ready. Put yer horse up and come on in."

She still did not say anything about the horses and dog. I wondered if she expected me to.

Teddy Blue had tied two large burlap bags across the pommel of his saddle. He fiddled with some leather ties, separated the bags and dismounted with a bag in each hand. I was naturally curious about the bags, but Teddy carried them in the cabin without a word.

I took the bay through the gap in the fence and down to the lot, unsaddled and fed him. I walked to the back of the barn lot and looked down in the field, but it was too dark to see the dead horses. I walked back to the cabin, my mind in a muddled state.

Mavis dished up tin plates of fried potatoes, fatback and cornbread and poured tin cups of black coffee. Discussion around the table quickly got around to Papa's murder, and the killing of Brownie and the horses. Teddy Blue sat quietly eating and sipping coffee and did not say anything or change expression. Mavis said something though. "We got Statin and Decker problems. Ole man Statin was here agin today."

"Lazarus Statin, here? Hell, ah thought thet ole bastard would be dead by now. What'd he want?"

"Wants to buy this place," replied Mavis. "Wants hit bad, I kin tell. Had a hard lookin man with him named Crow."

"Neil Crow?"

"Yep, thet's him. He's the one rode up here with Kel Decker day after Papa was kilt, and now he's been up here twict with ole man Statin."

"Ah knowed Crow in Texas," said Teddy Blue. "Ah chaste 'im fer a spell. Ah wondered whar he went. He's a dangerous man. You'ens be keerful round him. Mavis, he won't thank twict bout killin a woman. Ye didn't say anythin bout me bein home did ye?"

"Not a word," I said.

"Well, we'll jist let it be our little sur-prise."

We sat quiet, eating our supper, lost in thought. My thoughts turned to Brownie and the horse team. A tear or two welled up. Mavis was thinking along another line.

"Grandpa Abbott started hit years ago. He was mean, Mama said, and he didn't take nothin off nobody. Allus into it with the law. Papa, hisself, had some run-ins up at the tradin post a time or two o'er thet thang, Teddy, ye got into back in '62'.

Papa got into drink heavy after Mama passed. He got mean, when he was drunk. He'd come home and take his ailin out on Chet and me. Ah thank what ailed 'im more'n anythin was he missed Mama. He used the razor strop on me a time or two fer no reason. Whupped me like a rented mule and me tryin to do the best ah could and even tried to whup Chet with hit, and Chet jist a baby.

Ah taken his meanness fer a spell. Ah was fourteen, near fifteen, he come in one day drunk and started on me and ah couldn't stand hit no more. Ah hit 'im with an axe handle and knocked im offen the back porch. Ah left 'im laid out'n the yard o'er night. Early summer, weather warm. He was a changed man after thet.

He'd eat whut ah put on the table afore 'im and hain't made no nasty comments bout my cookin, and he nary agin tried to tell me how to do my work. He hain't been a bother to me or Chet since. But, he busted his share a heads. He had enemies all right. Hit shocked me he got kilt, but it warn't no surprise neither."

"Drink'll do thet to a person. Make 'em onery I mean. Seen a lot of thet in Texas, specially the mex and injuns. Mex and injuns bad to drink."

I felt like I needed to jump in and make my contribution about Papa.

"Papa was funny in some ways though. A feller come up here one day ridin in a one-horse buggy. Was from thet country o'er the ocean: England. Talked funny. Caught a riverboat from Cincinnati, up in Ohio, down to Batesville. Had some time on his hands, he said, so he rented a buggy at the Batesville livery barn and come up this road. Stopped out there at the gate. Papa, jist in from the field, was on the front porch, smokin a cigar and drinkin outta his jug. The man asked Papa iffen his master was at home. Papa looked hard at 'im fer a spell and said, 'the sunuvabitch ain't been borned yit.'"

Teddy Blue chuckled. "Thet sounds like Papa. Ye couldn't make nothin off 'im."

"He did have friends though," said Mavis. "He had his siders since his two sons went off to war, one on either side. Hit set real well with a lot a people round here thet Henry got kilt in Tennessee. Papa was held up high round here a spell o'er thet. Teddy, ye was his favert. Ye know thet?"

"Nah, didn't know hit. Ah loved 'im. So did we all. Ye couldn't not. Thet was all there was to it."

"They's plenty a union people up in this country" said Mavis. "They liked the fact, Teddy, ye was on they side. Ah thank thet was part a what started Papa drinkin heavy. He couldn't make up his mind, who was right."

We stopped talking and sat thinking and sipping coffee. Occasionally, Teddy Blue reached over to the dish of Mormon Johnny Cake and pinched off a little piece.

"Say somethin bout the mill, Mavis," I said. I was hoping Teddy Blue would be against it.

"Whut mill?" asked Teddy Blue.

"The Statins want this place real bad," said Mavis. "They want it so's they can crost o'er to the bluff and git at them ore deposits, but ah also thank they want to build a grindin' mill out there in the creek, whar them falls are, cause they hain't no grindin' mill left up in this part of the county. But they hain't goin to do it, cause ah'm gonna do it. Papa got the idee to build a mill up here. Ah thank he was waitin til he got nough money together. He'd go out to the crick at night, sit on thet rock o'er the blue hole and stare at the falls fer hours smokin and thankin. He first started gettin real nervous bout it, when Polk Bayou flooded in '67, and washed away a half-dozen mills and nobody built back. Ah thank he was near havin nough money to do hit."

Mavis paused, sipped some coffee and stared across the kitchen at the wall of warped and gapped pine boards, nailed over a framework of pine logs. I could see she was gathering her thoughts for another outburst. Teddy and I could not get a word in edgewise. I never knew of Mavis talking so much at one time. Her words turned hard. I detected more bitterness than usual.

"Maybe iffen it works out, Chet and me won't ave to work this damn crick bottom no more. We kin live offen the mill profits and rent this farm out to the Ulbrick's or somebody. We'uns'll be millers and live like human beins fer a change."

I stole a glance at Teddy Blue, but he never gave a sign for or against or said anything, and I never said anything, but my ears sure perked up, when Mavis mentioned renting the place out. I never cared much for the idea of building a grinding mill, but if it meant not having to work our old hardscrabble homestead anymore, I was all for it.

"Ye mentioned something about ore in thet bluff crost the crick," said Teddy Blue.

"Say somethin bout the minin people, Mavis," I said.

"Whut minin people?" asked Teddy Blue.

"Ye tell 'im Chet. Ye know more bout hit than me."

Teddy Blue looked at me. I took another sip of black coffee and began to collect my thoughts. I was sorry I mentioned it. I never cared a lot for talking and was not very good at explaining things.

"Well?" said Teddy Blue.

"Eagle Carter said a man from Cushman, knows somethin bout minin, was down here lookin at thet bluff crost the crick. The man tole Eagle the bluff is full a manganese iron ore. Says hit's a real rich vein."

"Thet's whut they mine over to Cushman. Makin steel out a hit up north. Is it the same stuff?"

"Same."

"That bluff's on Statin land, or was," said Teddy Blue.

"Still is," I said. "But, they can't git crost the ravine from the south side with heavy minin quipment."

The conversation ceased on that note. Mavis began clearing away the table. Teddy Blue and I sat drinking coffee and staring off into space. Teddy Blue broke the silence. "We're gonna ave to burn 'em horses tomorra. Hit'll be a damn mess down in the field, iffen we don't.

Teddy Blue got around to telling about meeting a Pinkerton Detective Agent at Cushman. The agent and he checked out a lead on the direction the James Gang took after crossing into Missouri. He guided the Pinkerton man to the Missouri border, and returned to Cushman and telegraphed the Pinkerton Agency in Springfield, Missouri, informing them what he knew of the James Gang's direction of travel, and that their agent was heading north.

"Ah don't ave no authority in Missouri and ah'm tard a chasin 'em men. They didn't git a lot off thet Texas train anyway, a few bags a coins."

I looked at Mavis cleaning a pot and could see the side of her face. A little smile picked at the corner of her mouth, but she did not say anything.

"Chet, ah hate to hear bout yer dog, and 'em horses," said Teddy Blue. "Ah beleve thet was the finest team a horses ah ave ever saw. We'll replace 'em with mules. They's a big mule barn o'er at Cushman. They use a lot a mules o'er there to work the mines. As fer dogs: they must be five hunnert dogs tween here and Cushman. Ah was barked at all crost thet country. We'll git nother one or two. You allus need a good huntin dog and watch dog round a place. Ah know why the horses was kilt, but whut concerns me more is why the dog was kilt."

Mavis cut in. "Hit wouldn't surprise me none iffen we don't ave some night visitors soon, like tonight. They know we hain't got no watchdog now, but they probly don't know we've already found Brownie. They gonna come quick afore they thank we'll miss Brownie and know somethins up. Ah'd already planned fer me and Chet to lay out on the porches tonight."

"Mavis, thet's good thankin," said Teddy Blue, "but first let's git some thangs outta the way. Chet, go in the bedroom and brang them two sacks a stuff ah brought in."

Mavis cleared the kitchen table. She placed the tin plates, cups, eating utensils, and greasy bread pan in a small tub of hot water heating over the fireplace coals. "Let 'em soak a spell."

She always boiled out the Dutch Ovens that by filling them with water and bringing the water to a boil with a bit of lye soap thrown in. She would later rinse everything out in the back yard with cold well water.

I brought the burlap sacks, one in each hand, and carried them into the kitchen. Teddy placed them on the floor at his feet. He took a pocketknife and cut the tie strings on one sack, pulled clothing from the bag and placed it piecemeal on the table. He reached out to me with a pair of heavy jeans and a black leather belt with *genuine cowhide* stamped on the inside. Next, he handed me two long-sleeve blue shirts and a pair of black leather boots and a felt hat.

"Well, ah hopen thet fits. Yer kind a skinny. Ah guessed the size. Maybe Mavis can alter 'em, need be."

"Lord won't ye look like somethin in church," Mavis said, with a little giggle. "Elsa'll be tryin to snuggle up close, ye kin bet on hit."

Teddy Blue smiled. I felt myself blushing and blurted, "Ah don't give a hoot-n-hell bout Elsa Ulbrick."

"Germans?" asked Teddy Blue.

"German family down the road bout a mile," said Mavis.

"Big German girl'll keep ye warm in the wintertime," said Teddy Blue, eyes twinkling.

I quit paying attention to the ribbing about Elsa. I was too busy trying on my new boots. Teddy Blue picked up cuts of colored cloth and a strip of fine lace and two pretty dresses. One dress was light green and the other black. Mavis did not break down, but she came close. She ran her hands over the cuts of cloth and a tear or two trickled down her cheeks. She dabbed at her eyes.

"Ah jist sware, ah don't know whut's wrong with me."

Teddy Blue picked up a pair of women's black high-top shoes, with laces, and several pairs of gray cotton stockings.

"Teddy, whut ave ye done? This musta cost a purty penny. Ah got clothes to ware. Me and Mama ware the same size, but these dresses, oh my."

Teddy took a small stack of clothes for himself. Heavy denim jeans like the ones he gave me, blue cotton shirts, and a new pair of tanned leather brogan shoes.

"Ah can't be a Arkansas farmer in Texas boots."

He picked up the other sack from the floor and I heard metallic clinks, as he chunked down five boxes of .44 caliber pistol shells on the table. The he pulled out a dyed-black leather cartridge belt with matching holster and handed it to me. I did not think I could speak so I held my tongue. I ran my fingers over the new leather, held the rig up to my nose and smelled it. I felt hot tears well up in the corner of my eyes, but I hid them pretty well by turning back to working with my boots.

I finally pulled my boots on. They fit snug. I walked around the kitchen, into the front room and back, stretching my toes, trying to work out the stiffness of the leather. I had been wearing Papa's old shoes, but I outgrew Papa in height and shoe size, and found it necessary to cut holes in the toe of the shoes for a little wiggle room. I came back to the kitchen table. Mavis was not saying much. The new clothes mesmerized her. She held the soft dress cloth up to her face and softly rubbed it against her cheek and made little murmuring sounds, like the purring of an old cat. I sat down, picked up a box of shells and began studying the writing on the side.

"Can you read it?" asked Teddy Blue.

"Some. I know hit's .44 caliber and Remington."

Teddy Blue pulled a cardboard box out of the sack and it clunked when he set it on the table. The box held a Remington black metal .44-caliber revolver with mother-of-pearl handles. The big gun glistened in the light of the coal oil lamp.

"This is fer you Chet. After everythin thet's appened round here, ah spect ye better start wearin this on a reglar basis. The Deckers and Statins won't hesitate to kill, iffen they think it'd shorten the time fer 'em to git they hands on this place. Ah spect the cowardly bastards hired Crow to do they killin fer 'em."

Mavis sat quiet, watching and listening, a look of contentment showing in her eyes. She stood and scraped back her chair. She never said anything, as she gathered both hands full of her new things and walked into her bedroom. She reappeared shortly with a lit coal oil lamp. She set the lamp in the middle of the kitchen table with the kitchen lamp and turned down the wicks until both lamps went out leaving only light from the dying embers in the kitchen fireplace.

"We better git ready," she said. "Probly gonna be a long night, and I thank a starm is brewin in the southwest. Ah feel rain in mah bones. Ah ache all over."

"Ah'm goin to the barn," said Teddy Blue, "git in the loft. Ah kin watch the barn, and from the loft see the rear and both sides a the cabin."

Mavis was over her weak spell. She started getting bossy again.

"Chet, ye go to the front porch and watch the road, but ah spect iffen they come, they'll come through the gap in the hills east, and up through the field behind the barn. Ah'll take the back porch. Thet way I kin watch the back a the cabin and both sides a the barn.

I stood, strapped on my new gun belt, took the Remington .44, opened the breach and started loading the chambers from one of the ammunition boxes on the table. Mavis went to her bedroom and came back with her seventeen-shot Henry .44 caliber rifle. She picked up another box of shells and began loading the magazine.

"Whut do ye thank they'll try to do?" I asked.

"Most natural thang," said Teddy Blue, "is fer 'em to try to burn us out, and kill the animals and us too, iffen they git a chanct. They won't come fer a while though. They gonna be a full moon tonight. They'll come in the moonlight, probly after midnight, so they won't need torches."

I got my thirteen-shot Remington .44 carbine off the antler rack we had nailed up over the front door. I made double sure I filled the magazine and levered a shell into the firing chamber. I eased the hammer down off full cock and laid the carbine on the kitchen table.

I had holstered the big Remington .44 pistol. I pulled it, cocked the hammer and spun the six-shot cylinder. I loved hearing the metallic clicks. I lowered the hammer on an empty chamber. Between the pistol and the rifle, I had eighteen shots. Surely, I could hit something with that many.

Teddy Blue sat off to the side of the fireplace, sipping coffee from a tin cup and watched the cool detached way Mavis and I handled our firearms. All Abbotts knew how to handle guns. Papa always made sure we had plenty of guns and ammunition on the place, and we all knew how to shoot. Mavis, many a time, sat in a cane-bottomed chair on the back porch, with a .22 caliber rifle and off-handed, without a rest, shoot dried seeds from the limbs of the peach tree standing to the left of the barn fifty yards away. She embarrassed me. She seldom missed, while I counted myself lucky to hit three out of five.

Mavis won two turkey shoots at the Sandtown Trading Post, when she was sixteen and again at seventeen years old, shooting against all comers. By 1875, she was not shooting much, because shells were expensive and we did not have money to burn on target practice. There were a few times when she walked down to the creek with her Henry rifle and stood on the big rock hanging over the blue hole and shot pine cones off the trees across the creek. Her hand was steady when it came to shooting without a rest or a brace, steady as anyone I ever saw including Teddy Blue.

"Chet, iffen shootin starts out back, don't come through the cabin and out the back door. They'll be lookin fer thet. Come round the north side of the cabin and stay in the shadows. Make yer way o'er to the corncrib and git inside. You too, Mavis. At least, ah'll know whar ye are. Anythin else movin out there, ah'll drop."

Mavis got up from the table and in the dark walked back to her bedroom. She came right back with a quilt and a pillow, picked up her rifle off the kitchen table and walked out on the back porch. I poured myself a fresh cup of coffee and followed her out. Teddy came out behind me, rifle in hand. He stepped off the porch and headed for the barn. The moon peeped at us from over the barn. Teddy Blue wore two side arms, the left-hand pistol butt forward--a spare. He could shoot with either hand, but he shot right-handed when in a hurry. He disappeared inside the barn like a heavily armed ghost.

Mavis fixed her pallet on the porch next to the back wall of the kitchen. Even in bright moonlight, she was nearly invisible in the porch roof shade to anyone approaching the cabin from the barn. She lay down, stretched out, head on pillow, rifle beside her. I heard her fingers drumming cadence on the rifle stock. Far off to the southwest, thunder rumbled low. A cool breeze wafted over the falls carrying the promise of rain. I thought Mavis's bones must have been right. I was not expecting Mavis to say anything.

"Ah wonder whut hit might be lack to dress up and go to a dance."

I did not know what to say, because I had never once gone to a dance and was not sure how one went about it. I doubted she wanted my opinion anyway.

"Ah hain't been to a dance in a long spell, at least since ah was twelve or thirteen. Ludi taken me once or twict afore Mama died."

I could see the new clothes caused her to remember and put her in a talkative mood, notwithstanding we might be attacked any minute. I sat down on the end of the porch next to her, my legs dangling.

"Mavis, whut appened with ye and Ludi?"

"Mama died is whut appened. Ah didn't ave the time and spirit fer courtin after thet."

I knew Ludi had married a young girl from over near Cushman in 1864, and his wife lived only one year. Some people said Ludi never got over it.

"Ye ever meet Ludi's wife?" I asked

"Nah, nary did. Died afore ah got the chanct."

"Whut kilt her Mavis?"

"Nobody knows fer shore, but her stone o'er in the graveyard at Lee's Chapel has *died of consumption* chiseled on it. They allus write *consumption* on the marker iffen they don't know whut else to put."

"At's a awful big word fer a grave marker."

"I know it."

The rising full moon yellow creamed the barn and landscape. The ghostly black mulberry tree sheltering the gravestones up on the hill at our little family graveyard stood like a silent round sentinel. Moonlight was good enough so I could make out Mama Ida's white granite marker, the one on the right. My Uncle Lester and Aunt Eunice's markers were on the north side of the crest out of sight. Papa's grave marker was a dirty flat sandstone rock. I planned chiseling some dates on it and finally got around to it several months later. Some years later, I bought a single white granite marker for Mama and Papa from a funeral home.

I wanted another cup of coffee. Mavis had quit talking and was breathing heavy. I thought she was asleep, so I got up and tiptoed across the porch and into the kitchen. I thought I would go out and check the front, and go back and wake Mavis. I hated to. I knew she was tired.

I eased through the darkened cabin up to one of the two front windows. The little log church was clearly visible across the road. I wondered about the possibility of someone setting an ambush from inside the church. If they did, it would probably be the last one they ever set.

Copperhead snakes denned under the floorboards, some big around as my arm. I imagined the copperheads had already come up through the cracks in the floor and were crawling around the pews. A field mouse that wandered into that church never left.

I tried to get my mind on something besides church mice and copperheads. I thought about Brownie murdered and buried across the creek and became agitated. I eased back through the cabin onto the back porch.

"Mavis."

"Ah hear ye," she whispered. "Be still. Somethin is movin on the hill. Maybe foxes. Maybe somethin else."

I walked over to the edge of the porch, but never stepped out of the shadow of the porch roof. I looked up the hill. Something was flitting about among the stones. Foxes. A pair often played on the hill at night and slipped down around the barn looking for a rabbit, possum, or a big rat.

Mavis sat up on her pallet, her back against the kitchen wall. She picked up her rifle, brought her knees up, put the stock to her shoulder, and laid the rifle across one knee. She sighted in on one of the foxes. I knew she was not about to shoot a fox. She was practicing lining her front and rear sights on a target, in the moonlight; a practice I did many a time hunting at night.

I sipped my coffee and watched the foxes scampering around the graveyard. Both, clearly visible in the moonlight, came out in the open, on the brow of the hill and sat on their haunches side-by-side. They showed interest in something behind the barn and commenced high-pitched yipping.

"Mavis, 'em foxes see somethin."

"Could be a cat, bear, or anythin," said Mavis.

"Reckon Teddy Blue knows it?"

"Probly, but he's up in the loft, and ah can't see 'im, so don't know."

"Mavis, recken whut we ort to do?"

"Don't go off the back porch in the moonlight. Go back through the cabin and up the road aways, maybe fifty yards, and turn up the hill."

I remembered Teddy Blue's instructions.

"Teddy Blue said fer us to go to the corncrib."

"They's been a change a plans," said Mavis. "Listen to me now. Stay in the shadows all ye kin. Go up to the graveyard, so ye kin see down behind the barn. Ah'll stay here so's ah kin watch both sides a the barn. Hurry up, hit's gonna git dark purty soon. A thunderhead is gettin ready to hide the moon."

My role was not entirely clear to me. "Mavis, whut do ye want me to do, iffen ah spot somebody?"

"Well hell Chet. Cut down on 'im, son. Hain't nobody got no business ahind our barn in the middle a the night. Now go on. Watch out fer Teddy Blue."

I drained my coffee cup and set it on the kitchen table, as I passed on my way through the house. I eased out on the front porch, stopped, and listened. I could still hear the foxes yipping. As I stepped off the front porch, I heard a clicking sound behind me. The hair stood up on my neck. I whirled around, gun up, but it was only Mavis. She had followed me through the house and bolted the door from the inside. I was coffee nervous--nervous as a long-tail cat in a room full of rocking chairs. I wondered if I could even hold a rifle steady enough to hit anything.

In the southwest, lightning streaks crisscrossed heavy clouds reminding me of a red spider web; although, I do not reckon I ever saw a red one. A heavy cloud darkened the woods on the hill across the creek. Little time remained before the advancing thunderhead covered the moon. As I slipped through the front gate, the thunderhead's shadow crept across the creek and followed me up the road.

I stayed out of sight of the barn by walking north several yards up Batesville Pike, stepping over the rail fence, and circling graveyard hill, coming up on the north side. The foxes spotted me and stopped barking. They slipped silently away to the northwest, as the thunderhead covered the moon and a charcoal darkness settled over the land.

As I climbed the north side of the little hill, I considered the possibility someone behind the barn might notice the foxes had quit barking and look up the hill. It was pretty dark, but they might spot me against the sky. I stayed below the brow of the hill until I came to the whitewashed fence. I dropped down and crawled around and through the gate and in among the gravestones. I felt strange about possibly killing someone and me lying among the dead.

A light bobbed behind the barn. I figured a pine knot torch. Another torch flashed farther back in the garden. They meant to fire the barn. I heard Teddy Blue's voice carrying up the hill, low like. I could not hear what he said, but the torch closest to the barn was either dropped or thrown down. The boom of a six-gun reverberated from inside the barn followed by a yelp. One torch still bobbed and weaved toward the barn. I opened on it with my carbine.

I fired three times in quick succession and heard another yelp. A crease in the cloud cover allowed enough light, so I could see the back porch of the cabin. Mavis stood in the yard with her rifle up. She hollered out, "Hit's time to tune the fiddle and start the dance."

A lightning flash revealed three shadows running for the creek. I watched the skedaddle and out of the corner of my vision picked up Mavis. She snapped a shot at the lead runner, who had waded out on the far bank. He threw up his right hand and fell face down in a patch of bitter weeds. She snapped off two more shots, but I could not tell if they took effect. Big drops of rain splattered the gravestones around me.

A close lightning strike spurred me off the hill and away from the old mulberry tree previously struck twice by lightning splitting the bark down both sides. Some people do not think lightning will strike twice in the same place. That is a foolish notion.

Continuous lightning flashes lit the landscape bright as day. I ran for the corncrib twenty yards northwest of the barnlot fence. Once inside, I looked through a gap between the logs. I saw Mavis coming across the yard. She shielded her face from the rain with one hand and carried her rifle in the other. I held the door open against a strong wind. She was soaked to the skin by the time she got inside.

"Shoot," Mavis said, and laughed. "My hair's soppin, if ah had a bar a soap, ah'd go ahead and lather up. Nothin better fer yer hair than soft rainwater."

I did not have a reply, but I thought about it. Bullets flying everywhere and her talking about washing her hair and me shaking in my boots. I did not know if my shakes were from nervous excitement or fear. I finally decided I was scared near witless. I do not know why. As far as I could tell, no one had shot at me yet.

Through a crack, we watched a gunman at work. Teddy Blue, clearly visible in chain lightning flashes, pistol in hand, eased around the barn to the creek side. When Mavis was shooting from the back porch, some of the fugitives made it across the creek and dove for cover in the weeds. Now, with the storm bearing down, they must have thought it time to make a run for the cover of the woods twenty yards beyond the creek. Two shadowy figures jumped out of the tangle of weed cover and scampered for the woods. Teddy Blue's right hand came up, left hand fanned the hammer, and five shots rolled off so fast it became one long rolling boom. Someone squalled out. They disappeared. I could not tell if they fell or made the cover of the woods. Teddy Blue stood for a moment, watching the woods, turned and jogged through the barn lot gate toward the back porch and called to us.

"Mavis, Chet, come on in."

We gathered on the back porch, as sheets of hard driving rain swept the home place. We backed up under the porch roof against the kitchen wall out of the wind, guns held ready. Teddy Blue reloaded his pistol with cartridges out of his gunbelt. If we talked at all, we whispered. Nothing moved at the barn or across the creek.

"Let's go in," he said. "They ain't gonna be nothin more goin on tonight. 'Em ole boys run into a buzz saw they nary spected. Ah'm purty shore they's one or more down behind the barn, at least one in bad shape crost the crick. But, we'll stay put till mornin, look, when it's light. Mavis, let's git some coffee."

CHAPTER EIGHT

Billy bleated from the back porch.

"How'd thet damn goat git outta the lot?" asked Mavis.

"The gates open," said Teddy Blue, "Left it open, when ah run through it last night."

After the shooting stopped, the three of us spent the rest of the night in the kitchen with no light except from fireplace embers, over which Mavis baked biscuits. About daylight, while I buttered a biscuit at the kitchen table, Teddy Blue went out on the back porch and sat outside the kitchen door in a straight-backed cane-bottomed chair propped against the wall, biscuit in one hand, coffee cup in the other. He sat watching the sun breaking through light cloud cover over the eastern hills. He had a clear view of the barn lot, creek and the strip of woods between the creek and the bluff. Everything was dripping. The yard was a mess. Rivulets streamed down from graveyard hill across the clay-baked yard, to the creek, turning it brown.

"Chet, better git the gate closed," said Mavis. "Ah don't want them nannies gettin out afore they git milked."

Teddy Blue chuckled. Billy not six feet away was staring him down. Any open door was an invitation to Billy, but a stranger blocked this one, and he seemed hesitant about what to do. He lowered his head and considered his options. "Danged, if ah don't beleve this goat is bout to charge me," said Teddy Blue.

Teddy Blue stood, took a quick step and kicked Billy sprawling off the porch into the muddy yard. The little gray goat scrambled to his feet, bleated, switched his tail and eyed Teddy Blue standing on the porch above him. He was clearly outclassed, and he knew it. He turned reluctantly from the back porch and ambled around the cabin toward the front yard. I knew he would go to the front porch hoping to find the front door open.

I walked down to the barn lot. In the act of closing the gate, I happened to look back. Billy had discovered the budding rosebush next to the cabin wall, and not any rosebush, the rosebush planted years ago by Mama Ida. The climbing thorny vines clung to trellises and covered half the south side of our cabin. Mavis knew how her mother had loved roses and lovingly tended that bush. Spring, summer and fall, she weeded the flowerbed around it and watered the rosebush in dry weather. She worried all winter if that bush would come alive the next spring. Mavis, too, loved the big red roses that bloomed every April, roses as big as her bony hands.

Billy eyed the rosebush for a moment, evidently having forgotten several past whippings and one severe beating over the bush. But Billy, like all goats, had a short attention span. He moved in on the bush and had eaten several of the sweet red buds by the time I made the run from the lot and got to him. I grabbed him by the horns and drug him bleating back to the barn lot. He bleated at me through the lot gate, as I made my way across the muddy yard to the back porch.

Teddy Blue, after watching me walk across the yard through mud, removed his shoes and socks and rolled his pants legs up a turn or two. A little late--my shoes were already mud caked--I removed my shoes and socks and set them on the porch. My britches legs were already halfway to my knees without rolling.

Teddy Blue was tender-footed, I could tell. He eased into the yard, wiggled his toes a little, pulled his pistol and as a matter of habit checked the loads, spun the cylinder and reholstered.

"Come on Chet. Brang yer carbine. Hit's light nough. Let's go see whut we got. Mavis, ye stay on the porch and watch the woods crost the crick."

It was warm for a spring day in the hills. Steam rose from the ground and off tops of bushes. Puddles of water stood in the yard. The creek normally clear, or blue-green in the deeper holes, ran a muddy brown. Rainwater continued dripping from the black walnut tree on the north side of the cabin. Trees glistened in the strip of woodland between the creek and the bluff. Homesteaders loved the warm damp freshness of a spring rain. It meant growth.

I glanced over my shoulder, as I squished through the mud toward the barn. Mavis, rifle in hand, came out on the south end of the porch. Teddy Blue, a few steps ahead, pulled his pistol, as we curled around the barn to the garden. I held my carbine in my right hand cocked with thumb on the hammer, barrel pointing skyward resting against my right shoulder. I could drop the barrel and fire all in one motion.

The garden was soggy. The heavy rain had obliterated all footprints, but a dead man was left behind, sprawled across two rows of green onions. He stared wide-eyed at the sky. A small man, not five and a half-feet, maybe one hundred pounds soaking wet. He had a strange look on his face: surprise, I think.

It looked like Teddy Blue's pistol shot knocked him flat of his back. He had flung his arms straight out, no sign of struggle. He wore brown corduroy pants and a red plaid shirt. An old soggy gray felt hat lay near his head. Black hair and beard were matted with mud and plant matter. He wore brogan shoes, no socks. He held a torch clinched in his right hand made from a length of a pine tree limb with a pine knot on the end. Last night's rain had quickly extinguished the blackened torch. A gagging stench from a bowel release strengthened in the rising heat.

Teddy Blue stuck a bare foot under the thin shoulders and nudged him over on his side. The man was shot through the belly. The slug entered above the belt buckle and exited the back, leaving a hole the size of a silver dollar.

"Thet's one a 'em carryin torches. I got 'im through a crack in the logs. You know this galoot?"

I studied the man, but couldn't place him.

"Nah, don't recken ah ever seen 'im. He's shit hisself ain't he?"

"Yep. Forty-four slug in the belly'll do it evah time."

I looked around for some evidence that I had actually shot someone. It soon became obvious I was not going to find it in that muddy garden. When I first looked down on the barn from the graveyard, I was not sure I wanted to shoot anyone, but the vision of Papa lying in the road, in his bloody pink long handles, flashed in my mind, and I was instantly consumed with an internal fire. When the torch flared, I opened up--too fast--and expect I overshot. You will tend to overshoot firing from above like that.

"Let's wade the crick and see whut's o'er there," said Teddy Blue.

I looked down the creek across the plowed field. Buzzards, maybe a dozen, were already circling Ned and Ted. It always amazed me how quickly turkey buzzards found the dead.

We went over to the creek, usually running at knee depth, but still running a little high and brown from the night's downpour, rolled and pulled our britches legs well above our knees and waded across. A red squirrel chattered out in the woods. Pine and cedar scents stood out on that fresh wet morning. A light misty band of fog hung low over the creek, spread out toward the woods on the south side, and out into our fields on the north side. A redtailed hawk, low over the treetops, wheeled in a tight circle looking for a rabbit on the move. A high-pitched shriek rent the air. Teddy Blue and I dropped to one knee.

"Thet's the biggest chicken hawk ah ave ever saw," I said.

The big bird dropped from the top of a tall pine over by the bluff and turned at a right angle right over our heads pushing east up the creek.

"Thet ain't no chicken hawk," said Teddy Blue. "Thet's a eagle. Must ave a eight-foot wingspan. Better watch fer thet thing. Kill it, ye git the chance. Hit'll carry off a good-sized goat, and they'll eat a dead man. Ah seen 'em do it down in Texas. Ah thank thet eagle and 'em buzzards and thet hawk up yonder has got their sights set on more'n 'em dead horses."

The eagle had unnerved me a bit. I was just getting over my tingle when a horse nickered out in the woods. I dropped hard and banged my knee on a rock. It jarred me through and through and hurt like the devil. The hair stood up on the back of my neck. I felt like squalling out, but I bit my tongue. Behind us came answering nickers from the barn lot. Our mule team came out of their stalls to have a look at the strange horses they smelled. The mules stood side-by-side looking over the barn lot fence in the direction of the woods. Teddy Blue's big bay nickered and walked over to the fence and stood beside the mules. The mules began braying, and the goats began bleating. It seemed like every animal on the place found it necessary to join the chorus.

Across the creek, a large cedar glade, mostly moss-covered shale rock, lay like a green island in a sea of hardwoods. Cedar trees sprouted from the cracks in the shale and made a dense evergreen thicket, so thick you could not see man or animal standing, except to look underneath, where the drooping limbs did not quite touch the ground. I had often found deer that way, by first spotting their legs.

We cautiously approached the glade. My knee hurt and I was trying not to limp. I looked for the horse and saw it silhouetted through the heavy boughs. I whistled. The horse had been watching our approach. It nickered again and pushed through the brush.

A little sorrel mare walked into the open. She came toward me, head bobbing, reins loose and dragging, steam rising from her wet back and rain-soaked saddle. She suddenly danced to the side, snorted and looked at the ground. I eased forward. A man with half a head lay face down in a small patch of wild mustard weeds. Teddy Blue came up and took a quick look.

"They might be more," he said.

Teddy Blue pushed on into the cedar growth, pistol cocked. I caught up the reins of the little mare. She was a friendly little thing. Not the least bit scared. She nuzzled up to me like a big dog. Out of the corner of my eye, I caught movement to my left. I swung around and leveled the carbine, thumb on the cocked hammer. Another saddled horse walked out of the woods twenty yards upstream, ambled over to the creek and lowered its head to drink.

"Another horse upstream a bit."

"Good," said Teddy Blue, as he came back through the undergrowth. "Give 'em ole boys somethin to ride home on."

We examined the horses, saddles and saddlebags. The horses were not branded. The saddles were unmarked, saddlebags empty. I wanted the little sorrel mare and said so. I did not have anything to ride, but the mules. We did not even own a saddle.

"I bleve we ort to keep at least one of the horses and a saddle since they ain't brand one on 'em anywhar, finders, keepers."

"Well, ah guess there's somethin to thet ole sayin bout lookin a gift horse in the mouth. Ah was thinkin we was gonna ave to dig a couple a graves, but looks like we can jist tie both 'em ole boys crost the big horse and send 'em to Batesville in style."

Lester Tibbets swept out the jail and performed other odd jobs for the sheriff. He told me some years later about observing the meeting with Deputy Kel Decker and Two Toe Charlie Cole the morning following the shooting at our place. An axe glancing off a hardwood block had sliced into Two Toe's right foot neatly taking out the middle three toes, leaving only the big and little toe. Two Toe Charley went barefoot a lot and people always marveled at the visual result of his digital mishap.

Kel Decker addressed Two Toe Charley Cole, "Whut do ye mean, ye didn't burn it?"

"We run into a hornet's nest. One of the boys, ah didn't see which one, is gut-shot behind the barn and nother fell in the edge a the woods. Bill Train is bein patched up down at Doc Turner's. Hit in the leg, bone shattered. I got creased long my back. It's a wonder any a us got out alive, with all 'em bullets flyin."

"Well, who was doin all the shootin? They ain't nobody there, but thet ole girl and thet brother a hern."

"Nah. They's three anyway, maybe more. Somebody was inside the barn. Somebody opened on us from the hill north a the barn--thet was when I was hit--and I heerd a woman yell somethin from the back a the cabin. She opened on us whilst we was a crossin the crick. One of the boys was hit--ah couldn't tell which one--it was dark, rainin like hell, and he didn't ave much of a head left. We went to ground in some weeds on the far bank a the creek and layed still a minute. We jumped up and made a run fer the woods. Thet's when the shooter in the barn come around and opened on us with a pistol or two. Train took one in the leg. It's like they knew we was comin."

Decker looked at Cole, eyes not really focusing, looking through him. He did not know about Teddy Blue being home and could not comprehend how four men, in the middle of the night got themselves ambushed and shot up on the Abbott homeplace. His plan, worked out with his cousin, Jack Statin, was to approach the homestead from the rear, burn the barn, driving the mules out into the open lot, where they could be shot down, a five minute action, ten minutes--tops. The men would wade the creek, mount their horses left tied in the woods and ride a mile east up the creek and pass through a trough in the hills.

To be on the safe side, Decker and Statin provided horses without brands so they could not be traced in case they were shot and left behind and indeed two of them were missing. The men recruited for this job carried no identifying information, nor did they carry anything in their saddlebags traceable to the Decker or Statin families.

"Ah got to go see brother Clay. Ye better git down to Doc Turner's and ave thet back looked at. It's still bleedin some through yer shirt. Charge Doc's bill to this office and get the hell away from here."

"Ye know the ole doc. He's nosey. He's gonna ask how I got this," said Two Toe.

"Jist tell 'im it was a huntin accident, or somethin. Hell, make somethin up. Who are 'em other boys thet didn't come in with ye?"

"Billy Hix is one. He was down here from Cave City, lookin fer work and the tother one come in on a train from St. Louis last week. Ah thank he was down here runnin from somethin up there. Whut are we gonna do bout 'em?"

"Well, iffen ah know thet ole Abbott girl, I spect we'll see 'em comin into town afore long not likely settin straight up."

We Abbotts knew the Statins and Deckers were behind the burnout attempt. They had killed our horse team that evening and no doubt planned to burn the barn and kill the mules when they came out in the open. Common sense tells you homesteaders cannot farm without a barn and draft animals. We would lose the homestead for failure to pay our annual taxes to the county, something old man Lazarus Statin had already warned Mavis about. Clyde Decker, the sheriff, was also the tax collector for the county and was quick to notify Lazarus Statin of property taxes in arrears, so Statin could pay the taxes and take possession of the property. Statin, in collusion with Sheriff Decker, became owner of significant acreage in Independence County.

Right after the attack on our place, a Cushman mining official, in the process of selecting future mining sites, stopped in at the Sandtown Trading Post. Eagle Carter later told us the official said Sheriff Clay Decker assured him that mining engineers would soon have access to the ore laden bluff along the south side of Cave Creek. The official said he told Decker the mining company must have access soon, because one phase of a mining operation west of Cushman was near completion, and if the company could not gain access to the Cave Creek bluff, the engineers were going to open another large manganese vein northeast of town. That operation would last three years or more, depending on the depth and richness of ore deposits.

The story goes that Sheriff Clay Decker's rheumatism was acting up. His right knee was badly swollen, Gout was the diagnosis; although, Doc Turner did not have a clue. Decker kept scalding wet cloths on his knee. The skin blistered, peeled and itched, and people said he was danged irritable all the time and resorted to strong drink on a regular basis. He planned a train ride to a specialist in St. Louis, if he could get the mining operation worked out to his satisfaction, but we Abbotts were in the way.

His bad attitude only got worse, when his brother, Kel, came in to relay the news the raiding party was shot all to pieces, and as far as Kel knew the Abbotts and all their buildings were still intact and standing.

"Find Neil Crow," said the sheriff.

I kept the little sorrel mare and saddle. Teddy Blue and I removed the saddle from the other horse, a good-sized bay. Teddy decided to keep the saddle. It was not marked in any way, and we could use an extra saddle. He hung it inside the barn, in the tack room.

We fed the two found horses. Afterward, we took the bay around the barn to the garden and picked up the little gut-shot fellow. We had to fight a heavy swarm of green flies for him. A lightweight that Teddy Blue and I had no problem throwing across the horse. I knotted the end of a rope around his feet, ran the rope under the belly of the horse, knotted it around the fellow's hands, and cinched the rope tight. My intent was to keep him from sliding off under the belly of the horse. I do not know what difference it would have made. It might have made a difference to the horse.

We threw the other man up behind the little man and timed him on the horse in the same fashion. I do not think the horse was too happy with what he smelled. I know I wasn't. I led the horse out onto Batesville Pike and down across the creek now running normal depth, half way between my ankles and knees. I pointed the horse toward Batesville and slapped him on the rear with my hat. He crow hopped a couple of times and settled into a slow trot.

I stood in the middle of the creek washing the mud off my feet and watched the horse until it topped a rise in the road a quarter mile down. Going back to the cabin, I thought about the two dead men, bouncing across the horse, maybe all the way to Batesville. Teddy Blue was hardened to the killing business. The sight of dead men did not bother him, but it bothered me. I may have shot one of our attackers, but it was not either of those two. Teddy Blue and Mavis shot them. Mavis did not seem to care either. I think living through the war and the hard times afterward made her hard as stone.

From the front porch, Teddy Blue had watched me start the horse south. He spoke as I walked up. "Well, iffen somebody don't stop 'im thet horse'll probly make it all the way to Batesville. Iffen somebody does stop 'im, they can figure out whut to do with 'em ole boys. Let's go see iffen Mavis is got a fresh pot a coffee."

CHAPTER NINE

Teddy Blue walked into the kitchen, where I sat with Mavis drinking coffee. He carried two boxes of Winchester .44 caliber ammunition.

"Mavis, me and Chet are gonna take the mules and go down in the field and burn the horses. We'll be all morning cuttin timber and draggin it out a the woods. It's gonna take a big brushpile and a big fire to burn 'em. While we're foolin with thet, we'll do some shootin. Chet's purty good with the rifle, but he needs to learn to use a pistol. He can't carry a rifle everwhere he goes, but he kin strap on thet pistol ah brought in and carry it anywhar, includin the field."

Teddy and I walked down to the barn, harnessed the mules, picked up a chopping axe and a crosscut saw, a can of coal oil and headed for the two black mounds. The sky was black with buzzards. Some had already taken up residence in the treetops across the creek. It was just a matter of time before they were on the ground and tearing at the horses. I hated to think about it. I especially hated the thought of having to burn those beautiful animals, but that was better than having buzzards, wolves and foxes having at them.

We worked for two or three hours cutting, hauling, and stacking logs around the horses. Thankfully, the breeze was out of the southwest, so the stink would blow away from the homeplace. We splashed coal oil around on the logs and lit the fire. We watched it take hold and flare high. We drove the mule team back to the barn, unharnessed them, and went back out to the creek. I was looking forward to trying out my new pistol. At least, it would get my mind off the horses burning in the field.

I knew my way around pistols. I had proved a fair shot on occasion with Papa's old Colt Navy .36, but I didn't get to practice much because of a shortage of .36 caliber ammunition and more importantly: the shortage of money to buy it. I still thought ammunition was too expensive to waste, but Teddy Blue did not.

By 1875, ammunition was getting more reliable. Papa's old Navy Colt required paper cartridges with a load of black powder in one end of the cartridge and a lead bullet in the other; a percussion load requiring a percussion cap be set in each chamber of the cylinder, so the hammer striking the cap caused a spark exploding the powder in the paper cartridge. It did not work every time and a person could get in a tight, if the percussion cap failed to spark. Misfires resulted in a number of disappointed people, a disappointment usually short lived.

The Winchester Company introduced metal bullet casings sometime before 1873, with built-in percussion cap and powder charge. The hammer pin struck the center of the shell casing creating an internal spark exploding the powder. Metal casing cartridges did misfire occasionally, but not like the old percussion-cap paper cartridges.

Teddy Blue picked up a handful of rocks and set them on the ground a foot or two apart along the creek bank. He wore his gun belt with right-hand holster tied down. A notch cut out of the leather at the top front of the holster exposed the hammer. When he dropped his hand on the pistol, his thumb automatically locked on the hammer. He could jerk, cock and fire all in one motion.

He never asked me to help, as he methodically went about setting targets, not saying anything. I kept quiet, feeling it best not to interfere with his concentration. He placed the rocks, turned and walked back toward me. I could see he was silently counting steps. He paced back where I stood, stopped and looked at me a second. There was a spinning blur, the gun came out and thundered. Even though I was watching and halfway expected him to make a move, it happened so fast, I jumped. Pieces of rock flew everywhere. He was fast--fast as a copperhead's strike. His left hand was a blur fanning the hammer on the Remington .44, and it looked like he could hit anything he wanted, regardless of how small the target. He did not miss anything, as far as I could tell.

"Good God Almighty," was all I could get out.

We started working to improve my speed. Teddy Blue demonstrated his method of drawing and cocking the pistol in one smooth action. He showed me how to draw, cock the hammer and snap it on an empty chamber, calling it dry firing. I did it so many times I developed a blister on my thumb, and my whole hand began to cramp.

"Thet's a good exercise. Keep at it and it'll improve yer speed thout wastin shells."

Teddy placed more stones along the creek bank, and we both shot at the targets. The booming sound rolled up and down the creek and reverberated off the bluff across the creek. Mavis said it sounded like thunder.

We had quit shooting by the time Junior Ulbrick, carrying a rifle, came riding up on the Ulbrick's saddle mule to see what all the shooting was about.

Teddy Blue and I were sitting on the front porch smoking Mexican cigarillos. Mavis favored chewing a plug of tobacco from time to time. I guess her chaw was getting out of control. She walked out on the front porch to spit in the yard. A dung beetle was busy at its work and caught Mavis's eye. At ten feet, she sprayed the beetle pretty good. She was always amazed me with her accuracy.

I introduced Junior to Teddy Blue and cautioned Junior about telling it around that Teddy Blue was home. Later, after Junior left, we were at the kitchen table.

"Can thet German boy be trusted to keep quiet bout me?"

"Nah, he can't," replied Mavis. "Germans don't talk a lot, as a general rule, but Junior's eyes got big as silver dollars, when he found out who ye was. He'll tell his folks fer shore, and hit'll spread from there."

"Well, it'll be all right ah guess, word's gonna get out sooner or later," said Teddy Blue.

He sipped his coffee down to the bottom of the cup and chewed the grounds.

CHAPTER TEN

A glorious clear breezy Lord's Day followed a dawn rain shower. Rain-washed layered-slabs of shale rock surfacing the Batesville Pike glistened in the sun. The sky resembled glazed porcelain, deep blue decorated with an occasional cotton puff of cloud. I walked across the road to clear the copperheads out of the church.

I put on my boots and watched my step. Brownie was not there to help. The copperheads denned under the church floorboards, and generally kept quiet in hibernation during the winter months, but when the weather warmed in spring, they began stirring, particularly late in the afternoon. The copperhead infestation had gotten to the point where I stayed clear of the little church, except on Sunday.

The church floor was a construction of unseasoned rough oak planks laid over logs and nailed down. The planks, over time, had dried and shrunk leaving large gaps, which seemed an open invitation for the big thick brown and gold patterned snakes to join the congregation. I assigned myself the responsibility of removing them before the parishioners arrived for services; a responsibility for which I received considerable encouragement and thanks from the entire community.

Brownie and I had been a good copperhead team. He found them, and I dispatched them with a shovel. I looped each over the shovel blade, transported the venomous creatures behind the church, dug a hole and buried them. Every Sunday, I dug a fresh hole. Little burial mounds behind the church resembled a small graveyard.

Our pastor, Whistler Lewis, arrived humped over on his saddle mule. He dismounted with an arthritic grunt and tied the mule to a hitch rack on the south side of the church. He took a minute to loosen the cinch strap and spotted me behind the church patting down a sizable dirt mound over a new grave.

"How many this time?"

"Five."

"Got to do somethin bout thet."

I propped the shovel against the back wall of the church and followed Whistler. He walked across the road straight through the open front door of our cabin and passed on back to the kitchen. Coffee was black and steaming in a pot sitting on the kitchen table. From a dutch oven, Mavis produced a biscuit the size of a ceramic saucer that she served with sorghum molasses and goat butter.

Whistler said he always liked coming to Mavis's kitchen and enjoying what he found. Mavis was quite at ease with the way Whistler walked right in, uninvited, and sat down at her table. She thought it her Christian duty to make a preacher welcome, and anyway she liked Lamont Lewis.

"Hungry, Whistler?"

"Ah could eat the runnin gears offen a bull moose."

"How's the ride o'er."

"Soft mornin, hard mule."

Mavis laughed. Whistler had funny sayings, which he often injected into his sermons. His sayings and the way he whistled through his teeth made his sermons something to behold.

Whistler had done some horse-trading in his time and was sharp at it. He sold one fellow a blind horse and justified it with scripture. Some disturbed people approached Whistler wanting to know how a preacher of the gospel could do a man that way. Whistler said, "Well, biblically speaking, he was a stranger and I took him in."

"The Wilsons are a comin. They ort to be here dreckly. They was a gettin ready to load the wagon, when ah come by. Looks like the old man, and woman, and Ludi and Lois all comin."

"Wonder why thet is," said Mavis, "since they been goin o'er to Lee's Chapel."

Whistler smiled and looked up at Mavis through bites of buttered biscuit and sorghum molasses.

"Ah spect it might ave somethin to do with Teddy Blue bein home, don't ye recken? Word is out, ye know. Ah speck more people'll show up today than we're use to avin. Some people know 'im, like the Wilson family, others ave heerd the stories and want to git a look."

Teddy Blue clumped into the kitchen, wearing new store-bought overalls over a faded gray cotton shirt and new pair of store-bought brogan shoes, coal-black hair slicked down with water and chin whiskers trimmed. He looked less the desperate character, than when he first rode up to our front gate.

"Whistler, it's been a spell. Ye still preachin 'em hell and damnation sermons?"

"Still tryin, but the far is bout gone outta mah belly. Ah'm gettin too long in the tooth to be makin these rides o'er here. Too stiff in mah joints, and mah ole mule ain't no spring-board buggy."

My eyes were on Teddy Blue from the time he entered the room. I was just an ignorant old kid and easily influenced by notoriety and fame-- and he was my brother. Teddy Blue smiled at Whistler's remark, picked up the coffeepot and poured a big tin cup. He sat down at the kitchen table with Whistler, Mavis and me. After some small talk, Whistler stood up and said it was time to go over to the church and get ready "to give 'em hell."

Teddy Blue and Whistler started for the front door with Mavis behind. I lagged back. I was not looking forward to sitting on a split-log bench. Those benches sure got hard after an hour or so of a Whistler sermon. Sitting through a church service really was an endurance test more than anything. I would rather have walked the 24 miles to Batesville and back, than endure a church service conducted by Whistler Lewis. I would not normally say such a thing, but Whistler is dead now and not likely to take offense.

Mavis paused to take down her fiddle hanging on a wall peg in the front room, and continued across the road behind Whistler and Teddy Blue. She told me once that she selected hymns to play, while walking from the cabin over to the church. I knew she would probably start with "Amazing Grace," which was always good, easy to play on the fiddle, and the congregation liked singing along. She would line up three or four others in her mind and usually ended the service with a rendition of "Fire on the Mountain," that was not a hymn exactly, more of a hoedown, but it got the congregation to stomping their feet pretty good.

All the stomping livened up the copperheads under the floorboards, which never was a good thing, because sometimes here would come one right up through a crack, and that is when the stomping really got lively. But a good rendition of "Fire on the Mountain" usually caused the congregation to leave the service in good humor, even if they sometimes left in a hurry.

When I walked out on the porch, a sizable crowd had already gathered across the road. It began to look like some folks were going to have to stand. The Ulbrick family came up in their wagon. The Crisler family walked in from their cabin a mile or so behind our barn. The Switzer family arrived in a wagon from the other side of the Ulbrick's--all German immigrants. The Germans were primarily of the Lutheran persuasion; but in the hill country, they made do with a Methodist preacher and did not seem to mind.

The Wilson family arrived in a wagon; Eagle and Rachel Carter in their buckboard; several single riders on horses or mules. Everyone hitched his animals to the long hitching rail along the south side of the church or to the short rail in front.

The parishioners, for the most part, mingled in the churchyard. A few straggled into the church to find seats. The Wilson family brought word of old man Newton Cole's passing, so the Cole family would not be coming. Mr. Cole was over one hundred years old when he passed, according to his family, but even they did not know for sure. I remember Mavis saying, "One-by-one the ole folks are passin o'er Jordan, and they hain't a comin back."

I would miss Old Man Newton Cole. Newt Cole told the story every Sunday morning--if he thought of it--about the time during the war, when a Texas soldier passing through the county stopped for the Sunday meeting at the Cave Creek church. Services were underway, when the soldier, in Confederate gray, appeared in the doorway. Whistler Lewis, facing the door, spotted him first. Whistler left the pulpit and walked to the door. The congregation murmured in surprise and turned to stare.

"Whut army do ye belong to?" asked Whistler.

"Ah belong to the Tenth Texas Regiment, Van Dorn's Army," replied the soldier. "Whut army do ye belong to?"

"Ah belong to the Army a the Lord," Whistler solemnly declared.

"Well friend," said the soldier, "Ye are a long way from headquarters."

Eleven a.m. was the usual starting time and the service usually ran to nearly one p.m., sometimes longer, depending on Whistler's mood, and how much Mavis had suppressed his appetite prior to the service.

A hush settled over the crowd. Necks craned. Eyes settled on the trio crossing the road. Teddy Blue was the center of attention, like it or not. Eagle Carter fronted him, said something soft, and smiled. Rachel Carter took him by the hand. Mr. and Mrs. Wilson, who knew Teddy Blue from the day he was born, came over. Ludi sidled over, and slipped more toward Mavis. Lois Wilson looked on, but stood apart, as she usually did where crowds were concerned.

Low-toned conversation and laughter hummed through the congregation. Everyone seemed in good spirits. I think some people may have been disappointed in Teddy Blue's appearance. He was not the giant people expected from his legend. I was two or three inches taller. Dressed in farm clothes, he looked nothing of the part of a Texas Ranger or western desperado. Eagle Carter said loud enough for all to hear, "Teddy Blue, ye don't look like a Texas man in them garments. Ye must spect to do a little farmin."

Teddy Blue replied to the question looking straight at Lois Wilson standing a few feet away. "Ah'd like to set on the porch a spell and watch a farmer's daughter rock in her chair and scratch her elbows."

Laughter rippled through the crowd and a pink blush settled on Lois Wilson's face. She looked at the ground and self-consciously toyed with the tight bun of dark-brown hair on the back of her head, while she made little scratch marks with the right toe of her high-topped shoe.

Whistler Lewis looked around silently counting heads--taking attendance. Satisfied of his figure, he turned for the church door. Rachel Carter, with Teddy Blue in tow, followed Whistler.

Loud singing echoed up from the creek and stopped the procession. Two horsemen, swaying drunkenly in their saddles, crossed the creek and cantered up to the hitch rail. The Statin brothers, Jack and Billy, dressed in their Sunday best, black long coats over black trousers and boots, dismounted, giggled, and held onto each other and the hitch rail for support.

I stood near the church, took a long look at Billy Statin, and thought about whipping his ass. Billy, a year older than me, was a bullyboy, when a member of his family was around to back him. He always tried bullying me, when he caught me out, like up at the trading post. Billy Statin or I was not old enough to remember anything about the Pine Hill shootout in 1862, which left Billy's oldest brother dead, but Billy heard about it enough over the years and had worked an evil intent in his mind toward all us Abbotts.

At age twelve or so, I was rawboned, near six-feet tall and weighed one-hundred-fifty pounds on the produce scales at the Sandtown Trading Post. I was hard as iron from having worked in the fields since I was big enough to walk. One day Billy caught me at the trading post and tried to brace me over a trifle. A faulty memory hampered his ability to reason.

We had fought one time before at the trading post. He had his brother to back him when he called me a hog thief. I layed into him pretty good and was getting the best of him, before Eagle Carter jumped in and separated us. This time he forgot he was at the trading post by himself. I stood his agitation for a while. I finally got enough of his mouth, particularly when he said something about Abbotts being hog thieves. Eagle sold axe handles out of a barrel. I selected a nice ash handle and before Billy knew what was happening, I trapped him in a corner and beat him severally about the head and shoulders. He lowered his head and tried to rush me, but I split him above the right eye. Blood went everywhere, but Billy didn't. He hit the floor hard, and after I stomped him a few times, Eagle Carter took him home in a wagon. No love was lost between Billy Statin and me.

The Statin brother's attendance at a Cave Creek Sunday service was their first and only one, as far as I know. Everyone knew they had not come for the preaching. They came to get a good close look at their nemesis, the absentee focus of their hatred for so many years: Teddy Blue Abbott--their brother's killer. And they found courage to do it in a fruit jar of mountain mist. I guess they felt safe with spectators around.

The crowd came in and filled the split oak benches. Some men and boys, including me, stood along the back wall. I planned to slip out the back door, if given the chance. Mavis and Teddy Blue took a seat on the right front pew. Mavis always sat near the front because of her participation in the music program. The Statin brothers took seats to the left rear. They continued to embarrass with their giggling. Some men at the rear were taking hard glances at the two, and I expected to hear more than a sermon before long.

Whistler Lewis stepped up to the lectern, an old Civil War rifle-packing box turned on end. From where I stood, I could read the word Winchester printed on the side of the box in faded black letters. Whistler reached under his long coat, pulled a Navy Colt .36 from his belt, and laid it on top of the box, his common practice. He stood a moment, eyes sweeping the congregation, settling for a time on the Statin brothers. He startled the congregation with an announcement: "We are gonna burn this church."

The congregation stirred uneasily and looked at one another, trying to make sense out of Whistler's statement. Eagle Carter cleared his throat and started to stand, I suppose to ask for clarification, when Whistler continued, "Too damn many snakes."

Whistler Lewis moved through the service with the mechanics he always employed and the congregation came to expect. He welcomed the members of the congregation and visitors, and went to a prayer. He prayed for so long that I began to wonder if the prayer had an end. After he prayed for everyone and everything under the sun, he asked Mavis to step forward. She stood, turned and faced the congregation with her fiddle tucked under her chin and played "Amazing Grace." The congregation sang along. After the hymn, Mavis sat down, and Whistler went right to the sermon. I do not remember the subject, but it had sin in it everywhere. We did not have a communion service like they have in some churches, or did Whistler bother to pass a collection plate. Most people did not have two pennies to rub together. Whistler once said his congregation was so poor God was going to have to figure out another way to manage his money. He was not going to get a lot of help from the Cave Creek bunch.

Finally, at 12:30 p.m., after a lot of twisting and squirming on the hard oak pews and after a couple of men got up and went out to the outhouse back of the church, Whistler called on Mavis for a final tune. I stayed inside, because I thought the Statin brothers might cause a scene. I was disappointed. Both went to sleep midway of the sermon, slumped over, with heads in their laps. If not standing, I probably would have gone to sleep too. As it was, I stood so long in one place my feet went to sleep and my legs began to cramp. Mavis obliged with the crowd favorite: the foot-stomping "Fire on the Mountain." As expected, the copperheads stirred under the floorboards, and a couple of the big motley snakes poked their heads through a crack. Whistler alertly stepped off the pulpit and stomped on one of the snake's head with the heel of his brogan. Both snakes ducked for cover. We all started to get nervous and I, for one, kept looking through a crack in the floor boards between my feet. Whistler, after a lengthy prayer, dismissed the congregation. Everyone made a beeline for the exit, but with some caution about where they stepped. As we passed through the door, Whistler admonished, "Some of ye men hep me set this place a far. We need a new church buildin anyhow."

Mavis walked across the road to our cabin saying something about getting some dinner on the table, but she, like me, was watching the Statins and so was Teddy Blue. I thought Teddy Blue was unarmed, but I should have known better. He had on a belt under his overalls and stuck one of his pistols in the belt. The bib of the overalls covered the gun, but he could reach inside the bib and get it out quick. He was making conversation with several people crowding him, including Lois Wilson, but he was closely watching the Statin brothers.

The Statin brothers were not showing weapons, but I am sure a pistol or two were in their saddlebags. Mavis disappeared through the front door of the cabin, as the Statins went over to their horses at the hitch rail, but she soon reappeared on the porch with her Henry rifle.

Mavis's actions were not lost on Jack and Billy Statin. When they mounted their horses, they looked at her, and rode closer to Teddy Blue, surrounded by a knot of people. The knot untied of its own volition and faded back.

"Ye gonna be farmin here are ye?" asked Jack Statin.

"Nah," answered Teddy Blue, "never keered fer farmin as sich."

Jack Statin showed a glimmer of relief, a slight smile, for he did not expect that answer.

"Goin back to Texas?" Statin asked.

"Nah, gonna hang round a spell," replied Teddy Blue.

I stood a few feet off to the side next to Lois Wilson. Lois seemed nervous and twisted her fingers. I could see Teddy Blue's black eyes. He reminded me of a timber wolf, the way he took in everything, and yet never took his eyes off the Statin brothers. He kept stealing glances at their heavy brown leather saddlebags. I also noted the Statins kept stealing glances at Mavis standing on our cabin front porch, rifle in hand.

A blast of heat caught us all by surprise and broke the tension. The little log church went up in flames forcing us back toward the road. Whistler also fired the outhouse behind the church. I never considered copperheads being under the floor of the outhouse, and the thought chills me to this day.

Jack Statin's eyes narrowed a bit. He kept looking at Mavis and whiskey blinking in the midday sun. Billy Statin, sitting his horse next to his brother remained steady in the saddle, silent, and noncommittal.

"Yore sister spectin trouble?" asked Jack Statin.

"Nah, don't thank Mavis is spectin trouble. Spect she plans on killin a snake, should one try to git out a the far and crost the road."

Jack Statin showed a little crooked smile displaying tobacco-stained yellow and black teeth.

"Ye thank she kin hit one from there?"

"Yeah. She usually hits whut she shoots at, from up close or far away."

"Any problems up here, day or so back?" Billy Statin asked the question this time. He stepped his horse forward enough so that he looked across the neck of his brother's horse directly at Teddy Blue.

Teddy Blue caught the slight change in the speech pattern. Billy Statin was better educated than the rest of his family and spoke differently. Lazarus Statin educated Billy in the little Soulesbury College in Batesville. The college teachers, recruited mostly from St. Louis, tried to take the hill accent out of Soulesbury students. It worked some on Billy.

"Nah, recken not," replied Teddy Blue. "What kind a trouble?"

"A bareback horse walked into Batesville," said Billy, "couple days back, two dead men tied on. One of them had his head blown half off, at least what I heard."

"He musta had his head whar it shouldn't a been. Happens."

Teddy Blue looked directly into Billy Statin's eyes. Billy tried to hold the stare, but like a dog, he could not. Teddy Blue noted his weakness.

"Come on Billy," said Jack Statin.

He pulled his horse around and nudged the animal into a walk toward the road. He turned slightly in the saddle and addressed Teddy Blue. "Whut are ye gonna do Abbott, ye ain't gonna work this place?"

"Oh, ah'm gonna work this place all right. Mavis wants to build a grindin mill out there o'er the falls."

He hung it out to dry, as we like to say in the mountains. No use concealing our intentions any longer. If the Statin and Decker factions were going to try to take our place, the ball might as well open.

"A mill?" Jack Statin questioned, surprise showing. Thin lips tightened over his teeth.

"Thet's right. Ah aim to be a miller. Ah'm tard a rangerin."

Whistler Lewis sat his mule close to the church fire and watched for escaping copperheads. He now rode over beside Teddy Blue and caught the tail end of the conversation.

"We'll be a buildin back this church," said Whistler, to all in the general vicinity. "Ain't no better place fer a church."

He directly addressed the Statin brothers. "Ye boys are welcome to come hep us. We'll be a startin on it purty soon. I thank we'll build the church and the mill at the same time. Ye boys'd like to hep on thet wouldn't ye?"

"Go to hell ye psalm-singin sunavabitch," said Jack Statin. He kneed his horse and moved on toward the road, Billy Statin followed.

"Boy, cussin a preacher ain't no way to git close to God," said Whistler.

Neither Statin brother bothered to reply. We all watched, as the Statin brothers walked their horses down the road and through the creek.

"Ah'm afeerd them boys is on the road to perdition," said Whistler.

CHAPTER ELEVEN

Monday morning Teddy Blue and I worked in the field back of the barn. I chopped weeds out of the young corn with a goosenecked hoe. Teddy Blue worked the mule team and ran a middlebuster through the corn. At noon, he unhitched the mules from the plow and turned them loose. They headed for the barn without prompting. Mules do not need a lot of driving when they are heading for the feedlot. I am a lot that way myself. When Teddy Blue and I walked in for our dinner, we were not far behind the mules.

I anticipated something good. At breakfast, I had noticed a large pot of purple hull peas soaking in water. I did not know what Mavis planned serving with the peas, but I was sure cornbread would be one thing and that was good enough for me. I could make a meal out of purple hull peas and cornbread anytime.

"Somebody's been watchin the cabin," Mavis said, when Teddy Blue and I entered the kitchen off the back porch.

"Watchin? From where?" asked Teddy Blue.

Mavis nodded toward the kitchen window with a view across the creek.

"In the road, back in the cut, crost the crick. Ah was down to the crick washin. Ah barely could see 'im back down there in the shade."

"You recognize 'im?" I asked.

"Not real good. Probly thet Crow feller, but he didn't look quite like Crow neither. He come down there bout mid-mornin. He acted like he didn't want nobody to see 'im. He kept lookin at the barn and the cabin. Ah spect he was lookin fer you, Teddy, tryin to see who ye was."

"Ye need be keerful with Crow, Mavis, if thet was him." "Ah had mah rifle with me. Ah taken my washin and rifle, come on back in, and watched through the kitchen winder. Iffen he'd made a move to turn down in the woods, ah'd'uv come out behind the barn and got yore notice, but he didn't. He turned back down the road."

"He's lookin fer an openin. He knows whut appened to thet last bunch thet come in here--may ave been a part a it--and he ain't anxious to close in daylight. Ah'll start sleepin in the barn. Ain't use to sleepin inside no ways, and besides, ah like the smell a hay."

Someone knocked. Teddy Blue and I stood and with some apprehension turned toward the front door.

"Now, who'n hell is thet?" Mavis said.

"Jist goes to show ye. Anybody kin walk right up on us thout a dog round," I said.

"Well, at least they's knockin," said Mavis.

She held in front of her, in both hands, by the bail, a fire blackened cast iron pot full of stew taken from where it hung in the fireplace.

Teddy Blue, barefoot, padded silently to the front window.

"Hell, it's jist Ludi Wilson. He's rid o'er here with two dogs on ropes and a team a mules."

Teddy Blue opened the door and invited Ludi in. Ludi tied the dogs and the mules to a front porch post and came in with hat in hand.

"Ludi, come on in and take dinner with us," said Mavis. "The food's already been blest, so jist dig in unless you got some personal business needs takin care of."

She reached up on a shelf by the fireplace and took down a tin cup and a tinware plate. She poured out a cup of black coffee and filled Ludi's plate with rabbit stew, purple hull peas and a chunk of cornbread.

"Whar'd ye git the rabbit," I asked, when I discovered the stew's main ingredient.

"Plinked 'im outta the garden early this mornin with mah twenty-two."

In addition to our heavier rifles, we used a single-shot, .22-caliber Remington around the house on snakes, rabbits, squirrels, groundhogs and other varmints.

"I recken I ort to warsh up a little," said Ludi, "lot a dust in the air today."

"Bucket a water and warsh pan on the shelf on the back porch. Hep yerself," said Mavis.

Teddy Blue eyed Ludi. A slight smile creased his lips. I had heard, when I was a young boy, Ludi and Mavis had been fairly close, and that eventually turned out to be true. Sometime later, Teddy Blue related that when Ludi was fourteen and Mavis thirteen he remembered hearing Mama Ida say they might marry. I was born not long after that prophecy. Teddy Blue said he did not recollect ever hearing Papa Austin state an opinion on the subject.

Ludi indeed proposed marriage to Mavis. I could not for the life of me understand how a fourteen-year-old proposes marriage and considers raising livestock, crops and kids. But the proposal came too late. Mama Ida died suddenly. Mavis told Ludi she had too much on her plate to think about getting married. Ludi quit coming to church and started taking an interest in social activities in the Cushman area. Cushman was twelve miles from Cave Creek, as the crow flies, fourteen miles or so by road, too far away for Mavis to participate.

Ludi married soon after Mama Ida's passing. His fourteen-year-old wife died within a year of the marriage. People said Ludi became quietly detached after his young wife's death. I think mental detachment must have run in the Wilson family. I think I have suffered bouts of detachment.

Through the years, I met Ludi occasionally, usually at the Sandtown Trading Post. He seldom talked to me, but he always studied me, when he thought I was not looking. Sometimes I would walk over to one of the front glass windows and make out like I was looking outside. If the light was right, I could see Ludi behind me in the reflection. He would be staring at me. When I turned around he would always look away. I could never quite read his eyes. He just acted strange and out of sorts.

Ludi had suffered something emotional, for which there was no known cure. But the previous Sunday, during church, Ludi and Mavis stayed close before and during the service, and their eyes seemed to come alive. I expect they were remembering from a long time ago.

"Ah brought you'ens a couple a dogs and a team a mules. I heerd Sunday somebody kilt yer dog and yer big horse team," said Ludi, as he entered the kitchen and took a seat at the table.

I did not look at the dogs or the mules when he came up, being too busy with purple hull peas, cornbread and rabbit. And too, I became interested in a cockroach that appeared over the edge of the table and trundled toward me, antennas searching. No one seemed to notice but me. I sat quiet, did not say anything and thought about it. The cockroach approached a glass pickle jar in the center of the table, encountered its own reflection in the jar and froze.

I lost interest in the insect after that and decided to go out and see what Ludi had brought us. A large black shorthaired dog, weighing sixty pounds or more, lay sound asleep in the yard. Ludi had tied him to a porch post with a rope. A black and white spotted fiest hardly knee-high, not weighing ten pounds soaking wet was tied around the neck with another piece of rope and sat on the porch watching the front door. And standing hip shot, tails switching at green flies were two medium-sized thick-chested red mules. They looked to be a hand higher and a couple of hundred pounds heavier than our little brown team. When I opened the door, the little fiest sprang to his feet, barked at me, and did a little dance.

I watched for a moment, as he danced for me. I shut the door and went back in the kitchen and sat down for another plate of purple hull peas, cornbread and rabbit stew. "What do ye spect us to do with thet little feller?" I asked.

"Well, he might be the best a the two, 'cordin to the Wilkins fambly, whar ah got 'em. Mr. Wilkins says he's jist a pup, but he's got the makins of a top-notch squirrel dog and they ain't nobody gonna come up round this place thout 'im lettin ye know bout hit. The big dog is eight months old and shows some signs of bein mean. His daddy was a bear dog, went in a cave with an old boar bear, and nary come out. Mr. Wilkins says Blackie is like his daddy. He don't cotton to strangers, but iffen you'ens feed him a time or two, ah bet he'll make friens." "Well, sounds like the big'uns been named, but whut bout the little feller?" I asked. "Ah don't know," replied Ludi, "call him Shorty, Little Bit or somethin'."

"What bout 'em mules?" Mavis asked. "We hain't got money fer mules."

We actually did have money enough for a team of mules, but Mavis was playing her finances close to the vest.

"Em's mama's mules. Said she wanted you'ens to ave 'em, at no cost. We got two other teams."

"Them's yer mammy's mules?" I was a little bit incredulous. Mrs. Wilson was an old woman. I could not imagine her behind a team of mules.

"Yep. Mama use to plow with 'em, till she got the gout or rheumatize in her knees. She can't walk good no more. She'd be pleased iffen you'ens would take 'em and use 'em. She knows you'ens take good keer a yer stock. They's bout eight-years-old. Got some good years left."

Ludi stopped talking, took a sip of coffee, picked up a pewter fork and started mashing cornbread into his rabbit stew. He seemed a little embarrassed by the length of his statement. Ludi was not used to talking. He usually only answered questions posed directly to him from family members and since his family did not talk much either, Ludi did not often get to hear the sound of his own voice. It seemed to me he was trying to think of something nice to say about the stew, but he could not think of how to put it. I volunteered. "This stew is awful good, Mavis. Ain't it Ludi?"

"Doggone good, ah'd say," blurted Ludi. He immediately dropped his head and took a strong notice of the contents of his plate.

Mavis seemed embarrassed by the compliment on her cooking.

"Oh heck, Ludi, hit's jist some stuff ah throwed in the pot."

Teddy Blue had a problem keeping a straight face. He turned away and looked at the wall like he was studying something important. He sobered and turned back around.

"Ludi, ye jist didn't come all this way to brang us dogs and mules, did ye?"

Ludi took a moment to form a reply. He did not want his mouth to outrace his brain, which as far as I could tell was not much of a challenge.

"Nah," replied, Ludi, who was gradually getting used to his new conversational skills. "Ah'm a little at loose ends. We got the crops in. Finished the tabakker yestiddy. I thought ah'd come and see bout gittin started buildin a new church, since we burned the old un, and I don't see no reason we can't get to work on the mill, if you'ens are a mind to."

"Well, ah'm a mind to," said Mavis, and said no more.

"We'll do the church floor different this time. We'll use a lot of cedar in the floorboards, keeps the snakes out. Snakes don't like cedar."

"Snakes don't like cedar," said Mavis. "I hain't nary heerd a sich a thang in mah life."

Before Ludi could defend his statement, Teddy Blue came to the rescue. "There's some truth in thet Mavis. Injuns know it. Ye never see a copperhead or rattler in a cedar glade. Deer and cattle like to bed down in cedar, and ah allus look fer a cedar glade to bed down in when ah'm caught out in the woods."

Mavis considered Teddy Blue's statement for a moment. "Well, ah'll be go to hell," she said.

Mavis never put up more of an argument, but I could see she thought how she could test it. Mavis did not like being bested on knowing something as simple as a snake's aversion to cedar.

"You folks kin start on yer buildin projects, but ah got some bizness in Batesville needs tendin to," said Teddy Blue. "The plowin can wait a little; we're almost caught up anyway."

"What kind a bizness?" asked Mavis.

"Like the livery barn. Ah aim to find out who brung Papa's mules to thet barn."

"What are ye gonna do, ye find out?" I asked.

"Ah'm gonna make it real hard on thet person, should he still be round, and ah'm gonna start right now. Does Eagle Carter ave dynamite at the tradin post?"

"Yep," I said, "He usually carries a little, but ye don't need to go up there to get it. They's a few sticks in a box under the corn in the crib. Papa allus kep some on hand fer blowin stumps and rocks outta the field."

"Ye got fuse and caps?" asked Teddy Blue.

"Yep, they's a roll a fuse and a box a caps in the tack room in the barn."

"Well, ah thank ah'll hep myself to a stick or two. Can't nary tell when ye might need to blow up somethin."

Teddy Blue got up from the table and went into the bedroom to change clothes. A little later, I heard him exit through the front door and say something to the dogs, and I heard him whistling a lively tune, as he walked around the cabin toward the barn lot.

Mavis, Ludi and I were still at the kitchen table drinking coffee, when Teddy Blue brought his big bay through the barn lot gate and passed the cabin. I looked out the kitchen window. He wore his Texas outfit, but had added a dark-brown leather-vest over a long-sleeve shirt. Mavis had washed and ironed the shirt and pants, the day after he got home and complained the jeans were so stiff with sweat and dirt they could stand alone in the corner. His weapons naturally drew my attention. He had tied down the Remington .44s on crossed cartridge belts, the left holster reversed, gun butt forward. A Winchester .44 rifle fit snug in the saddle scabbard.

Mavis pushed back from the table and walked out to the front porch. I went out behind her, interested in what she was going to say. Ludi came out behind me. Both dogs were out in the yard, the black one still asleep and the fiest sitting next to him taking everything in. I did not want to be critical to Ludi's face about a gift, but I wondered about that black dog. The little fiest yipped at Teddy Blue's horse. The big bay snorted, stomped a front foot and the fiest ran under the porch.

"Teddy don't ye want somebody to go with ye?"

"Don't worry Mavis, ah'll be okay, but since ye mention it, why don't ah take Chet along. The experience'll do 'im good. We got some trouble comin ah spect. Chet needs to git hisself prepared for some tight scrapes he might git hisself in. We'll do a little scout after sundown and come on back in sometime roun midnight. Don't set them dogs on us, specially thet fiest. Ah'm not shore thet black one is alive," he said and laughed.

I got goose bumps, when I heard him say he wanted me to go. I started for the barn to saddle my little sorrel mare, but stopped short to listen, when Mavis voiced an objection.

"Teddy, ah don't want mah boy hurt."

My boy. I thought it strange the way she said it, but in the excitement of the moment let it pass.

"He'll be alright Mavis. We'll be goin into Batesville after dark, and there won't be nobody spectin us to visit."

I waited a moment for a rebuttal, but Mavis did not say anything more. I ran to the barn and saddled my horse. At the front gate, Teddy

Blue, sitting his horse in the road in front of the house, said to me, "Hey Bub, ain't ye forgot somethin?"

I studied the situation a moment and realized I did not have weapon one on me. I was embarrassed, having to dismount, and go back in the cabin for my rifle and pistol belt. I knew Mavis would not let me get away without a sharp rebuke. Mavis noted my coming in through the front door.

"What is hit?"

"Ah forgot mah gun."

"Ah'll jist swear Chet, whar's yer mind? You'd lose yer head iffen hit weren't screwed on."

I took a handful of cartridges from a box of Winchester .44 caliber and put them in the pocket of my jeans. The rest of the box went in one of my saddlebags. Mavis and Ludi were still sitting at the kitchen table, when I passed back through the cabin to the front porch. I heard Ludi ask Mavis, "What do ye thank he aims to do?"

"He aims to hurt somebody real bad, I spect," said Mavis. "Trouble's comin. Ye kin count on hit, and ah fer one want to see hit come."

CHAPTER TWELVE

Teddy Blue surprised me with his route selection. We did not take the Batesville Pike, instead, we crossed the pike and rode west through a narrow flat strip of grassland bordering Cave Creek. I didn't question his choice though, realizing he planned riding to the juncture of Cave Creek and Polk Bayou and taking the old Indian trail running south down the east side of Polk Bayou into Batesville.

Originally, a buffalo trail, the narrow track, hardly wide enough for a team and wagon, was little used. Osage Indians were the earliest settlers in our county, and early on started following the buffalo trail along Polk Bayou down to White River. The trail followed the line of the Polk Bayou creek bed for the most part but sometimes wandered off and cut the angle, where the creek made sharp turns.

My little sorrel mare followed Teddy Blue's bay through sagegrass, bitterweed and briar patches like one dog follows another. Teddy Blue's Texas horse found unfamiliar smells in the Arkansas hills and was difficult to hold in check at times. The bay pranced, tossed his head and snorted, likely smelling black bear or panther. My little sorrel rode easy and did not seem to find anything strange in the air. She had smelled it all before.

Teddy Blue kept quiet the half-mile ride to Polk Bayou. When we got down to the big creek, he turned south along the east bank. I had hunted those woods over the years. Familiar squirrel and raccoon den trees, bee trees, and bear caves bordered the creek.

Teddy Blue amazed me. Absent from the area for thirteen years, he still remembered obscure den trees and other landmarks. Boulders higher than our heads often sat in midstream. The boulders, through some mysterious force, had turned loose from their moorings on the hillside and crashed down, coming to rest in the creek, practically damming it in places. I could tell he remembered climbing on top those boulders and waiting for a deer, elk or bear to come along, for I had done the same thing.

Teddy Blue hunted the area in his youth usually with one or more of Chief George's Osage boys. The Osage boys taught Teddy Blue to read sign and showed him other mysteries of the land. Mysteries, Teddy Blue said served him well and saved his life more than once on the plains of West Texas, when he was hunting Kiowa and Comanche.

When I hunted along Polk Bayou, I never paid much attention to the surface of the old trail, because the big game animals that once traveled the road like buffalo and elk were killed out long ago. But, Teddy Blue studied the trail looking for shod horse and mule tracks.

"Are ye a tracker?" I asked.

"Ah'm a trackin fool. Ah kin track low flyin birds."

"What do ye see?"

"Not a damned thang."

Riding quietly along the creek, a thought occurred to me: Papa's killer probably took the trail down Polk Bayou into Batesville since Mavis and I had not found any evidence of the mule team at the Osage camp father to the southwest. The killer crossed Polk Bayou and headed for the Osage camp, but evidently turned east, recrossed the bayou and followed the old trail.

A man from Texas, like Neil Crow, would not know about the trail, unless someone showed it to him. If someone showed him that trail, they had mischief in mind.

I rode up beside Teddy Blue, when the width of the trail permitted, and voiced my assertion.

"Thet's good thinkin Chet."

I looked off down the creek trail and remembered something Papa had said one time.

"Old timers say a white man has been ambushed ever mile of this crick a tween here and Batesville."

"I heerd thet. Looks like they woulda learnt to stay away from hit."

We had ridden a little farther when Teddy Blue made a comment I will never forget: "Ah wonder iffen it was Crow thet kilt Papa. Don't matter none though. Crow needs killin anyway."

We occasionally clattered across shale rock slabs, which magnified the sound of our iron-shod horses.

"Let's git offen this shale fer a spell," he said. "We'll come back to the trail on down the crick aways."

He pulled the bay left into a heavily forested woodlot of black oak, willow oak, elm, pine and sycamore trees, interspersed with cedar glades. Strong odors of pine and cedar mixed with fainter odors of moldy plant life, toadstool and lichen. We were not fifty yards off the trail, when we heard the clicking sound of a horse walking on shale rock. Teddy Blue, pulled up, signaled for quiet, dismounted and waved me down off my horse. He motioned for me to hold my hat over my horse's nose and eyes like he was doing with his bay. I realized he wanted to distract our horses from smelling the other horse and from making any noise that might attract the rider, or his horse.

Teddy Blue had pulled his bay in behind an ancient oak. I lined my little sorrel mare behind the bay. We watched through the brush. A rider passed north along the trail. I thought it might be one of the Osage boys going up to the trading post. If the rider happened to be someone I knew, I wanted to ask if he had seen someone recently leading two mules through the woods. But I do not believe Teddy Blue wanted to be seen by friend or foe.

Teddy Blue struggled with the big bay. The horse did not care to have a stinking hat held over his eyes. He pranced and fidgeted. My mare stood quiet and looked at me out of her left eye, while I held my old hat up close to her nose. She was so quiet, in fact, I began to wonder if she was sick, but she wasn't. She just had less tension in her than any animal I ever saw. I do not know how old she was, but she lived until 1890, and was lively right up until the day she died.

We bent low trying to see the rider underneath the overhanging branches. I thought surely that it would be someone I knew from either church or the trading post. The heavy undergrowth blotted out everything but the legs of the rider and bottom half of the horse. Teddy Blue could not see any better than I could, but he noticed something I didn't. He noticed the wide skirt of the saddle, and the extra thick pommel, made for roping and holding cattle. What he saw caused an immediate change of plan.

"Chet, thet's a Texas saddle."

We waited for the rider to pass. Eventually, the sound of the horse walking on shale rock passed beyond our hearing. Teddy Blue waved his hand at me and swung into the saddle. I followed suit and followed him, as he turned his horse back north through the woods for several hundred yards before angling back, to the creek trail. I was beginning to wonder what he was up to, when he leaned close and whispered that since the horse ahead carried a Texas saddle, the rider was probably Neil Crow

. "If thet's Crow, ah want to know whar he's headin. He could be goin to the tradin post, but ah doubt it."

"Maybe he's headin fer our cabin," I said.

"Thet's what ah'm thankin. We got to get back and warn Mavis and Ludi."

The narrow trail along Polk Bayou made ambush a distinct possibility and Teddy Blue knew it. He took an oblique angle away from the trail and pushed through heavy timber angling northeast toward our homestead two miles away. We were now south of Cave Creek and needed to cut across the hill above the bluff that bordered the creek, near a mile uphill at a steep angle through heavy cedar growth, stunted pine trees, persimmon and oak saplings. The terrain plateaued on top of the hill for several yards before descending sharply another mile east, where a steep drop-off at the bottom could throw an unwary rider headfirst onto the Batesville Pike.

Teddy Blue decided to give the horses a quick breather, when we reached the plateau. An eagle, in all his majesty, never had a better view that we did from that hilltop, Cave Creek Valley and our entire homestead in full view. The undulating green sea of treetops smudged occasionally by a brown square, where a farmer--Indian probably--had once cleared ground to plant a patch of corn or tobacco. The old fields, long abandoned, were now grown up in briar patches and sage grass.

The sun reflected off a scattering of thunderheads stretching like gigantic white columns from earth to heaven. I wondered if Papa Austin and Mama Ida were on top of one of those big white fluffy clouds watching Teddy Blue and me.

Visible at five miles, on the northern horizon, on a hilltop above Dry Creek, stood the Sandtown Trading Post. Looking across that magnificent space, I thought of the eagle and wondered what it must be like, to loose our earthbound ties and soar free over the mountains. I wished I could, if only for a little while.

Teddy Blue reined in his horse close to the edge of the bluff. I rode up beside him. With a good running jump, I felt I could leap far enough out from the bluff to land in the silver shimmering waters of Cave Creek below.

"Come o'er here Chet and hep me look fer thet rider. He's down there somewheres."

I calculated the rider would be somewhere along Polk Bayou past the Cave Creek juncture and I concentrated on a stand of heavy timber bordering the bayou, dark green in color, almost black. The big oak trees, cottonwoods and persimmons hugged the water and flourished in the driest weather. The bayou ran like a black snake curling back through the hills. I followed the snaking turns and quickly spotted our man on horseback. He broke from heavy cover a hundred yards upstream from where Cave Creek joined the bayou.

As we expected, the rider turned northeast away from the bayou toward the dogwood grove that lay over a gentle rise in the valley floor.

Using the cover of the dogwood grove, he headed straight for the back of the burned out blackened remains of the church.

"He's headin fer the cabin head-on," said Teddy, "thet way he'll less likely be spotted. My guess is Mavis ain't payin much mind with Ludi there. We'd better git on down."

"Look yonder," I said, pointing.

Two figures left the back of the cabin and walked out toward the creek. Mavis and Ludi had decided to inspect the falls area of the creek.

Ludi had evidently promoted himself to chief engineer for the mill project, and I suppose wanted to determine the best method of laying the foundation for the mill. No doubt Mavis and Ludi, standing on the big rock above the blue hole, made perfect targets for a rifleman from anywhere close to the site of the burned out church. "Let's go, we ain't got time to lose," said Teddy Blue.

We lost sight of the valley and the homestead, as we pushed our horses through heavy timber down the hill's sharp eastern slope. We struggled to hold our horses in check, when they stumbled and skidded on rocks. When we reached the final fifty yards of the forty-five degree slope, our horses began squatting and skidding and came out hard over a six-foot drop-off onto Batesville Pike. Teddy Blue nearly lost the saddle on his big bay. I hung on to my pommel with both hands, hugged the little mare with my knees and made it.

We slammed into the pike a few yards south of the creek and took a few seconds to check for injuries to the horses and ourselves. Except for minor scratches, we came out unscathed. We cantered up the road until we reached the creek crossing. Teddy Blue pulled up before crossing the creek and told me to turn back west along the base of the bluff and flank the dogwood grove on the south side.

"As soon as ah warn Mavis and Ludi, ah'm circlin north on foot and will come round the grove from the northwest, so watch fer me. We'll have Mavis and Ludi with rifles in the cabin on the east, ah'll git round to the north and west side, and you'll be on the south side. If he breaks from cover, he'll head fer the creek. Don't wait for me. Kill him. If ye don't knock him out of the saddle on the first shot, kill his horse. I want him on foot. Got it?"

I was stunned by the implication of what he said and did not answer. I had never shot at anyone and I knew that horse and doubted I could kill it.

"Got it?" He repeated.

"Yeh, I got it."

Well, I did not know if I *got it* or not. One minute I was on my way to Batesville participating in a clandestine night raid; the next thing I knew I was on Cave Creek setting up an ambush that placed me in a position to shoot someone off a horse. I told myself that was Papa's killer in the dogwood grove, but I was not sure about it. The only thing I really felt sure about: Teddy Blue meant to kill Neil Crow.

Masked by heavy timber, I led my horse down the south side of the creek about two hundred yards. Not wanting to get my feet wet, I mounted the sorrel and waded her across the creek. After dismounting and tying up to a sapling, I crawled to the edge of a thicket and took a position in heavy brush from where I could look out across the open strip of grassland to the dogwood grove.

Mavis and Ludi stood in plain sight on the big rock overlooking the falls. Ludi waved his arms and pointed, doing most of the talking. Mavis, holding a rifle, seemed to be doing most of the listening. I knew Teddy Blue had turned east along the bluff and would be about even with the cabin, and sure enough, while I watched, Mavis and Ludi seemed attracted by something across the creek. Mavis immediately turned toward the cabin with Ludi right behind. Not trying to be obvious, both glanced toward the burned-out church, and acted unhurried. I breathed a sigh of relief, when they stepped on the back porch out of my sight. Mavis and Ludi were safe inside the cabin. I knew two rifles would be looking through the front windows of the cabin.

Teddy Blue, on foot, entered my field of vision. He walked between the barn and the cabin, headed for the backporch, and out of sight of a shooter in the dogwood grove.

The hair stood up on the back of my neck and I broke out with a serious case of chill bumps, when I realized I was now closer to Crow than anyone. I turned my attention to the dogwood grove and checked for movement. My palms beaded with sweat; my heart thumped against my ribs. I tried to gain control of my emotions and was not entirely successful. I felt faint and had a great need for a hot cup of black coffee.

I expected Teddy Blue, once inside, would tell Mavis and Ludi someone was stalking the cabin from the dogwood grove and would show them my general position and explain his plan.

The dogwood grove and the cabin were in my field of vision. I was scanning the dogwood grove in my front when movement to the right caught my eye. Teddy Blue left the back porch and trotted back to the barn, keeping the cabin between the dogwood grove and him. Where were the two dogs Ludi brought? I found out later Ludi had locked them in the corncrib to keep them from running off, until we fed them a few times and they got used to our place, a good move on his part, the way things turned out. We did not need a pair of dogs mixing in.

Teddy Blue next appeared on the north side of the barn. He jogged northeast toward graveyard hill. I knew he planned circling the east end of the little hill, using the hill to mask his movements from anyone in the dogwood grove. After he passed around the hill, he would turn west and cross the Batesville Pike maybe a quarter-mile up, and pass around the dogwood grove on the north side, eventually coming in behind the grove on the west side, all told, a march of over a half-mile. But, I expect he did not think Crow, or whoever, was going anywhere soon.

I decided to change my position and move farther west along Cave Creek toward Polk Bayou. I did not think anyone would see me. The fellow in the dogwood grove was not expecting anyone on his flank, and heavy woods hid me. I wanted to see Teddy Blue when he came around the west end of the dogwood grove. I eased back to my mare, caught up her reins and led her along a path bordering the creek.

Reins in one hand, rifle in the other, I eased along. Crackling and thrashing in the brush startled me. I flung myself face down in front of the little mare, expecting gunshots at any second. Relief swept over me, when I discovered our goatherd feeding along the edge of the timber on the north side of the creek--an unexpected development.

I got to my feet a bit shaky, caught up the mare's reins and continued along the creek path trying to be quiet, hoping Billy wouldn't spot me. Billy could get me killed, because I knew, if he saw me, he would likely bleat and make a run for me and reveal my position. One or two of the old nannies raised their heads and looked at the mare and me as we passed, but paid little attention. Billy, on the far side of the herd, eating his way through a briar patch, did not see me.

I passed on down the creek well past the goatherd and reached a position, where I felt comfortable. I loosely looped the reins of the little sorrel around a sapling. Rifle in hand, I slipped across the narrow band of timber bordering the creek, dropped down on hands and knees and crawled out to the edge of the timberline. I looked out across a narrow belt of flat grassland to the dogwood grove.

Low-hanging cedar branches masked my position that was directly across from the southwest corner of the dogwood grove. My field of vision included our cabin to my right, the south edge of the dogwood grove and the grove's west end. A saddled horse stood hipshot tethered to a dogwood tree at the rear of the grove. The rifle scabbard was empty. Ten steps beyond the horse and about a hundred steps from my position, a gigantic knarled hundred-year-old oak tree stood apart--a majestic observer.

I lay on my stomach facing the dogwood grove, rifle pushed out in front. Could I shoot a man off a horse? At first, I hoped it would not happen, but I had a vision of Papa shot to pieces lying in the road in his tattered long-handled pink underwear, Mavis cradling his head in her lap. My feelings hardened, and I hoped it would happen. I quietly levered the breech partially open and made sure a shell had chambered. Now, all I had to do was just cock the hammer and pull the trigger.

I had no sooner settled in under the cedar when Mavis did a remarkable thing. Scanning the edge of the dogwood grove for signs of the intruder, I happened to glance at the cabin not expecting to see anyone, but the front door opened and Mavis, bold as you please, stepped out on the front porch with a broom in her hand and began sweeping. Ludi told me later he thought she had lost her mind. I thought so too.

She had reason for her perceived madness not readily apparent, at least to Ludi and me. If the bushwhacker concentrated on her, she reasoned he would not likely see Teddy Blue when he crossed the road north of the cabin on his way to circle around the north side of the dogwood grove.

Something was odd about the way she moved. Although she made the pretense of sweeping the porch, she swept in the same spot. I finally realized she was keeping one of the large oak porch posts between the grove and her. A bushwhacker might get a shot, but Mavis was not presenting much of a target.

She moved quickly to the north end of the porch, behind another post, and casually looked up the road. Once she saw Teddy Blue cross the Batesville Pike, she started sweeping back toward the front door. She stopped dead still behind a post. I expected to hear a rifle shot any moment. But I am guessing the bushwhacker wanted a sure shot and waited for her to walk out in the open on the edge of the porch, but she never did. All of a sudden, she disappeared through the front door. I let out a sigh of relief and realized I had been holding my breath.

No birds sang. No squirrels barked. No crows or blue jays shrieked warnings. Everything was quite. In the strip of pasture between the woods along the creek and the dogwood grove, new sprigs of spring grass broke the ground along with a variety of weeds. Oddly enough, bunches of bright yellow daffodils were scattered helter-skelter.

I was considering the possibility an Indian maiden a long time ago planted the daffodils, when Teddy Blue came into view at the rear of the dogwood grove. He held a 44-40 caliber rifle in his right hand, finger on the trigger, the long barrel straight up beside his right ear. He spotted the tethered horse, stopped, dropped the rifle to firing position in the crook of his left arm and watched the rear of the dogwood grove for a moment. He raised the barrel up beside his right ear and approached the horse from the rear like a cat walking on hot rocks. I remember thinking all he needed to do was drop the barrel, cock the hammer and drop it on the bushwhacker.

The roan detected Teddy Blue's approach. Its head snapped up and around, ears snapped forward. It pulled the reins taut. The tie held. Teddy stopped and said something. I could hear his voice but could not understand the words. He was trying to sooth the roan with soft words and not have him snort or nicker, alerting the bushwhacker to danger in his rear.

Teddy talked low to the horse and eased forward. The roan shied, but Teddy Blue kept inching forward and eventually caught the reins, worked his way up to the bridle and began scratching the horse behind the ear. The roan immediately quietened and began nuzzling Teddy. I remember thinking the roan was a nice big horse, one I would not mind owning. About that time, matters got complicated.

While Teddy Blue caught up the horse, Billy and the goatherd unwittingly entered the impending conflict. For some reason, known only to goats, Billy decided it was time to feed on the new leaf growth of the dogwood trees. Billy knew, and it may be assumed the other goats knew too, the tree limbs hanging close to the ground were heavy with new leaves putting them in easy reach of the small animals, without their having to stand on back legs and stretch for their forage, which Billy, for one, did not enjoy. He had been experiencing difficulty with his lower back ever since Mavis slung him through her kitchen window, and Teddy Blue had added to his discomfort, when he kicked him off the back porch into the muddy yard.

Billy had my full attention. I knew Mavis was watching, and probably giving him a pretty good chunk of a cussing. She said later that she thought about killing him. Billy led; the rest of the herd strung out behind. Billy stopped and seemed take an interest in something in the dogwood thicket. The other goats bunched around Billy and looked into the thicket. Billy flicked his tail a time or two and entered the dogwoods.

Neil Crow had made a deadly miscalculation. He did not make a proper scout and was unaware the church and the church outhouse had been burned to the ground. Two hundred yards of open space now separated the east edge of the dogwood grove from the front of our cabin. I am sure Crow counted on the burned log church to screen from the cabin, which would have allowed him to close to within easy killing range.

He faced a dilemma. He could make a sudden charge across the open space, coming at the cabin head-on, and hope he wouldn't be seen, or he could try to work his way north through the dogwood thicket and hope to cross the road and come at the cabin from the north side. Of course, Crow did not know he was already spotted and surrounded by Abbotts and was not slipping up on anyone.

The goatherd entered the grove and headed directly for Crow. They were friendly goats and enjoyed human companionship. Billy was the friendliest goat of all.

I heard a grunt, a smack, and a bleat and presently Billy burst out of the dogwood thicket with a hat in his mouth. He danced into the open, flicked his tail a time or two, while vigorously chewing Crow's hat. Goats will eat about anything, and I suppose nothing taste better to a goat than a sweaty Texas hat.

I spotted whom I assumed was Crow crouched low at the edge of the thicket. He looked like he wanted to get his hat away from Billy. I lay dumbfounded, not believing what I was seeing. It is strange how attached some people are to their hats. I am a lot that way myself.

I was not real sure it was Crow, until he burst into the open, rifle in hand, and made a dash for Billy. I guess he felt no one knew he was around, so he could take a chance and try to retrieve his hat, but Billy did not cooperate. He liked the hat and was not going to give it up. Crow charged Billy. Billy dodged aside, hat in mouth, and bolted for the creek.

Crow ran about ten steps into the open. When Billy bolted, Crow turned back toward the grove. I finally came to my senses, realizing the man was in that dogwood grove trying to kill an Abbott.

I shifted my body and was bringing my rifle to bear, when Ludi opened on Crow from the cabin window with a rifle. Ludi was not much of a shot. Mavis gave him hell about it later, but Ludi never was much for using firearms, and I could not fault him. Some people are simply better at it than others are. When Crow and the goat ran into the open, it startled Ludi, and he fired before he was ready. Puffs of dust kicked up around Crow's feet, and he dove back into the cover of the dogwood grove. Ludi's bullets ricocheted off the hard ground and cracked close by me. Scared me, when I realized I was in the line of fire. I flattened out against the ground, scooted backward like a crawdad enough to get the trunk of a cedar tree between the cabin and me.

Billy still had Crow's hat in his mouth, chewing away, when he entered the timber along the creek about seventy-five yards east of where I lay. When the firing started, the rest of the goatherd bolted out of the thicket and chased after Billy. When the goats loped across the clearing between the dogwood thicket and the creek, Mavis stepped out on the porch, bold as anything. She fired her Henry four times. One of the heavy slugs cut a dogwood branch in two directly between Teddy Blue and me. I was safe enough, but I flinched anyway. Crow, lying low, did not return fire. He knew the game was up. I am sure his main thought was survival. He needed his horse bad.

I looked left away from Crow's position. Teddy Blue stood beside Crow's horse. He removed the saddle and bridle, took hat in hand and slapped the roan on the rump. The horse jumped, made a few quick steps, and trotted down the hill almost directly toward me. Teddy Blue carried Crow's saddle and bridle uphill a little way, to the old oak tree, laid the saddle down at the foot of the tree, sat on it and leaned back against the trunk, rifle across his knees. He pulled a cigarillo and a match from his shirt pocket, lit the cigarillo and eased his head back against the tree, pushing his hat slightly over his eyes. Blue tobacco smoke curled into the branches. Crow's horse passed to my left and snorted when he smelled my little sorrel down at the creek.

I turned my attention back to the dogwood thicket. I knew Crow was on the move. Spotted and shot at, he would be desperate to get out of rifle range. I caught glimpses of him on his feet, crouched and headed to the rear of the thicket. He did not know his horse was gone.

I tried to get a bead on Crow, but remembered Papa's teaching early on about making sure of your target. I could have snapped some shots into the dogwood thicket at the running man, but I might not have hit him, and it would have given my position away, something I did not want to do with Teddy Blue waiting patiently smoking a cigarillo.

Crow moved fast and made a lot of noise like a frightened deer thrashing through a heavy thicket. Teddy Blue heard him coming. He shifted slightly to his left and brought his Winchester loosely to his shoulder, letting the barrel rest across his left knee. He took a couple of quick draws from his little cigar, reached out and carefully laid his smoke on top of a small flat rock.

Crow burst out of the thicket into the open. He looked wildly left and right for his horse. He held his rifle with his right hand over the trigger guard. He looked down at an empty holster and slapped at the holster in disgust. Teddy Blue watched from twenty yards.

Crow's horse had passed on down to the creek behind me. I heard him in the water splashing, drinking. But the drama unfolding before me drew my full attention. Teddy Blue sat unmoving on Crow's saddle at the base of the oak tree with a cocked rifle, pointing at Crow, set firmly against his shoulder, barrel resting across his left knee.

His horse nowhere in sight, Crow realized death was at hand. I saw the strength leave his legs; his knees buckled. He froze in step, like he was about to take a step, but changed his mind, rifle in his right hand, barrel pointing down. He sensed he was not alone and turned his head slightly to his right. Out of the corner of his eye, he caught the dim outline of Teddy Blue sitting in the deep shade of the ancient oak. He did not have to look hard to know Teddy Blue's rifle was looking at him.

A screeching eagle flew low down the creek, right over my head. I heard rustling as the goatherd made a dash inside the heavy brush cover along the creek, the nannies bleating for their kids. A cool southwest breeze brushed across the hillside bringing the smell of fresh-budding forest flowers. A jay from the haven of heavy timber screeched at the passing eagle. A frantic squirrel barked in the timber along the creek.

"Nice day," said Teddy Blue.

I heard the words, plain as anything like little clasps of thunder rolling downhill.

"Yeah, seems so," replied Crow, still looking toward my position, toward the creek.

"You Crow?"

"Yeah. You Abbott?"

"At yer service."

"I don't like this place," said Crow. "Can't see no further'n the next hill. Not like Texas. Could see fer miles any direction, not git slipped up on."

"Awful, hot and dry, though."

"Texas?"

"Yeah."

"Was thet."

Conversation ceased; a deathly stillness hovered over the land. Crow seemed fascinated with something on the ground. He made marks in the dirt with the toe of his right boot. Teddy Blue broke the silence.

"You the one kilt the ole man back up the road aways?"

"Nah, warn't me, did thet."

"Who was it?"

"Can't say."

"Can't say, nor won't?"

"Either way don't make no difference does it?"

"Nah, guess not."

Another moment of silence passed. Crow brought his left hand up slow-like and wiped his brow, the right arm still extended straight down, hand over the trigger guard. He was not even close to being ready to go into action, and he knew it.

"Is thet a Mexican cigar ah smell?" asked Crow, buying time on credit.

"It tis. Ah brought a couple of boxes from Austin."

"Damn, whut ah wouldn't give fer a good Mexican cigar right now."

"Well, iffen they got Mexican cigars in hell, yer in bizness," said Teddy Blue, and he dropped the hammer on the Winchester.

I was not ready for the explosion. I must have jumped clear of the ground even though I was lying flat. The brow Crow had wiped flew off his head in a spray of blood and brains. He nose-dived into the dirt and lay still, not even a quiver. I lay in shock, as a little cloud of dust rose over Crow like some ghostly apparition, caught the breeze and was gone. I wondered if I had seen Crow's brown soul leaving on its way to hell.

Teddy Blue still sat on Crow's saddle. He reached down, retrieved his cigarillo and took a puff. He looked toward me, but did not say anything. I walked out in the open and waved toward the cabin. Mavis and Ludi immediately appeared on the porch. I waved them on, and angled over to meet Mavis and Ludi, as they passed down the side of the dogwood thicket.

"He's kilt Crow," I said.

"Ain't no surprise there," said Mavis.

A few steps and we were in full view of Teddy Blue standing over Crow. Mavis, Ludi and I walked over to Teddy Blue. No one said anything. Teddy Blue turned away, walked back to the oak tree, and examined Crow's saddle.

The top front of Crow's head was missing. Blood pooled on the ground with a mixture of red and white brain tissue. Green flies were already swarming. Ludi looked, turned away and began gagging.

"Ludi, fer gawd's sake, git a holt a yerself. Hain't ye nary seen a dead person afore?" asked Mavis.

Ludi did not answer. He was taking short breaths, bent over with his hands on his knees.

"Chet, thet's a good saddle and bridle," said Teddy Blue," as he came back from making his inspection. "The saddle ain't marked, and ah don't beleve Crow's horse down there at the creek has got a brand. Ye kin ave 'im, but ye need to git 'im up to the barn and take Pa's little double A iron and brand 'im on the neck behind the base a the left ear, leastwise thet's how ah member Pa doin it on the stock. Brand thet saddle while yer at it. Crow lost his pistol out there in the grove. Ah beleve iffen ye was to backtrack 'im, ye'll find it. Ah spect it's a good'un."

"What are ye gonna do now, Teddy?" asked Mavis.

"Goin back to the cabin, git a cup a coffee and somethin to eat and head back to Batesville. Chet go git the bridle and go find the horse. Ludi, carry the saddle on down to the barn. It'll take yer mind offen yer troubles. Ludi, when ye git down there, git a shovel and a pick and come back up here and plant Crow right where he lays--good a place as any. Ye git 'im buried, two, three foot down, scatter some heavy rocks o'er the grave, keep the coyotes off. Don't want 'im gittin dug up, jist yet."

"Ye thank he's the one kilt Papa?" asked Mavis.

"Said he warn't," replied Teddy Blue.

"Ye talked to 'im?"

"Some."

"Ye beleve 'im?"

"Yeah, ah do. Warn't no reason to lie. He knowed he was a dead man. Ah thank a man would hate to lie on his way to hell. We're lookin fer somebody else."

I picked up the bridle and headed for the creek, where I had tied my little sorrel mare. Crow's roan had found her and both were standing side-by-side drinking. I spoke softly, eased up to the roan and held out the bridle. He nodded, and came to me and I slipped the bridle over his head. I rode the mare down to the barn and led the roan. He was not shy. He had been to our cabin before. A first-rate animal. I knew it the first time I saw him. Mavis would get the little mare.

Teddy Blue went directly to the kitchen, drank a quick cup of coffee and found a biscuit left from breakfast. I walked into the kitchen in time to hear Teddy Blue inquiring about rope.

"There's some rope looped o'er a stud in the corn crib. Whut are ye gonna do with rope?" asked Mavis.

"Don't know yit. This bizness with Crow has got me to thankin. May ave to hang somebody. Ah've found during serious interrogations ye kin git good results iffen ye put a rope round somebody's neck."

Mavis let the statement pass. She knew he was capable of anything, including hanging. Teddy Blue got up from the table and passed me on his way out the back door. I was thinking about what was left of Crow's head and felt a little queasy. I poured a tin cup of steaming black coffee and walked back out on the porch.

Coffee always settled me. I still did not feel like saying anything. I had watched my brother kill a man as cold as anything you would ever want to see, and I knew he had done it a lot.

Teddy Blue entered the corncrib and came out with a roll of rope looped over one shoulder. He looked at me.

"Git yer coffee drunk and git yer horse. Take the sorrel. We don't want nobody seein Crow's horse, jist yit. Let's go to Batesville."

Two hours of daylight remained for the two-hour, twelve-mile ride down the Polk Bayou Indian trail. We passed Ludi Wilson walking up the slope beside the dogwood grove with a shovel in one hand and a pick in the other. Ludi, head down, dragged along. His upper body seemed like it wanted to go forward, but his lower half seemed like it wanted to go in the opposite direction. I do not think he liked the idea of having to bury Crow, and I guess Mavis must have thought the same thing, because I looked back and saw her following Ludi, I suppose to give moral support. I think he needed it.

When Teddy Blue and I passed the west end of the dogwood grove, I glanced up the hill at Crow's body. Green flies already swarmed. I glanced at Teddy Blue, to see if he would look. He didn't.

Passing down the east bank of Polk Bayou, we discovered remains of four grinding mills wrecked by the 1867 flash flood. (Lazarus Statin's mill, one mile north of Batesville, was the only mill to survive that flood.) Teddy Blue said to remember the locations, because some of the heavy oak timbers appeared to be in good condition, and we ought to salvage several timbers for our mill project.

We walked our horses through lengthening shadows. Along the trail, we occasionally passed circles of stones--old campsites, and at least one rotted down log contraption, built by hunters. Settlers were afraid to build permanent cabins close to the big creek because of flash floods. Faintly outlined, the old road, mostly bare rock and red clay, paralleled the meandering bayou. Bayou peepers hushed constantly before us and commenced behind, as if we moved in a void of sound. I was still jumpy from the evening activity and occasionally spooked at shadows but the road only held shapes of things. We passed up the trail without incident. Near Batesville, we kicked our horses to a trot. At dusk, we walked our horses to the edge of the woods bordering the mill site, dismounted and observed the mill from a place of concealment.

The mill wheel, locked down and raised clear of the water, looked like the paddle wheel on a riverboat. That it was locked down did not surprise us, since little milling was done in the spring. Heavy milling began in early fall, when homesteaders harvested corn and wheat.

Lantern light shone through a side window of the mill office. A shadow passed in front of the window, the light dimmed and went out. An elderly man, in workman's overalls with galluses buckled over a faded shirt, wearing a blue and white striped train engineer's cap, stepped through a side door. He turned at the door, slid a heavy metal bolt in place and turned a lock with a large brass key hanging from a small silver chain around his neck. Producing a can of tobacco and a package of cigarette papers from the bib of his overalls, he took time to roll a smoke, and proceeded across the mill yard toward town.

We watched until the man disappeared over a rise in the road a hundred yards south, and walked our horses out of the woods across the mill yard up to the edge of the creek and let them drink. Teddy Blue studied the mill construction. He said he could not remember seeing a grinding mill anywhere in Texas. They had them obviously, but he had not seen one, not powered by flowing water anyway. As a kid, he went to local mills with Papa, but never paid attention to the mill's operation. Now he felt the need to know, especially if he was going to help build one, and he wasn't going to have the Statin mill to study much longer, because, when the time was right, he intended blowing it to smithereens. But blowing the mill would take more than the four sticks of dynamite he carried in his saddlebags.

Teddy Blue remembered Mavis saying that Mr. Wilson had given her his mill construction blue prints.

"We might as well try to foller thet design," he said.

All the grinding mills that I ever saw were of a log construction framework overlaid with heavy planking. Logs for our mill would come from our own property--the woods across the creek from our cabin. Heavy oak planks would be hauled in by wagon from the sawmill northeast of the Sandtown Trading Post, to supplement the timbers we planned salvaging from the flood-destroyed mills back up Polk Bayou. Teddy Blue also wanted to fortify our cabin at the same time we built the mill and the new church. Several logs in the cabin's walls were decayed at the corners and showed signs of potential collapse. I believe Teddy Blue, in considering the building projects, thought he was helping salvage something of his parent's dreams.

The sun had dropped behind a mountain west of the O'Neal Settlement, five miles or so up White River. Night shadows crept over the landscape. Foxes and coyotes hunted along the edge of the woods and crossed in front of us, sometimes stopping to investigate the intrusion into their territory before scooting off into the brush.

We walked our horses down a road that widened enough for team and wagon. Lamplights twinkled in homes and businesses of the town of fourteen thousand. On the west side of Polk Bayou flickering lamplight revealed locations of log cabins and clapboard houses scattered around the hills and along the banks of White River.

We passed behind the billiard hall and saloon on our way to the livery barn. Everything was quiet; it was suppertime. A steam-powered paddle wheeler docked at the river landing a quarter-mile downstream; a light flickered through a window in the pilot's cabin; otherwise, the steamboat appeared deserted.

We reined in at the lot gate of the livery barn. Teddy Blue dismounted and unlatched the gate letting it swing wide and led his horse through. I followed on foot leading my mare. I spotted movement inside the barn and flinched a bit. A liveryman forked hay into stalls lining either side of a wide central passageway beneath the loft.

Teddy Blue's bay nickered at the smell of livestock. My little sorrel did not make a sound. Snorting and shuffling sounds came out of the barn along with a middle-aged man with a pitchfork in his hand.

"Ah is jist bout to lock up and go to supper," he said, manner gruff and irritable.

I glanced at Teddy Blue's face in near darkness. It was not friendly. The liveryman stabbed the pitchfork tines in the ground; the pitchfork handle stood straight up quivering. Teddy Blue stepped down out of the saddle and walked right up to the man.

"Ah'll take jist a minute a yer time. Week, ten days ago, somebody brought two small gray mules in here late in the day. Was ye here?"

"Ah don't recollect."

"Maybe this'll hep some."

Teddy Blue stepped forward and with a strong backhanded blow slapped the liveryman so hard his hat flew against the barn wall ten feet away. The man grunted and went down on one knee, grabbed the handle of the pitchfork and came up fast holding the pitchfork low with the tines toward Teddy Blue. "Ye sunavabitch, I'll--."

He stopped short, for he was looking into the barrel of a Remington .44, and the metallic clicking of the cocking mechanism sounded like a roll of thunder in the quiet of the evening. I involuntary took a step backward, half expecting to see another man get his head blown off.

"I ain't got a lot of time and less tolerance," said Teddy Blue. "Now, who brung them mules in here and ye better not stutter or ah'll blow yer head clean off."

The liveryman dropped the pitchfork and developed a bad case of the shakes. The string went out of his legs. He sunk down on both knees.

"Go easy mister. I ain't here all the time. Somebody might a brought mules in, when I warn't here. We get a lot of mules comin and goin. Some of 'em come offen them riverboats." He nodded toward the river.

Teddy Blue took the coil of hemp from around his saddle horn. He dropped his left hand, gripping the rope, so the liveryman could get a good close-up look.

"Well, ah tell ye whut ah'm gonna do. Ah'm gonna give ye the benefit a the doubt, fer now. But iffen ah find ye was here, when thet little gray mule team come in, ah'll be back to hang yer sorry ass from one a them barn rafters. Get on yer feet."

The liveryman put his hands down in a motion to push himself up, but he could not rise. His legs seemed to have lost all strength.

"Mister, ah don't thank ah kin git up, jist yit."

That scene froze for me in a moment of time, implanted in my memory everafter. Neither man spoke. Teddy Blue looked down on the liveryman. The liveryman looked at the ground. I stood a few feet back, but the liveryman never looked at me. On his knees, when he did look up, staring directly into the barrel of that big pistol, I saw his mind working, dwelling on the shortness of life. I expect his life passed before his eyes like they say it does in times of dire stress.

Teddy Blue held the gun steady on the liveryman's head. Teddy Blue's bay took a step forward. The liveryman glanced at the horse.

"Thet's the third'un ah seen lately."

"Third whut?"

"Texas saddle."

"How'd ye know it's a Texas saddle?"

"Thick leather-bound wooden horn. Heavy horn made fer ropin. Stirrups made a wide steam-bent wood and wide fenders and thet bridle with the split-ear headstall is a rig we don't see here much."

"Man smart nough to know saddles, ort to be smart nough to member a pair a little gray mules."

Teddy Blue's thumb slid off the cocked hammer of the Remington. It scared me a little. I knew that gun had a hair trigger. A question crossed my mind: what if that gun goes off and blows the top of the liveryman's head off? The answer came in right behind: I did not think Teddy Blue cared one whit, and I think the same question and answer crossed the liveryman's mind too. Dealt a hand his turn to play, he spoke right up.

"Man brought them mules in was settin a Texas saddle, but don't tell nobody I tole ye. Ah'd be kilt fer shore, and ah got fambly at home."

Teddy Blue, looked down, studied the man. The stable hand dropped his eyes taking a great interest in Teddy Blue's boots like he might want to buy them. I halfway expected him to make an offer.

"Ye got a name on thet feller?"

"No name, but he's a Statin hand. Ah thank he's stayin up at the old Statin home place with Jack's fambly."

"Thet's Neil Crow--and he's from Texas awright. He's one mean sunavabitch. He's handy with a knife. Iffen he finds you tole me bout this, he'll cut yer gizzard out."

Of course Teddy Blue withheld the news that Crow was freshly dead and buried. The liveryman struggled to say something. He opened his mouth, but his throat locked up. He coughed and started taking short breaths. Teddy Blue took a step forward.

"But, who's settin tother Texas saddle?

"Nary laid eyes on thet feller. Kid come down one night from o'er there at the saloon and billiard hall leadin a horse and give me six-bits. Said a man sent him and fer me to put the horse up. I did thet and the next morning, when I got here, the horse was gone."

Teddy Blue took a moment to study the liveryman, who still looked at the ground. Teddy Blue knew the liveryman was not lying. He had questioned too many scared men.

"Git on up, when yer a mind to. Go on home to supper. Fergit bout this talk we are a havin. It ain't somethin ye'd want to member, savvy?"

The man coughed. "Yessuh."

"By the way, take yer time and tell me who owns this barn?"

The liveryman took some time to speak, and when he did a quavered voice measured words to get them just right.

"Decker fambly--owns it. Deckers and Statins."

"Ah thought so. Ye kin go on home now. Ah'll be watchin."

Teddy Blue lowered the hammer on the Remington and spun the big gun into the right-hand holster. He turned to the bay, grabbed the pommel and swung up in the saddle in one easy motion, guided the bay through the open gate with me following. I glanced back at the liveryman, as I passed through the open gate. He was still on his knees.

When we got far enough up the Polk Bayou road, where darkness hid our movements, Teddy Blue turned toward a heavy stand of weeping willow trees lining the bayou, round sentinels wearing green leafy hoop skirts. We rode our horses in under the drooping branches of one of the larger trees, dismounted, tied the horses to the trunk, and lay flat down side-by-side masked by the branches, but with a good view of the road.

Presently, the liveryman came at a trot, lantern bobbing. He broke into a hard run when he passed our position, heading home in a hurry. I wondered what he was going to tell his wife at supper. We watched him pass and kept quiet until we could not see the lantern, making sure he did not veer east toward the sheriff's office. We rode back down to the barn, opened the gate and went inside, opened all the stalls, shooed all the horses and mules, and one cow, out of the barn and through the lot gate. They wandered off in every direction.

Inside the barn, two pitchforks leaned against a stall gate. The pungent smell of fresh cut hay drew us to a hay pile near the back wall of the barn. We began forking hay into small piles at several places throughout and around the barn. Satisfied everything was ready, Teddy Blue reached in his shirt pocket and pulled out a small pack of Mexican cigarillos. He took one, gave me one, and we lit up. We took a few drags from our little cigars and began lighting hay piles, finishing with the large one inside the barn.

We saddled up and watched long enough to make sure the barn timbers were fired, and we rode up the bayou a little way, turned east on a side street, and rode past the saloon and billiard hall to Main Street. We turned north on Main and walked our horses past the sheriff's office and jail. A light shone through the window of the sheriff's office quite bright.

I thought it one of those newfangled electric lights, I had heard about. I did not see anyone through the window.

After we passed the sheriff's office, we kicked our horses up to a canter. We were a mile out of Batesville when we heard the fire wagon bells and some kind of loud horn, probably the docked riverboat. We pulled up and looked back. A bright light shone in the southwest. I immediately thought of Lot's wife in the Bible and how she turned to look back against good advice and immediately turned into a pillar of salt. Knowing I had sinned, I wondered at the possibility, but I felt all right. After a minute or so, Teddy Blue pulled his horse around.

"Looks like a fire a some kind," he said.

The barn burning did not bother me. The owners of the barn knew who killed Papa and probably had a hand in it. Teddy Blue still did not think it was Neil Crow. His thoughts turned to the man riding the third Texas saddle.

The aroma of boiling coffee filtered into my bedroom, stirred me. I lay still and considered the sliver of yellow light creeping under the door, an escapee from a lamp in the kitchen. I wondered how long I could lay there before Mavis came for me like an angel of death snatching an unborn from the womb. A long tiring day followed by a Batesville night excursion left me hoping Mavis would not have a lot for me to do. Hope without hope.

Dead tired, I threw the covers off, rolled out of bed and pulled on my overalls. Barefooting into the kitchen, I beelined for the coffee pot. Mavis and Ludi sat at the kitchen table discussing the mill and church building projects and paid little attention to my intrusion.

"Ludi, the best thang ah know to do is ave an old fashioned barn raisin, cept we'll build a mill and a church house."

"The way ah'm thankin," said Ludi, "we're gonna need a lot a hep. Havin a mill raisin would be the way to do it."

Mavis observed me rattling around in the cupboard searching for an old biscuit.

"I heerd you'ens come in. Real late it was, some after midnight. Whut appened?"

"Nothin much. We went to the livery barn, to see iffen we might find who brung our mule team in, but didn't ave any luck."

I decided to omit the incidentals of our Batesville visit. Knowing our encounter with the liveryman and how we burned the barn were not subjects I felt Mavis needed to know. Anyway, like all towns in those days, Batesville had many wooden buildings, and many fires. I ignored Mavis's stare, walked over, and looked out the kitchen window, while I sipped my coffee. Ludi spoke up and relieved me of further interrogation.

"Ah'll go up to the tradin post and put word out thet a week from Satidy, gawd willin and the crick don't rise, we'll start buildin the church and mill. Ah'll ask Rachel Carter bout her brothers. She's got plenty. Them ole injun boys won't hardly hit a lick at a snake, but maybe they'd like to make a dollar or two, to buy 'em some of thet good brewery beer outta St. Louie."

Ludi stood spoke no more, walked through the front room, collected his hat off a deer horn rack and went out the front door. I followed, curious as to what he was about. His saddled horse stood hipshot at the front gate. Mavis and he had been up awhile.

Where had Ludi spent the night? Detouring slightly, on my way back to the kitchen, I discreetly surveyed Papa's room. The bed did not look slept in, but Mavis could have straightened it, and I would not have known. He did not sleep in my bed that was for sure. Mavis brushed by me and went out on the front porch encased in early morning shadow. Day was breaking behind the barn. A shard of sunlight hit the very top of the rise behind the burned out church and reflected off the pearly-white dogwoods, giving the little hill a silver crown.

"Ludi, when ye comin back?"

"Tomorra, with a team and wagon. We got to start haulin mill lumber, and we got to start cuttin timber and gettin it in place. It's all got to be ready week from Satidy."

A smiling Mavis sat down on the front porch and let her feet dangle on the ground. She smoked one of Teddy Blue's cigarillos and sipped mountain mist from a tin cup. A smile was an uncommon feature on Mavis's face. She did not smile much in the morning or any other time. I pulled a Mexican cigarillo from a pack I discovered on a front room windowsill, went out on the front porch and took a seat behind Mavis in a cane-bottomed chair. I leaned the chair back against the wall and savored my cigar and coffee.

I could tell Mavis felt good. I think she anticipated rising above the misery of her life on that hardscrabble farm. She was going to be a mill owner and operator, at least someone was going to operate it--maybe me. I felt important just thinking about it.

Billy eased around the side of the cabin looking for me. He peeped around the corner at Mavis. She happened to glance toward the creek and spied the pesky goat. The little goat knew Mavis was giving him the evil eye. His mysterious goat instinct alerted him to the fact that it was not a good time to seek human companionship. He backed out of sight.

"Chet, we're gonna ave a mill and church raisin week from Satidy. Me and Ludi done decided. Lot a work got to be done afore thet, like gettin everythin in place, logs, mill plankin, tools and sich. Ah hain't been to but one, back when ah was jist a girl and it warn't a mill, but Ulbrick's barn thet got risen. Mrs. Ulbrick put on a good feed, iffen ye appen to like sausages and sauerkraut--which ah don't. But she made some sweets and German black bread, which hain't bad. Anyway, ah'm thankin bout barbeque."

"Whut kind a barbeque?"

"Goat."

Panicked bleating and pounding of tiny hooves caused me to get up from my chair and walk over to the south end of the porch. Billy, running full speed, plunged into the creek above the falls, dug hard to get through the pull of the current, exited on the opposite bank and disappeared into the woods.

"Mavis, kin a goat unnerstan human talk?"

"Nary heerd sich a thang."

"Which goats ye got in mind?"

"Well, we kin start with thet goat a you'rn and three or four a 'em kids thet hain't fit fer nothin cept suckin the milk out a 'em ole nannies, when I need hit fer my butter churn."

"Mavis, ye ain't gettin mah goat."

"Well, we'll see. Anyway, ah planned to buy a hog offen the Ulbricks. They got plenty. They got some big'uns. We need one'll dress out bout a hunnert and fifty pounds. Why don't ye ride down to the Ulbricks this mornin, try out thet new horse and saddle and see bout hit. Ah'm shore Elsa'll be innersted in yer new rig--and by the way, iffen yer gonna ride thet roan taken off Crow, I want thet sorrel mare. We'll need bout a three hunnert pound hog to get a hunnert and fifty pounds of dressed out pork. Ask Mr. Ulbrick how much he wants fer a hog thet size, and can Junior drive it up here."

"Mavis, some hogs can't be drove."

"If the drivin is a problem, tell him to kill it and haul it up here in his wagon. I'll pay extra fer thet. We'll clean and dress the hog up here. You'll ave to be up all night cookin the thang o'er hot coals. When you get back, go ahead and dig a pit behind the barn and start gathering hickernut wood."

I was not the only one that spent the next week at hard labor. Ludi, Teddy Blue, and I took crosscut saws, axes and awls to several large pines across the creek. We felled trees, trimmed away the branches and bark and used our two teams of mules to drag the timbers close to the waterfall.

"First thang we got to do is build a bridge crost the crick, o'er the falls," said Ludi.

Teddy Blue stared at Ludi a second.

"A bridge? The hell ye say."

Ludi's statement caused immediate consternation in my mind, but I did not voice an objection. I simply followed Teddy Blue's lead, took off my hat, wiped my brow and stared at Ludi.

Ludi seemed confident.

"Well, not zactly a bridge, but a platform crost the crick, to set the mill works on. We'll set large pine posts on both sides a the crick and lay crost some long logs. The logs'll be our cross timbers thet we'll overlay with oak two-by-six planks from the sawmill. When we're finished, hit'll look more like a bridge than most bridges in this country."

I supposed Ludi was right to make that statement, but I had never seen a bridge and wondered if he had--maybe in some picture book.

"Well yer the boss on this project Ludi," said Teddy Blue. Ah ain't got no idee bout building anythin, let alone a grindin mill."

Ludi puffed up at Teddy Blue's remark. I don't suppose he was ever boss of anything and maybe was beginning to feel important, a rare luxury in the hills.

"Once, the platform is built, we'll install the machinery right on top a it with the wheel in the water, and we'll build the housin o'er the machinery."

"Kin we do all thet in one day?" I asked.

"We kin, iffen we get several fellers willin to put in a full day's work, startin early, finishin late," replied Ludi.

"Well, we got to make shore thet everythin needed, is in place," said Teddy Blue.

"Hit'll be," said Ludi.

"We gonna build the church back, too?" I asked. I liked seeing and talking to someone other than family once in a while. A church house was a good place to visit, graveyard another.

"Yep. Might as well. Won't take much, iffen we git nough folks to hep on it," replied Ludi.

All the building material and necessary tools were in place on the appointed date. Teddy Blue and I had taken our mule teams over to Polk Bayou and scavenged several good timbers from washed out mills scattered along the creek. It took five trips in all to drag out the heavy oak timbers, many of which Ludi used during the construction to reinforce the mill platform around the heavy waterwheel gear housing.

Mavis baked several dried apple pies, at which she excelled. She thinly sliced dried apples, layered the slices in a crust covering them with goat butter, a good sprinkling of sugar and cinnamon, and baked the pie in a Dutch oven. I needed a doctor handy, when those pies came out of the oven, as I generally ate myself sick.

I was up all Friday night barbequing a hundred and fifty pounds of pork shoulder, butt, and ribs over a bed of hickory coals and trying to keep the flames down with an occasional dousing of water. I got good hickory smoke by soaking hickory wood chips in water and throwing them on the fire.

"We want hit smoked and seared good," said Mavis, "not burnt to a crisp."

I kept awake by visiting the kitchen periodically during the night for coffee that I kept boiling over fireplace coals. Sometime between midnight and sunup, from the garden, I noticed a light in the kitchen window. I walked up to the cabin and found Mavis in the kitchen preparing biscuit dough.

"Hit's gonna be a long day," she said.

"It's already been a long day fer me."

"Ah know hon, but yer young. Ye'll git o'er hit."

"I wonder."

But pork was all I had to worry with and that was a relief in itself. I was glad Mavis spared the goat sacrifice. I dreaded the thought of having to make the selections. I have often pondered the Old Testament story of Abraham and the choice he had to make between Isaac and the ram caught in the bush. I don't see how he did it.

Teddy Blue was the only one who got anywhere close to a good night's sleep. He slept in the barn as usual, was up, ready to go before daylight, and helped make extra coffee for the morning crowd. Mavis's biscuits smeared with generous amounts of goat butter and honey would require a lot of coffee to wash them down.

Our two new dogs announced the arrival of Ludi Wilson and his sister, Lois. I saw the handwriting on the wall, as far as the dogs were concerned. With all the strangers arriving, the dogs would be barking all day and a general nuisance. I locked them in the corncrib and fed them each a biscuit. I slipped them a little barbeque later.

The Wilson siblings, particularly Lois, emotionally affected by bad luck in the matrimonial department, hardly ever left the Wilson homestead. I believe they enjoyed their outing, chiefly for two reasons: Mavis and Teddy Blue, plus Ludi got to play boss for a day. Ludi, Lois and I were in the kitchen with Mavis, when she announced, "The Ulbricks are comin."

Puzzled by her statement, I asked, "How do ye know thet?"

"Ah smell sauerkraut and sausages."

I went to the kitchen window. Sure enough, the Ulbricks were crossing the creek in their wagon pulled by their Percheron horse team.

Mrs. Ulbrick brought several fruit pies, black German bread and of course a wash kettle full of sauerkraut and sausages. I ran out to help Mr. Ulbrick and Junior struggle with the sauerkraut and sausage kettle, wrestling it around to the back porch.

I thought about our Shires. They were big horses, but Shires were no match for Percherons. Mr. Ulbrick offered Ludi the use of his team. Ludi and Teddy Blue later made good use of the Percherons and our two teams of mules to move some of the heavier timbers into place.

"We couldn't a done it, thout the Ulbrick's big horses," Ludi said later.

Ludi was still in the kitchen when Junior Ulbrick came in to ask about his work assignment. Mavis gave Ludi a strong signal he could not ignore.

"Well, Ludi," said Mavis, "ye hain't gettin my mill built in here."

Ludi and Junior left immediately through the back door and headed down to the creek.

I figured Elsa would come looking for me, and I made a dash for the garden behind the barn, where I was supposed to be watching the barbeque pit. Someone put her on to me. Before long she came around the barn with Billy tagging along, Elsa's long blonde hair pulled back in a bun and tied with a blue ribbon. She wore a gray work dress, the hem of which flirted with the tops of ugly brown high-top shoes, laced all the way up.

"I followed my nose," she said.

I almost made an uncharitable remark about her nose I would probably have come to regret, but held my tongue. I sought to offset her intentions of closing on me by stating, "Ah've got everythin under control. Maybe they need ye in the kitchen."

But, if she heard me--and she did--it did not seem to register. She came up to the pit, where I was reddened from having spent several hours facing hot coals and acquired what appeared to be sunburn in the middle of the night.

"You're blistered," said Elsa. "I need to go get some butter to put on your face. Help take out some of the sting."

"Nah, it'll wait til night, and ah'll do it."

The last thing I wanted was someone spotting Elsa smearing my face with goat butter behind the barn. It would have been a difficult thing to explain to anyone, especially the Germans.

Eagle and Rachel Carter and six of Rachel's Indian brothers arrived in a wagon pulled by a team of black mules. Rachel brought a few jugs of fresh mountain mist, and some fruit pies. Her older brother, Charlie Two-Toes, already into the mountain mist showed signs of possibly not earning a day's wage set by Teddy Blue at one dollar.

Thirty men and women, or thereabouts, came for the raising. No one ever made an accurate count and years afterward when people talked about the church and mill raising at the Abbott place, and a guess was made about the number of people, "It must have been thirty," is what everyone always said.

Ludi Wilson took the majority of the men and started on the log platform over the creek. Whistler Lewis took a few men with him and supervised laying the log foundation for the little church. The inside width measurement of the church was set at ten feet and length sixteen feet. They built a small fireplace into the back wall, five feet behind the lectern.

The inventive Whistler found another Civil War ammunition box, five feet long and eighteen inches square, to stand on end and use for a lectern. According to writing on the side of the box, it once held .50 caliber cartridges from a factory in Springfield, Massachusetts. Turned on end, the box provided ample room for Whistler's bible. The bible would rest on a lace doily supplied by Mavis, a doily once belonging to Mama Ida.

Mid-morning, I was still in the garden watching the barbeque. Elsa was watching me and evidently did not intend leaving my presence. She wanted to talk, and I didn't. I kept busy poking the fire, and she kept busy talking. I had not realized Germans were so talkative.

Deputy Sheriff Kel Decker rode up to the front gate and looked over the activity on both sides of the road, particularly the construction of the mill. He dismounted, walked through the gate and down to the creek for a close up view. Someone in the crowd spotted Decker as soon as he crossed the creek and alerted Teddy Blue. Teddy Blue sidled off to the cabin, went through the back door, but in no time was back out on the porch wearing a strapped down black leather gun belt. Silver Mexican Conchos, inlaid in the holster and belt leather, sparkled in the morning sun. I decided it was time for a coffee break.

I walked toward the cabin with Elsa in tow, making the pretense of going for coffee, to get her from behind the barn and back to the cabin. I figured if I could get her in view of the women at the cabin, maybe one of them, hopefully her mother, would require her attendance in the kitchen, where she belonged, and not trying to smear me with goat butter behind the barn. When Teddy Blue walked out on the back porch, with gunbelt on and holster tied down, I thought I might see something exciting.

Mavis walked out on the back porch behind Teddy Blue. I watched her, Teddy Blue, and the deputy. I figured something was going to happen, but I was not sure what. Decker never said anything to anyone and wandered over to a log fire, where hung a big metal bucket of coffee.

He acted as if he owned the place, without asking anyone, picked up one of several tin cups sitting on a stump, and poured himself a cup. I poured a cup for myself and sat down on a log. Decker moved off to one side and watched the proceedings, sipping his coffee. He had not spoken to anyone since arriving and no one had spoken to him. Mavis came down off the porch and confronted him.

"Whut in hell do ye want?"

"Now now, Miss Abbott, don't git yer bowels in a uproar. Ah'm here on official bizness."

"Well, whut?"

"Ah'm lookin fer Neil Crow."

"Hain't seen 'im."

"Well, ye seen 'im onct."

"Onct, but not lately."

Teddy Blue had walked up on Decker's blind side and stood sizing him up, listening to the conversation.

"Maybe he went back to Texas," said Teddy Blue.

Decker turned slowly, as if to chastise the speaker, but paled, when he got the full force of the gunfighter staring him square in the face.

"W-W-Why would he do thet?"

"Cause, it kin be awful unhealthy fer a Texas pistolero to be messin round in these Arkansas hills," replied Teddy Blue.

Decker attempted to gain self-control. He was near throwing up.

"Ah heerd ye was back. Ye ain't here on no official Ranger bizness?"

Mavis backed away and stood quietly apart observing. A smile ticked at the corners of her mouth.

"None official, but ah'm makin it my bizness to find who kilt my Pa."

"What ye gonna do, ye find 'im?"

A few stragglers comin over for coffee began to sidle up close to pick up on the conversation.

"Hain't you fellers got somethin better to do," said Mavis.

They took their coffee and moved a few steps back toward the creek. She looked back at Decker with fire in her eyes. She took up his question.

"We aim to kill 'im, and anybody else thet had a hand in it, iffen we got time," said Mavis.

"We got law in this county," said Decker.

"Whut law?" Mavis snorted.

"Me. Ah'm the law."

"Ye hain't nothin but a dog turd," said Mavis.

Decker reddened.

"Watch yer mouth, Miss Abbott, or ye'll be in violation."

Mavis took a step toward Decker, speaking through teeth firmly clenching a cigarillo. "Violation a whut?--ye sorry bastard."

Decker flinched but did not respond. He turned, walked away toward some men who were struggling in the creek with heavy timbers. He said in a loud voice, "Anybody know the whereabouts of a man named Neil Crow?"

No one responded to the query, for the simple reason only four people present knew, and they were not saying. A horse nickered in the barn lot. The late Neil Crow's roan came over to the lot fence with ears up and forward, looking at Decker's horse tied to the front fence. The two horses knew each other having traveled together.

"Thet's Crow's horse," said Decker.

"Nah, it ain't," said Teddy Blue, "thet's my brother Chet's horse."

"Where'd he git it at?"

"Pa bought it offen a drummer, come through some time ago, so ah'm tolt."

Decker walked down to the lot fence. He looked the animal over carefully and spotted the little double-A brand I had burned on the neck of the horse behind the left ear. He knew the Abbott brand. He had seen it enough over the years in disputes over hogs running wild. Papa branded all his animals in the same place.

"Shore looks like Crow's horse," said Decker.

"Lot a horses thet color look alike," said Teddy Blue.

Decker turned and started walking to his horse. I was standing by the fire, sipping coffee. Decker gave me a hard look, and as he passed by Mavis and Teddy Blue, and casually observed, "How come yer little brother don't look like the rest a ye? He's a good bit taller than any Abbott I ever saw, and he's the spittin image of thet Wilson feller o'er there."

Teddy Blue gave me a quizzical look, and looked at Ludi, and back to me. He smiled softly as if he recognized something for the first time. Ludi Wilson must have heard his name, he came over to our little group. As Teddy Blue watched Ludi walk over, the small smile pulling at the corner of his mouth widened into a grin. I guess Ludi and I did favor. I suppose the resemblance was more noticeable, when seen together, but I had never given it much thought.

"Some folks don't allus favor they kin," said Mavis, "jist like goats and horses."

Mavis turned and walked toward the back porch. Decker didn't say more. He ambled back out to the road, mounted his horse, sat for a moment looking around as if measuring something, nudged his horse in the ribs and rode south.

Sundown: The new pine log church was finished, with a flooring of cedar boards laid over a foundation of cedar posts. Not only would the floor not rot, snakes would not den under the cedar because of the strong scent. The church was ready for Sunday services and Wednesday night singings, when people could get away from their farms and felt like singing. That did not happen often.

Mill work was still to be done. Mostly mechanical things Ludi could take care of without a lot of help. Minor adjustments for different grain would require minor adjustments prior to milling. Ludi and Lois decided to stay overnight and finish the mechanical work, as well as help replace rotten logs in the walls of our cabin, which badly sagged at the corners.

The working party started breaking up near sundown. People began gathering their tools, loading the wagons and buggies and made ready to head home. Something happened that bordered on the miraculous: Elwood Crafton came out on the back porch with a guitar, and Mavis stepped up beside him with her fiddle.

Mavis cut down on the old fiddle tune "Sally Gooden," and Elwood tried to keep up. Some couples made a pass at dancing, stiff straight-legged stepping out from having worked on their feet all day and, in some cases, having imbibed a considerable amount of mountain mist. They invented a new staggering dance step. A lot of shouting and singing messed up what was normally a quiet night along Cave Creek. It turned out to be an admirable end to a long day.

Elsa helped me hang coal oil lanterns to posts on the back porch. A full moon rose over the proceedings and finally about midnight festivities wound down. Most of the pork barbeque and black German bread was gone by midnight. The sauerkraut and sausage kettle was empty and the kettle washed out, in the creek. Leftover pastries, biscuits and cornbread started me thinking about breakfast.

Teddy Blue and Lois huddled on one side of the porch, shoulders rubbing. Mavis handed her fiddle over to Will Baxter and took a seat on the opposite side of the porch with Ludi Wilson. Ludi spoke in low tones and Mavis looked at him in a strange kind of way as if they shared a secret. Her eyes blinked more than usual, fluttered actually.

Elsa Ulbrick pestered me to dance, but I told her I did not know how. Even if I could, I would not, but I did not tell her that. Even though no dancing was involved, Elsa was very persistent about hanging on to me.

I was thankful when the Ulbrick's decided to go home and Mrs. Ulbrick told Elsa to get in the wagon. Elsa said she would walk home directly, but Mrs. Ulbrick was firm, saying it was late. She heard wolves, she said, howling back toward their homestead. The mention of wolves in the dark settled it for Elsa. She reluctantly crawled in the wagon, completely unsatisfied with her lack of opportunity for dancing or anything else.

CHAPTER THIRTEEN

A few days later, as the mood struck me, I stood on the big rock overlooking the blue hole late one evening and thought of Papa. I admit shedding a few tears. I was always on the sentimental side. I wished Papa could have seen the grinding mill in full operation with that big paddle wheel turning, throwing water. Mavis was so proud, I thought she was going to bust wide open. I caught her from time to time looking at the mill and crying. She made it happen, and I told her so.

I thought at the time the Abbott's hardscrabble days were over, but every endeavor requires work, and it is never over. We Abbotts knew trouble lay ahead. We highly suspected another gunman rode the county, but we did not have an inkling who it was, and it worried Teddy Blue. He spent a day scouting Jack Statin's homestead with the aid of a twelve-inch telescope brought in his saddlebags from Texas, the first telescope I ever saw. He slipped through the woods and fields to within a half-mile of the Statin house and barn, but did not spot anything out of the ordinary, particularly a Texas hat or saddle. Jack and Billy Statin and two hired hands were outside and around the barn, but no hired gun.

Teddy Blue had brought money from Texas, and he could get more by using the telegraph at Cushman. He sent a telegram to a bank in Texas and transferred funds to the miner's bank in Cushman. He split construction costs on the mill with Mavis, leaving her with quite a bit of money from the coins found in the fireplaces plus the tips left by the James Gang. We paid our bill at the trading post, and Mavis said she thought we could now pay our way. In midweek, she sent me to the trading post with a few coins to get some supplies, a short trip imbedded in my memory for life.

I rode Neil Crow's roan, carried Crow's pistol on my belt and my rifle in the saddle scabbard. Ludi Wilson got Crow's rifle.

"The least we could do for Ludi," said Teddy Blue. "He at least buried the feller."

Ludi had buried Crow and had superintended the mill-raising project. The rifle was the only pay he received. He never expressed dissatisfaction with his reward. Ludi was one of those people born with low expectations and was seldom disappointed.

I had backtracked Crow through the dogwood grove, from the spot where Teddy Blue killed him, and found his pistol, a gunfighter's pistol all right, like Teddy Blue thought. It was the latest model Colt .45, black metal with black onyx grips; the most beautiful handgun I ever saw.

As one would expect, Crow had used a file on the internal cocking mechanism giving the pistol a hair-trigger. The action was smooth as a dove's wing, but I did not have any .45 caliber shells. I figured Eagle Carter to have .45-caliber ammunition at the trading post, and I talked Mavis into giving me an extra two dollars for a box of fifty cartridges. I knew the ammunition would not cost quite two dollars. I planned having a little money left for some peppermint sticks, which I loved so well and still do.

A black horse, diamond-shaped white blaze on the forehead, stood hip-shot at the trading post hitchrail. I knew what a Texas saddle looked like, and found myself looking at one.

I should have turned around, went home and found Teddy Blue, but I had recently turned fifteen and was full of piss and vinegar. I threw caution to the wind, tethered my horse and went inside. Junior Ulbrick would probably be alive today, if I had just turned around, got on my horse and rode away.

Eagle Carter left Rachel alone to tend store and had ridden his horse to the sawmill, located a half-mile northeast. A gaunt figure sat at a table near the back wall. He drank moonshine whiskey straight out of a quart fruit jar. I tried to avoid looking at him, but from the corner of my eye, I knew he studied me. I wished Crow's pistol and gunbelt were in my saddlebags, particularly when he said, "Thet looks like Neil Crow's rig, and thet danged shore looks like Crow's hoss ye rode in on."

The voice, shallow, low, raspy, voice box burned out by years of drinking moonshine whiskey. I ignored him and went over to the counter.

An assortment of can goods filled the wall shelves behind the counter. One shelf contained boxes of ammunition of various calibers. Rachel came over and faced me across the counter. She never said a word, but her expression spoke volumes: you need to get out of here and fast. Too late. The stranger scraped his chair back.

"Boy, ah guess ye don't hear too good. Where'd ye git thet pistol and thet hoss?"

My stomach knotted. I felt nausea rising in my throat. My entrails were choking me to death. I searched for an answer and moved around the corner of the counter, trying to get behind it. Clicking boot heels on the floorboards tapped out a code, and the message I received was unfavorable.

"Ah found it," I blurted.

"Now whar did ye find my frien's gun, and ah guess ye jist appened to find the hoss, too?"

I never was good at talking my way out of anything, did not get to practice a lot. My mind raced for answers. The only problem, it raced in a circle.

"Damn it boy, are ye deaf and dum?"

I tried to think of something to say and not sound scared. Truth is, I nearly wet myself.

"Whose yer frien agin?" I asked.

"Neil Crow. He's got a black bone handled gun like thet. You seen 'im?"

My throat constricted. I could have used a drink of water. I jammed my shaking hands in my pockets.

"Don't know nobody by thet name."

Rachel, bless her heart, tried to save my bacon. "Chet, didn't I hear Eagle say you found a gun on the Batesville Pike down by Cave Creek?"

Right then I felt like kissing an Indian. I put on my boldest face, turned and faced the stranger. Thin and wiry, he stood near six-feet, wearing another one of those Texas hats pushed back. He had a high forehead, balding in front, thin bristled face, withered scarred skin, pockmarked. I guessed his age at forty and some. He wore two guns with mother-of-pearl handles, the right-hand gun tied down; the left-hand gun rode high with butt forward, in a reversed right hand holster. Teddy Blue wore his guns the same way. I had heard enough about shooters to know the left hand gun was a spare.

"What's yore name boy?"

I almost blurted out Chet Abbott, but something caught in my throat, and I held back.

"Chet."

"Chet, what?"

I do not know why I said it--some say divine providence--but as I was about to say *Abbott*, a sign on the back wall caught my eye: *Proprietor, Eagle Carter.*

"Carter."

I glanced at Rachel's round expressionless face and unrevealing round black eyes. The stranger looked past me.

"Thet's yore name, ain't it?"

"Yes," she said, calm as a frozen millpond.

"Ah heerd a squaw man run this place. Ah guess yer the squaw."

Rachel was not going to say more than necessary. She was always quiet, being Indian and all. I regained some feeling in my legs and thought to divert attention elsewhere.

"What's yore name mister," I asked.

He looked at me hollow-like, more like through me or past me, as if he was thinking whether he ought to say or not, but he did say: "Kyle Boone."

I very nearly soiled my clothes for a second time. One of my legs involuntary jerked, my toe tapped the floor. I kept telling myself to keep calm. We never got a lot of word back in the hills about what went on around us, but everyone knew that name. Kyle Boone was a Missouri bad man through and through, a renegade Quantrill Raider during the war, bank robber, and killer of men, women and children, not shackled by any moral concept known to man, a borderline animal. I thought he was dead, and I wished he was.

"Ye kin to this squaw?"

"Well, by marriage. Eagle is mah uncle. Mama's brother."

Did a lie get any better? I believe Boone had been warned to keep hands off Eagle Carter, because of his position in the community, and the fact Eagle had so many Indian brothers-in-law capable of raising cane, drunk or sober.

"Ye found the gun--whar?"

A lie already had me in a stranglehold, so I thought I might as well make the best of it.

"Four mile down the road, whar Cave Creek crosses, in the middle a the road at the water's edge. Musta fell out a his holster when his horse jumped the crick. Matter-of-fact, ah was brangin it up here to leave with Eagle, case somebody come lookin fer it. Ah ain't got no shells fer it no way. But the horse: we've owned it fer a long spell. Somebody said all roans look alike, maybe thet's so."

I thought I handled the inquisition as smoothly as possible under the circumstances. I managed to get my hands out of my pockets and was relieved to find my lies had calmed me. I pulled the gun out slow, went over to Rachel, and started to hand it to her, but like a damn-fool kid will do, I made a show, and twirled the gun as Teddy Blue had shown me--and

I had practiced--before handing it to Rachel butt first. "It's empty," I said in a voice too loud.

When I twirled the gun, Boone flinched and his hand brushed the handle of the right-hand gun. He was looking for an excuse, I think, to go into action. I believe he would have killed me on the spot if he had known I was an Abbott. I found later that the Statins brought him into the county for that specific purpose.

I thought I was out of trouble and turned to Rachel asking about some things for Mavis. Steel-shod hooves clattering on shale rock caused Boone to go to the open front door, and step out on the porch. Curious too, I eased over to a front window. Billy and Jack Statin were tying up at the hitch rail beside my roan and Boone's black.

My goose was not yet cooked, but the fire had gotten hotter, and I felt the heat. Once the Statin brothers saw me, they were sure to reveal my identity. I stood naked of any weapon, except a pocketknife, and a pocketknife sure was not going to do me any good with that bunch. Rachel came up beside me and looked out the window. She knew immediately the situation. "You've got to get out of here."

She handed me Crow's pistol and reached up on the shelf for a box of pistol shells.

"Head down to the creek. I'll tell them you decided to walk over and see Eagle at the sawmill, but you head the other way."

I skittered out the back door. My hat flew off my head, but I dared not stop. I figured I might not see the roan again, or my rifle that I foolishly left in the saddle scabbard. Running off leaving my horse and losing my hat would later have dire consequences for Junior Ulbrick.

Northern Independence County is full of watershed creeks running east to west, draining into Polk Bayou. The creek curling around the base of the hill, on which sat the Sandtown Trading Post, was called Dry Creek; I guess because it went dry nearly every summer. The sawmill was a mile northeast up Dry Creek, but I ran the other way. Once I reached the creek below the hill, I faced a hard run two miles west down the creek bank, to the bigger creek called Polk Bayou.

If I made it to Polk Bayou, I would try to hide inside the trees and brush lining the creek bank and work my way down to the juncture with Cave Creek, a half a mile or so from our cabin. I was looking at a roundabout march of eight miles. First, I needed to outfox the Statin brothers and Kyle Boone. If caught, I faced a hanging in the woods. Hanging men and boys in woods or along roadways and pinning warning signs on them contributed to Boone's legendary notoriety. I could count on the Statin brothers to hold my horse under the hanging tree while Boone tied the noose.

I ran, tripped, stumbled and tumbled down hill to the creek, rolling through heavy brush and out on the creek bank. I got to my feet expecting to be crippled, but I was still in one piece, the pistol in my belt and the box of ammunition squeezed in my left hand. I pulled the pistol and attempted to load it. It would not load. Rachel, in her haste, pulled a box of .36 caliber Remington loads off the shelf, for my Colt .45. I was unarmed.

I threw the box of cartridges in the brush and loped down the creek bank toward Polk Bayou. I kept the heavy pistol holstered. I do not know what I planned to do with it, except if caught in a tight, pull it and try to bluff my way out.

Two hundred yards downstream Dry Creek curved to the left, and the curve was the last place from where I could look back upstream and see the sawmill road crossing. The sound of voices carried down the creek. I dove under low hanging branches of a willow tree and looked back, as the Statin brothers and Kyle Boone splashed across the creek and whipped their horses into a run toward the sawmill. I thought I would have a half-hour before they discovered I had not gone to the sawmill.

The Sandtown Trading Post was like the hub of a wheel with several roads spoking toward every compass point. One narrow wagon-road cut through the timber from the trading post, crossed Polk Bayou, and continued twelve miles west to Cushman. The Batesville Pike ran almost due south from the trading post by our home place, to Batesville. I figured the Statin brothers and Kyle Boone would eventually split up. One would probably ride down Dry Creek, another would watch the Batesville Pike and the third would probably watch the Cushman Road. The one sure thing for me to do, being on foot, was stay clear of roads. Eventually, I would have to chance crossing the Cushman Road in order to get home.

In my panic, I had temporarily forgotten the Wilson family home place on Polk Bayou, three and a half miles southwest of the trading post. I ran down Dry Creek until a pain in my side forced me to stop and catch my breath. Bent over gasping for air, I gave myself a short talking to, about how to get out of my predicament. I remembered the Wilson homestead. At least I could get help and my hands on a gun. I did not think the Wilson family owned anything .45 caliber, but they owned several guns. I needed a shotgun in the brush and dearly wished for our old Greener double barrel ten-gauge and some double-ought buckshot loads.

The Sandtown Trading Post sat on the east end of a hogback, a long narrow ridge named after wild razorback hogs. The hogback ran east/west between Dry Creek on the north side and the Cushman Road on the south. On the west end, the hogback dropped abruptly down to Polk Bayou, which ran north to south across the base.

Trying to make time on foot along a creek winding through woods is difficult. A man on horseback could catch up to me in a hurry. I thought it best to climb the hogback and get away from the creek. Once on the crest of the hogback, I could watch both the creek side and the Cushman Road. Plus, I could hide among the many boulders, caves and animal den holes along the crest and below the brow of the hill.

I worked hard scrambling uphill for half an hour before reaching the crest. The timber thinned toward the top. A sun-speckled worn animal trail ran down the hog back. I turned west, walking fast. Often in sight of Dry Creek, I knew a rider traveling the creek bottom could see me against the sky, if he looked up the hill at the right time. Two red squirrels barked behind me. I stopped and looked back and could not see them. I did not know if they were barking at me or something else. I hunkered down behind a moss and lichen covered boulder and listened. The squirrels were really going at it and not because of me. An iron-shod hoof pinged on a shale slab. I eased my head above the boulder. Jack Statin rode straight at me.

Statin rode easy, rifle in the saddle scabbard, his left hand empty. His right hand loosely held the reins. He showed little concern, knowing I was afoot and probably unarmed. He rode too casual. I wondered if he was drunk.

I was not sure what I was going to do, but I was not going down without putting up a scrap. I looked around for a good-sized rock. If Statin rode close to my hiding place, I might get in a lucky throw and knock him off his horse. I picked up a second rock and took another peek. He was near fifty yards away, his horse picking its way through the rocks.

I figured to let Statin pass, charge him from his blind side, grab him by the belt, pull him down, and crack his head with a rock. A simplistic plan that maybe would have worked. I never found out.

A family of skunks changed everything. An old mother skunk and three little ones waddled out of a hole somewhere behind me, passed within ten feet of my hiding place and headed right down the crest of the ridge toward Statin. Statin's horse smelled the skunks, did a little dance and veered off downhill. Statin at first tried to pull the horse back along the crest, but spotted the skunks and let the horse have its head.

"I'm going back," Jack Statin yelled to his brother in the road.

I thought at first he was yelling at me. It shook me so that I almost made the fatal mistake of showing myself. I was in the act of standing when Billy Statin called from down on the Cushman Road. "Go on back. He's probably sneaked back and got his horse. Watch the Batesville Pike."

I dropped to the ground and crawled around the boulder, watching with great relief, as Statin turned his horse east back down the crest. I lay quiet, heart pounding, until Jack Statin disappeared in the timber. I got up and hightailed it down the crest of the hogback toward Polk Bayou.

The terrain gradually leveled, as I neared the west end of the hogback. Large boulders and rocky outcroppings detoured and slowed me. I kept working my way to the end of the hogback and before long I looked down the western slope. In the distance, Polk Bayou threaded its way through the hills toward the White River at Batesville.

Movement caught my eye. A horseman rounded the base of the ridge and was now positioned between Polk Bayou and me. I guessed Boone. I thought Boone would be a better tracker than either of the Statin brothers. The Wilson cabin, my destination, was across the big creek, only a mile downstream, but a lifetime away.

The rider to my right-front obviously had flanked me driving down Dry Creek and beat me to the western end of the hogback. I looked for a way out on the Cushman Road. Billy Statin rode it and Billy was methodical. He rode slowly, scanning the road for tracks and watched the woods on both sides. Occasionally, he glanced up the hill in my direction. I stayed hunkered behind a tree and contemplated my future, the pursuit of which was currently blocked.

They had me blocked. If I continued down the slope, I would end up between the two riders with nowhere to go. I decided to sit still until they met. I finally got a good look at the rider, who turned left around the base of the hogback and rode into the open. It was Boone all right.

I wondered where my horse and rifle were at that moment. I was desperate for a weapon and wanted my hat. I felt naked without it. I had made a mess of things by entering the trading post blind, while looking at a Texas saddle, and to compound my mistake, I left my rifle outside in the scabbard on my horse. Due to my ignorance, someone dear to me could get hurt or killed.

I wondered if Eagle Carter knew about my situation, and if he did, what would he do. He would probably make a run to our cabin and alert Mavis and Teddy Blue. If Eagle did ride to our cabin, both Mavis and Teddy Blue might leave the homestead unprotected and search for me. If either of the Statins happened by and discovered the place vacated, they would probably burn everything to the ground. I wished for dark, but the sun was still high, and seemed unmoving. The Old Testament's Joshua commanded the sun to stand still and it did. I commanded the sun to set and it did not.

Kyle Boone and Billy Statin met on the Cushman Road. They sat their horses close together and seemed to be discussing something. Boone took out tobacco makings and rolled a cigarette. At one point both men turned and looked in my direction.

I suppose they thought I might be on the hill, but the slope was too steep for horses, and I doubted either man would climb the hill on foot. They could afford to wait me out knowing I must cross a road somewhere to get home.

I considered reversing course and walking the ridge crest back to the trading post, taking the chance I could get inside without Jack Statin seeing me. I knew Eagle Carter would protect me, but Eagle might not be there. When Billy Statin pointed southwest, and Kyle Boone and he turned in the direction of the Wilson homestead on Polk Bayou, I decided to follow them.

Sounds foolish I know, but I thought the safest place was directly behind those two, the most unlikely place they would think to look. I waited on the hill until they turned south on the ancient Indian trail running down the east bank of Polk Bayou. The Wilson place was a mile south and across the bayou.

I scooted, stumbled and slid down the hill off the hogback into heavy brush along the Cushman Road. After making sure the road was empty, I crossed, hugged the left side of the road and ran hard down to where the Cushman Road intersected with the old Indian trail.

I jogged down the trail and foolishly rounded a curve in full view of Boone and Statin. They were walking their horses a quarter-mile ahead. Fortunately, they were not looking back. I dove into the brush at the side of the trail and watched, as they kicked their horses into a trot, ran off and left me. I stayed away from the trail and pushed hard for half an hour through brushy thickets and brier patches, while trying to keep the bayou in sight. I heard a low boom, like a heavy pistol shot, shortly two heavier booms echoed down the bayou—shotgun. I cut back over to the trail and headed on a dead run for the Wilson homestead.

In less than thirty minutes, I was within three hundred yards of the Wilson homestead and out of breath. I stopped and listened. I could not see anything out of the ordinary or hear anything. I decided to move down into the creek so the bank on both sides would mask my approach. I waded cold water knee-deep until I was in front of the cabin that set back fifty yards from the creek on a little knoll. The cabin was quiet. Nothing moved in the yard. Something was wrong though. The Wilson family owned hunting dogs, which should have been raising a ruckus. Where were they?

I slipped out of the creek, crawled up on the west bank staying concealed in the brush. From my position, the north side of the cabin and the fields west of the cabin were in view. Ludi Wilson and his father were coming at a fast clip, each riding a mule. Two dogs trotted alongside the mules. I remembered the Wilson family owned three dogs. I spotted their big black bear dog lying in the front yard. It looked asleep, not unusual for an old hound on a warm day, but with two horsemen on the premises and all the shooting, the old dog should have been on his feet and ought to have been telling about it. I finally decided the dog was dead.

My best move was no move at all, simply stay out of sight, watch and wait, until Ludi and Mr. Wilson came up. They both carried rifles, not unusual for the times. Only ten years after the war, a lot of renegades and bushwhackers still prowled the hills. An armed farmer working his field was a common sight.

The Wilson men disappeared behind the cabin. I hunkered down in the brush and waited. The front door opened and Ludi eased out on the porch with Mr. Wilson right behind, both held rifles. Ludi walked cautiously to the north end of the porch and his father to the south end. They scanned the brush along the bayou and around both sides of the cabin.

Lois and Mrs. Wilson came out. Mrs. Wilson held a double barrel ten-gauge shotgun I knew they kept loaded with buckshot. I eased out of the brush in full view of the cabin and quickly got their attention.

"Chet, whut in the world are ye doin here?" called Lois.

I walked on up to the cabin. Water sloshed out of my shoes, my britches legs were sopping wet, and I was bareheaded. I quickly related my predicament. We talked about it and reached the conclusion that since Kyle Boone and Billy Statin were unable to find me; they decided to do some mischief at the Wilson place. They would have known the Wilson family helped with the construction of our mill, particularly Ludi, the chief engineer.

Boone and Statin brazenly rode into the front yard. The big bear dog charged the horses alerting Mrs. Wilson and Lois. Mrs. Wilson-- shotgun in hand, and Lois, watched through the front window. Kyle Boone shot the dog, stepped down from his horse, went over to the woodpile, picked up the chopping axe, came back over and with one stroke cut the dog's head off. When I heard that, I knew it was Boone who had killed Brownie.

Mrs. Wilson did not waste any time. She shot through the open front door and put buckshot into Billy Statin and his horse. The horse began bucking and bolted back across the creek. Boone jumped into the saddle, pulled his pistol, meaning to pull down on Mrs. Wilson, but she beat him. She let go with the other barrel spraying Boone and his horse with a buckshot load. Boone's horse kicked up and began bucking. Boone hugged the horse around the neck and held on as it ran after Statin's horse.

"I hope she has kilt both them sons o'bitches," said Mr. Wilson.

As the crow flies, I was three miles from home and the sun was going down. Ludi offered to take me home horseback, but I declined. I asked for the loan of a rifle. They gave me a .44-40 rifle and a box of shells.

I thought I would be better off on foot. I knew the ground from hunting in the area all my life and would not have any trouble finding my way even after dark. I was afraid a horse might attract attention of a panther or wolf, or a bushwhacker. I thought Jack Statin might still be out in the brush somewhere.

I left my pistol and cartridge belt with the Wilsons. They did not have any ammunition for it, and I was tired of lugging the heavy thing around. Without ammunition, it was good for only cracking hickory nuts.

I cut east across woodlands and hit the Batesville Pike in a little over an hour. I walked out of the brush into the curve in the pike above our homestead at almost the exact spot where, a few weeks earlier, Papa had been bushwhacked. Several bad things had happened since. When I got home, I found another bad thing had happened.

No light shone through the cabin windows, but as I walked closer I made out a faint light down low on the front porch, a candle or a lamp with the wick turned down. Moving shadows and low voices caused me to halt and study the situation. A woman sobbed. Mavis said, "They musta kilt Chet, too."

I was about thirty yards from the porch. "Not yet," I said.

A small silence and a shriek split the stillness. Mavis charged down off the porch and through the front gate. "Chet, my gawd, is thet you?"

She ran up, grabbed me, nearly knocking me down. "Chet, ah've been scart to death. They've kilt Junior Ulbrick."

Elsa Ulbrick, from behind Mavis, came around and grabbed me around the neck, sobbing, face and hair wet.

"Oh Chet, my brother is dead."

I took her in my arms and patted her on the back. I could not speak. We stood like that for a moment, and Mavis tugged at us. I untangled from Elsa and caught her by the hand. Mavis took Elsa's other hand, and we walked back to the cabin. Elsa stumbled and cried, Mavis sobbed, and tears ran down my cheeks.

The Ulbrick's team, hooked to a wagon, was outside the front gate. Mrs. Ulbrick sat on the porch in a cane-bottom chair. She rocked back and forth, but the chair did not. She moaned low like an animal in pain, but no tears shone on her face.

Poor Junior lay on his back, completely covered with an old brown blanket, except for his head; his black curly hair disheveled. Junior lay, eyes closed, as if he were napping on the porch after a hard day in the field. I halfway expected him to sit up, but a fatal wound under the blanket had silenced Junior forever. Mr. Ulbrick, who sat in another chair, stood up and stepped over to me. "Help me with Junior. We got to get him home."

I remained silent. What could I say? Mr. Ulbrick went over to Junior, knelt down and removed the blanket. He took hold of Junior's shoulders. I moved around and picked up Junior's legs. Junior, not as tall as me, weighed more than I did. We struggled some getting through the gate and eased him into the wagon bed. Mr. Ulbrick placed Junior's head on a fifty-pound bag of seed corn. I felt a presence behind me; Mrs. Ulbrick held the blanket. I took the blanket, climbed up in the wagon beside Mr. Ulbrick and helped cover Junior. Dead people were supposed to be completely covered and that is what I did. Mrs. Ulbrick said, "Uncover his head and let him see the stars."

Junior had stayed behind and helped me bury Papa. I never did thank him for that. Now I felt the need to say something to his parents or at least to Elsa but words failed me, as they often did. Mute as a rock I stood, while the Ulbrick family climbed in the wagon and took Junior home. Junior was dead on my account, but I did not understand how it came to be until later.

The dark shadow of the Ulbrick's team and wagon crossed the creek and disappeared into the night. Mavis had remained silent on the porch, and now she was gone. A low slow mournful tune filtered up from the creek with such body that I looked for it in the night air. Mavis, in the soft golden light of a quarter-moon, sat with her fiddle in Papa's old cane-bottomed chair on the big rock above the creek.

I ought to have gone down there and sat with her a spell, but I was too tired to think straight. I stumbled through the cabin, to the well out back and pulled up a bucket of water, washed my feet in a pan of water on the back porch and went straight to bed. Music filtered through the log wall of my bedroom, while I tried to think of a short prayer to say for Junior. I formed one or two in my mind, but I was dead tired, so no prayer got said before I fell asleep, and it is a shameful thing to admit--not later either. I was never good at praying.

I did not sort out all of the details surrounding Junior's murder until I talked to Rachel Carter, after the burying. Junior had ridden one of the Ulbrick family Percherons bareback, which was his habit, to the Sandtown Trading Post on that fatal afternoon. He arrived shortly after I had run out the back door with the Statin brothers and Kyle Boone in hot pursuit. Rachel told Junior about my run-in with Kyle Boone, about the Statins riding up, and me running out the back door for the creek.

Rachel found my hat outside the back door, where I had ran out from under it. She told Junior I was on foot in the woods and she did not believe I would return to the trading post. She asked Junior to take my hat and horse, when he left, and leave them at our cabin and tell Mavis what happened. Rachel said Junior left the trading post wearing my hat, riding the roan and leading the Ulbrick's workhorse.

About sundown, the roan walked up to our front gate. Mavis went out to investigate and found my rifle in the scabbard and blood on the saddle. Teddy Blue had come in from the field and was at the barn. When Mavis told him what she found, he saddled his horse and rode toward the trading post thinking I was lying somewhere shot of the horse, but instead found Junior Ulbrick lying face-up in the road, shot in the back, with my hat on his head. The Ulbrick's workhorse was standing nearby. The roan, used to our feedlot and horses, evidently decided to walk on home.

Teddy Blue loaded Junior on the Ulbrick's horse and took him back to our cabin, and rode to alert the Ulbrick family. Mavis said he passed back by our cabin heading for the trading post. He was leaning forward in the saddle, holding his hat, his horse running full out.

Teddy Blue returned after midnight. I was sound asleep and he did not wake me. After searching until well after dark along Dry Creek, he rode on to the Wilson place and heard that I had passed by and about Mrs. Wilson shooting Kyle Boone and Billy Statin. He knew I would make it home, he said, as soon as he heard I was afoot in the woods after dark with a rifle.

I never doubted for a minute that Jack Statin killed Junior Ulbrick, mistaking Junior for me, because Junior was wearing my hat and riding my horse. I knew too, Jack Statin had turned back to the trading post, when he was near upon me on the hogback, and likely set an ambush for me on the Batesville Pike. I was reasonably sure it was not Billy Statin or Kyle Boone. Shot by Mrs. Wilson, those two had charged off to Batesville down the Polk Bayou Indian trail. They were too far away from the Batesville Pike to have been involved in Junior's murder.

We later learned Billy Statin and Kyle Boone visited Doc Turner in Batesville, who reported Statin and Boone talked of pressing charges against the Wilson family. They left the doctor's office and immediately spread the story around Batesville they were riding by the Wilson place, minding their own business, when Wilson's big bear dog attacked them, and someone from the cabin shot them. Teddy Blue and Mavis made sure those lying charges never got pressed.

July was the month and it was hot even in our little shady valley. We buried Junior Ulbrick the next evening. His burying was a well-attended event, for a workday, and Junior being a young boy my own age. I wondered if so many would have attended my burying. But a large crowd at one's funeral seems a cold comfort, particularly for the deceased.

I dreaded going to the burying, for fear Elsa would get emotional and attach herself to me, but she was very quiet and stayed close to her folks. They buried Junior in the Crisler German graveyard about a mile east up Cave Creek. The Crisler family homesteaded back up the creek and started the graveyard burying two of their children struck down by some unknown disease or fever. They buried old man Crisler there, killed by renegades during the war. Over the years, other German families had buried family members on that site, and now Junior.

After the burying, the German men gathered around Mr. Ulbrick and talked of taking up arms and marching on Batesville. I am not sure what they thought they would accomplish, but Teddy Blue convinced them to let him handle the situation.

"The sheriff's deputies and the Statins will shoot ye down like dogs. This is mah kind a fight. Ah'll take keer a hit."

Near sundown, Mavis, Teddy Blue and I returned home from the graveyard in our wagon, pulled by our little gray mule team. Teddy Blue handled the reins. He had ridden to the Wilson's homeplace at daylight and informed them about Junior. All four Wilsons had attended the burying and now followed us back to our homeplace in their buckboard, Ludi driving.

Teddy Blue and I sat on the wagon seat, Mavis behind, in a cane-bottomed chair. Teddy Blue said little, his face a blank, a blue light shone in his eyes. Mavis was mad as a hornet and doing most of the talking. She would cuss a while, and cry a while. She kept saying, "Thet was posed to be ye layin up there in the road, and right whar they kilt Papa. Them people don't give a damn who they kill."

When we arrived at our homeplace, Teddy Blue and I walked to the barn, unharnessed the team and put feed out for our animals. Teddy Blue went in the tack room and came out with his bridle and saddle.

"Ah'm goin to Cushman," he said "Ah need a box a dynamite."

CHAPTER FOURTEEN

Mavis asked the Wilson family to take supper with us. Mrs. Wilson was in the kitchen with Mavis fixing supper. I walked in the kitchen and told Mavis what Teddy Blue intended and went on out to the front porch to visit with Ludi and his father.

Teddy Blue and Lois strolled around the corner of the cabin, Teddy leading his horse and talking low. He mounted the bay in the front yard. Lois opened the gate, and he rode through, stopped, leaned down and said something to her. He kicked the big bay into a trot up the Batesville Pike. Lois stood a moment watching after him, and returned to the porch. A tear trickled down her cheeks. I wondered what in the world Teddy Blue had said. She addressed her brother and father. "Teddy said fer us to stay here tonight. He thanks hit might not be safe fer us to go back home right now, but everythin'll be all right in the morning."

Everything will be all right in the morning. I pondered what that meant. Mavis called us in for an early supper of fried green tomatoes, sawmill gravy, bacon and biscuits.

During supper, Lois related to Mavis what Teddy Blue said when he left. Mavis got quiet for a spell and stared into her plate as if she had spotted a bug. She never said anything, but rose from the table, left the kitchen, went into a bedroom and came back with Papa's old railroad pocket watch she kept wound and running. She said that as long as the watch ran and kept time, Papa was still with us. She sat back down at the table, opened the cover and laid the watch by her plate. Conversation ceased. Everyone looked at the watch, as if expecting it to take wings.

Her actions puzzled me because we paid little attention to clocks and watches. I was near thirty-years-old before I was awakened one morning by the ringing of an alarm clock and to this day don't remember the occasion.

Mavis looked me.

"Iffen Teddy Blue hain't back by eight o'clock thet means he's gone to Batesville straight from Cushman, and Batesville is whar ah'm headin."

"Ah'm goin too," I said, "Junior died on account a me. Ah owe him somethin."

"No, they hain't no debts involved in this. Ah don't want ye gettin in this mess. The good lard looked out fer ye onct. He might be lookin tother way next time."

No use arguing, the way she said it, and the way her eyes glistened, but I did not intend letting her go in alone. I might not be along side, but whether she knew it or not, I intended not being far behind.

Seven o'clock on Papa's watch and no sign of Teddy Blue. I still thought he might come back. I hoped he would. An hour remained until Mavis's self-imposed deadline.

Members of the Wilson family said little during supper. Everyone seemed lost in thought. A sense of foreboding hovered over us like a dark cloud. After Mavis, Lois and Mrs. Wilson cleaned up the kitchen, they came out on the front porch where Ludi, Mr. Wilson and I smoked cigars and drank coffee from tin cups.

Mrs. Wilson, dressed in a long black dress, sat down in a cane-bottomed chair close to me and lit up a cigar. The floorboards on the porch had dried out over the years and separated in some places an inch or more.

Mrs. Wilson, needing to spit, leaned over and studied a crack between her feet and spit through it. I guess she felt the need to explain. "I know Mavis don't take kindly to people spittin on the floor boards."

Lois, who did not smoke or dip snuff, sat down on the edge of the porch, feet on the ground. She kept looking north up the road for Teddy Blue, and she was not the only one. The strangest feeling came over me, sitting among the Wilson family. I did not understand it, but I felt close to them. A revelation coming forthwith would reveal the reason.

Mavis went inside and returned with her fiddle. She did not say anything, stepped off the porch and walked down to the creek to the big rock, where Papa's old weather-beaten cane-bottomed chair sat overlooking the blue hole below the falls. Crickets chirped, and a couple of whippoorwills called in their strange melancholy way from behind the new church building. Mavis began playing a slow haunting ballad she dredged up out of our Celtic past. The tune blended with the water rushing over the falls. Mrs. Wilson stared blankly across the road toward the little church, looking into another world, a last single ray of sunlight reflected off a golden tear trickling down her cheek. Dusk began a slow fade to black. The music stopped. Mavis came back over to the porch and said to me, "Hit's eight o'clock. Saddle the mare."

I never said a word and stood up.

"Ye need some help son," said Ludi.

It touched me, the way he said it.

"Nossir," I replied.

On the way to the barn, I puzzled over my response. I never, to my recollection, ever called Ludi, sir. Addressing your elders as sir and mam was a mannerly thing to do, but I was raised without manners for the most part.

An hour of daylight remained, except in our little valley shaded by western hills. I took a coal oil lantern from the back porch and lit it on my way to the barn. I went in the tack room and gathered up a bridle and saddle, caught up the little sorrel mare and saddled her. She seemed a bit frisky. She did a little buck and jig. I think she expected to run. During the time it took to saddle the mare and lead her to the front gate Mavis had changed out of her black mourning dress into a pair of Papa's old faded blue-gray dungarees and a long sleeve faded gray cotton work shirt. On a warm night, she would not need anything more for comfort. She carried her rifle and another coal oil lantern, which she handed to me.

"Chet, hold my gun and this lantern till ah git in the saddle." She looked over at Ludi. "You'ens keep watch and look fer Teddy Blue and me after midnight."

She turned back to me and gave me a long look, never said a word, but it looked like she wanted to. She put her foot in the stirrup and pulled up easy in the saddle. I handed up the rifle and lantern, and walked over and sat down on the porch steps until she crossed the creek and disappeared into the timber beyond. I stood with purpose and started around the corner of the porch.

"Whar are ye to bye?"

Where are you going boy? Mr. Wilson did not say much but when he did, something surfaced in his speech from far away and long ago. He was hard to understand at times.

"Ah'm saddlin the roan," I said. "Ah ain't lettin mah sister go in there alone."

"Better listen to yer mama, boy," said Ludi.

"Whut?"

"Yore mama. Mavis is yer mama. She hain't yer sister."

"Whut?" The string went out of my legs. I sat down on the edge of the porch.

Ludi walked over and put his hand on my shoulder. "Son, ah'm yer daddy, guess ye ain't nary been tolt."

Stunned by the revelation, I tried to understand and choked up. After a moment, my mind began to clear. No wonder Ludi and the rest of the Wilson family were kind to me over the years. I was one of them. Mrs. Wilson carefully laid the stub of her cigar on the floor beside her chair, stood and walked over to me. She reached down and laid her hand on my head.

"Ah'm yer grandmammy, on yer daddy's side."

An emotion-charged surge made me dizzy. I broke down and cried. Shameful. Lois came over to me, got down on her knees, hugged me and laid her head on my shoulder. She smelled of wood smoke, bacon grease and flour. "Ah'm yer Aunt Lois," she said.

Tears ran down my cheeks. I never was much for crying, did not believe in it and hated for it to happen. I sniffed a little. Lois reached in the pocket of her apron, pulled out a dishrag, and wiped my face. I sat like a fool.

"Why wasn't ah nary told?"

Grandma Wilson spoke up. "Thangs didn't work out fer Ludi and Mavis, with the war and Ida dying and all. We didn't want ye a growin up thankin ye was a bastard child and havin kids callin ye a woods colt, and Mavis a grass widow, thet sort a thang."

I had always believed Ida Abbott was my mother. An early rumor, quickly squelched by Mavis and Papa Austin, had it Aunt Eunice Abbott was my mother, and when she and Uncle Lester Abbott died shortly after my birth, Ida Abbott raised me as her own.

It took a while for me to sort things out. When Mavis was near to birthing me, Mama Ida sent her to stay with Aunt Eunice and told around Eunice was with child and needed help. Aunt Eunice kept me for a few months, until she and Uncle Lester suddenly died, and Mama Ida took me. I have no memory of Aunt Eunice and only faint recollection of Mama Ida, who died before I was fully housebroken.

For fourteen years, my real mother, Mavis, raised me, leading me to think she was my sister. After the killing of Papa Austin Abbott, I considered myself orphaned, left with only a brother and sister. Now, near struck mute at finding all this family, I was stunned.

Ludi walked over beside me and looked down the road. Lois stood. Ludi looked at Lois, and turned to me.

"Saddle up son and go on. We can't let yer mama go in there on her lonesome. Me and Lois'll foller in the buckboard."

By the time I got my wits about me and saddled the roan, Mavis was well down the road to Batesville, a good three mile lead. The roan was a more powerful horse than Mavis's little sorrel mare, and he wanted to run. I could have caught Mavis, but I hung back. I did not want to cause her a problem before getting to town.

The Ulbrick cabin was dark and seemed deserted, even the dogs were gone. Where were they? The thought occurred to me that Mr. Ulbrick and some of the Germans might take matters into their own hands regardless of what Teddy Blue said to them, and they did, but not in the manner I expected.

A train passing from Cave City to Batesville rumbled through five miles east. A long mournful whistle caused me to look, where a dull glow lit the early night sky, too early and too bright for the moon. The next day I learned the Germans had fired the Statin's wheat and cornfields.

The roan cantered, while I pondered the light in the east. Suddenly, a tremendous explosion rocked the ground. The roan jumped. I nearly lost the saddle and grabbed a double-handful of mane. By the time I wrestled my horse under control and got my bearings, another moon rose in the southwest. Teddy Blue had set off a whole case of dynamite and destroyed the Statin's grinding mill.

The two incidents so close together were too much for old Lazarus Statin. His wife reported his standing in the front yard of his fine big brick house, a mile east off the Batesville Pike, trying to understand why his fields were on fire, when the mill explosion shattered the front windows of the house. Mrs. Statin said old Lazarus stood in the yard turning in a circle, looking at the fire in the east, and the fire to the southwest. He pointed in both directions, tried to say something, suffered a stroke and fell down in the yard. Within a week, Mrs. Statin took him to St. Louis on a train--for medical reasons she said. She had long wanted to leave the Arkansas hills, now was her chance. Neither ever returned.

I kicked the roan into a lope. He took the bit in his teeth and opened in a dead run. He was fast, faster than any horse I ever rode. I grabbed my hat and held on. My plan was, once reaching Batesville, to head for the saloon and billiard hall on Batesville's southwest side, a known Decker and Statin hang out. I thought Teddy Blue would head for the billiard hall, after blowing the mill. I knew he wanted a final confrontation and would expect to find it in such a place.

I heard bells clanging from two miles out. The horse-drawn fire wagon was heading for the mill. Obvious from the light in the sky, the effort was futile, but I suppose they needed to make a show.

I passed Mavis somewhere. Evidently, she thought Teddy Blue might still be near the destroyed mill, and rode over to see if she could locate him. I did not know her whereabouts at the time and continued on to the billiard hall. I really was not sure what I was going to do once I got there, one of those famous bridges we all hear about you have to cross, when you get to it.

The Batesville Pike became Batesville's macadamed Main Street inside the city limits. Shopkeepers and such were out on the street looking and pointing toward the bright light in the city's northwest quadrant. I heard questions without answers bantered back and forth, as I passed. I turned off Main Street and passed between a hardware store and the Independence County Bank. I tied up to a hitch rail behind the hardware store and looked across a dirt street. Three horses stood hipshot at the long hitch rail fronting the billiard hall, but not Teddy Blue's horse. I was not surprised. I thought he would tie up to the rear hitch rail and enter through the back door.

I walked across the street to the billiard hall, passed around the side to the rear. Sure enough, Teddy Blue's horse, looking like he had been rode hard, fidgeted at the hitch rail with a couple of others. Teddy Blue had not loosened the saddle cinch strap, which meant to me he expected to leave in a hurry.

I eased up to the back door and slowly opened it. Deputy Sheriff Kel Decker's voice more high-pitched than usual, sounded strained, scared. He was jabbering, and I could not understand him. Two unarmed miners from Cushman, in work-stained clothes, sat on a bench by the back wall, fidgety and anxious. They wanted to get up and leave without attracting attention, but seemed unsure how to do it.

Teddy Blue, backed against the south wall, looked across billiard tables at Kel Decker, Sheriff Clyde Decker, Jack and Billy Statin and Kyle Boone. All stood except the old sheriff, Clyde Decker, who sat in a cane-bottomed chair, pushed back against a cue rack.

When I walked through the rear door with rifle in hand, conversation ceased for the moment. All eyes turned on me. Teddy Blue briefly glanced my way, but kept one eye on the men across the room, all armed as far as I could tell.

"Chet, whatta ye doin here?"

"Thought ye might want to shoot a game a billiards," I said, in a much braver voice than I felt.

"Ah don't beleve we got time," said Teddy Blue.

My stomach was in a knot. I caught myself taking short breaths. I tried to settle myself by taking a deep breath and letting it out slow.

Billy Statin postured a little, took a step forward looking at me.

"Another one of them filthy Abbott hog thieves."

I never replied, but I thought if shooting starts, and there was no reason to believe it would not, Billy had just promoted himself to the top of my list.

Kel Decker looked back at Teddy Blue, who was armed with two pistols, both holsters tied down, the left holster reversed, pistol butt forward. Decker was nervous. He did not seem to know what to do with his hands. He removed his hat and rubbed one hand through his hair, and he glanced at me again. I leveled my rifle in his direction and thumbed back the hammer. Decker looked like a scared rabbit. You could tell he wished he were somewhere else. I expect we all did.

Evidently, I had interrupted a heated confrontation now taking a fatal turn. Kel Decker began jabbering.

"He kilt Mr. Abbott awright and the Statins paid 'im."

I took it he meant Kyle Boone, who stood to the left of the group, a step from Billy Statin. He seemed to be looking for an advantage. Teddy Blue watched him.

"Thet's a lie," replied Jack Statin, in a loud voice. "He's makin it all up."

"And thet ain't all," said Decker, whose bladder had released. He seemed unaware of the spreading stain on the front of his pants. "It was Jack shot down the German boy. He was braggin up at the office."

"You lying bastard," said Billy Statin. "You're tryin to save your fat ass."

I immediately changed my priorities. Jack Statin went to the top of my list, moving brother Billy down one notch. I meant to put a bullet in Jack Statin, if it was my last official act on earth.

Old Sheriff Clyde Decker, sat stiffly quiet, seemingly mesmerized by Teddy Blue. Boone spoke low and raspy, the voice from the trading post; chills went through me. "Abbott seems like yer bitin off a big chew."

Teddy Blue shifted slightly toward the dangerous Boone. The Statins could pull and shoot all right, but Boone was the gunman. He had put some good men down in Missouri and Texas.

"So yer Boone. Ah looked fer ye down in Texas."

"Whut fer?"

"Meant to kill ye. I got Crow."

"I wouldn't pull on Boone, Abbott," said Sheriff Decker, straining to get the words out.

Teddy Blue shifted slightly. "Decker, you squirrel-headed-sunuvabitch, you've lived too long.

The old sheriff opened his mouth, but nothing came out. Kyle Boone slid two short steps to his left like he was doing some kind of dance, and separated himself a little more from Billy Statin. Kel Decker discovered his wet pants. He looked down, face reddening, right cheek twitching. He scratched his chin with his right hand, keeping the hand well away from the gun on his hip. The tension was such it seemed a knife could cut it. I knew Teddy Blue would pull on Boone, regardless of who pulled first.

Things got a little more complicated and considerably more dangerous. The front door swung open. Mavis stepped through holding a rifle in her right hand, barrel leveled waist high, stock locked under her right elbow. She carried a lit coal oil lantern by the bail in her left hand. She took in the room. Teddy Blue glanced at Mavis, but kept his eyes on Boone.

"Mavis stay back."

"I reckon not," she said. "Chet, git outta here."

I never said anything. To satisfy her, I actually did sidle toward the rear door, but I was not about to leave. The two Cushman miners sitting at the rear of the billiard hall took my move as an opportunity to ease up off their bench and slide past me through the open door. I walked out behind them, turned and stood on the steps with full view of the interior.

Mavis walked slowly forward, rifle leveled at Boone, hammer thumbed back, the coal oil lantern swinging in step. I am not sure what she intended, but I think she meant to gut-shoot Boone close up. Lips drawn in a sneer like a snarling dog, Boone lunged at her. I think he meant to grab the barrel of the rifle, but Mavis was quick. She slung the lantern and smashed him upside the head. Lantern glass shattered, coal oil splattered, flashed up and set Boone's hair on fire. Her action caught me by surprise and very near fatally distracted Teddy Blue.

Boone made a squalling noise, threw up his left hand and pulled his pistol with his right snapping a shot striking Teddy Blue high along the left ribcage slamming him back and partially sideways. Teddy Blue, staggered, held his feet and steadied the pistol in his right hand. He leveled the pistol at Boone's nose. I clearly saw terror in Boone's eyes.

Teddy Blue dropped the hammer. The heavy slug caught Boone high in the chest. Boone spun, stumbled forward and butted the oak wall head on, bounced off and involuntarily turned back facing Teddy Blue. Teddy's revolver boomed again, the slug tore through Boone's throat, slamming him down. A wisp of blue smoke spiraled from his singed head.

The gun action froze everyone in place but Kel Decker. He took the distraction as an opportunity to slip away and headed for the back door where I waited. I did not want to shoot a deputy sheriff, but Billy Statin stepped in and saved me the trouble. Billy pulled his pistol and shot his cousin in the back from five paces. "Stay and get yours, you sunuvabitch," said Billy.

Mavis instinctively leveled her Henry firing from the hip taking off the top of Billy Statin's head. Blood mixed with brains splattered the cue rack. He hit the floor, bounced and never moved again. Billy's hat spiraled straight up, flipped once, and landed on the floor right side up almost on Billy's bloody head or what was left of it.

She levered another shell into the firing chamber. The reverberation of gunfire inside that hall followed immediately by the metallic sound of the lever action startled Jack Statin to the reality of the moment. Shocked by his brother killing their own cousin, and a deputy sheriff to boot, he froze momentarily, but pulled at a revolver that stuck in his belt. The heavy pistol's front sight hung in the lining of his waistcloth. He ripped it free, but too late. Mavis's big Henry Rifle boomed again blowing a hole though the middle of Jack Statin big enough to put a balled fist through. Reverberations again bounced off the walls, as Statin thudded on the floor. The room fogged with blue acrid gun smoke.

The coal oil from Mavis's shattered lantern, lying near the wall under the cue rack, flamed up and licked at the dried oak wall. Mavis levered another shell into the firing chamber. Teddy Blue and she turned their attention to Clyde Decker.

Sheriff Decker had not moved from his chair--could not most probably. His face had turned blood red. He tugged a small handgun out of a coat pocket and in the act of raising his hand; he gagged, choking on his own vomit. He tried to speak, grabbed his throat, and dropped his gun. A terrible stench rent the air. The old sheriff's bowels had released.

Teddy Blue weakened, slumped back and leaned against the wall, smoking gun in hand, barrel pointing at the floor. Mavis brought the Henry up and pointed it at Clyde Decker's nose. "Yore the root cause a all this, ye slobberin sunuvabitch. Ah aim to put yer lights out."

But she hesitated and saved Clyde Decker's life, if only for the moment. She could not drop the hammer on the gibbering stinking fool and took a step back, when Decker's head dropped in his lap. The front door swung open. Mavis and Teddy Blue turned to face a perceived new threat. Mavis brought her rifle up. Ludi yelled above the din, "Mavis, fer gawd's sake, hit's me."

I was back inside by this time and near Mavis. Her eyes had changed color. I knew she had reached that mental state, when intense stress causes a person's vision to turn red. It happened to me, when I discovered Papa murdered. Mavis kept her self-control. She lowered the rifle barrel.

"Ludi, whatta ye doin here?"

"Ah come to git ye Mavis."

Teddy Blue had slid down the wall almost to a sitting position, a dark red stain spreading on his left-chest. I put my arm behind him and tried to get him on his feet. He fell against me.

"Ludi," I said.

Ludi left Mavis, came over, and helped me with Teddy Blue.

"Come on, we got to git outta here," said Ludi, "this place'll burn quick."

Mavis went before us and held open the front door. Ludi and I managed to walk and drag Teddy Blue through the door, out into the road and into the deafening din of the town fire bell and the steamboat whistle blasting from the river docks. Townspeople ran in every direction, as flames engulfed the billiard hall and threatened buildings on either side.

I looked back. Mavis turned in the doorway, took a moment, and surveyed the interior of the flaming hall. I think she was satisfied everything was as it should be. She turned, walked across the porch, down the steps and out into the road. She had a look on her face I had not seen, the way death must look, when it is unshackled and walking free and easy among us. She never looked back, when one of the front glass windows blew out and shattered on the porch.

We walked across the dirt road toward the Wilson buckboard, where Lois fought to hold the horse in check. Eyes rolling, it reared, plunged and nickered, ready to bolt. The fire from the billiard hall silhouetted Lois and the struggling horse, projecting giant struggling shadows on the rear wall of the hardware store, a sight seen once in a lifetime and never forgotten.

Ludi and I pulled Teddy Blue into the back of the buckboard behind the springboard seat. Ludi jumped on the buckboard and took the reins from Lois. He began shouting commands to the horse and jerking the reins. The horse settled a bit. Mavis came around, opened Teddy's shirt and looked at the gunshot wound. Lois crawled down out of the buckboard, came around, and stood by me. We looked over Mavis's shoulder, as she examined Teddy Blue.

The wound was not as serious as I first thought. The bullet gouged a deep cut along his left rib cage exposing a small section of white bone. The left side of his shirt was soaked, but the bleeding had slowed.

"We need somethin to stop the bleeding til we kin git home. Lois, whut ave ye got on under thet dress?"

Poor shy Lois, startled by Mavis's question, stammered, "My-my petticoat."

"Well, we need some a hit. Chet, ye got yer pocketknife?"

I reached in my pocket, pulled out my pocketknife, opened it and handed it to Mavis. Lois stood quietly, as Mavis got down on her knees and reached up under Lois's dress and cut away most of the bottom half of her petticoat. The petticoat made a good bandage. Mavis packed the wound, and made a tie completely around Teddy Blue's chest.

"Thet'll hold til we git to the cabin. We kin put some coal oil on hit, and sear hit good with a hot poker so hit won't fester. Teddy, ye'll be awright. Ah've seen worse."

Teddy Blue, teeth clinched, did not say anything. I did notice his eyebrows flicked up, when Mavis mentioned the use of a hot poker to sear the wound.

"We need to git away from this fire. Ah'm gonna lose this horse in a minute." Ludi said.

Ludi was doing a good job holding the horse, but he could not hold it much longer before the animal took the bit in his teeth and left the premises. Lois climbed up in the back of the buckboard, and with Mavis helping, she positioned Teddy's head in her lap. Mavis climbed up on the buckboard seat beside Ludi. I ran over, untied my horse and Mavis's little sorrel mare at the hitch rail behind the hardware store and rode back over to the buckboard. The fire, smoke and noise unnerved my horse and he nearly threw me, but settled down once I turned him up the road away from the fire.

Someone untied the horses from the hitch rack at the rear of the billiard hall. Teddy Blue's bay tore around the corner of the burning building and turned north running full out. Mavis's little sorrel mare took off after him. We did not see either horse again until we reached home and found them standing at our front gate.

Flames licked up inside the billiard hall, clearly visible through the two front windows. Heavy black smoke billowed out between the roof and outer wall. Clanging fire bells, boat whistles and yelling added to the bedlam in the street. Townspeople from all over town dashed toward the billiard hall, some evidently intent on getting inside, but the fire was too hot.

As we started up the road, we met the city horse-drawn fire wagon coming fast. Mavis stood up in the buggy brandishing her Henry, as the fire engine came up.

"Don't bother with this." yelled Mavis. "Let it burn, save the other buildings."

"But ain't they people inside?" said the driver.

"Hain't nobody worth savin," said Mavis. "Do like ah tell ye, save the other buildins."

The driver, sitting high on the fire engine seat, I guess thought it best not to argue with a Henry rifle. He slapped the reins and pulled the engine to the next nearest building. Several men ran up to help. They yelled at one another, clamored around the fire engine, and began pumping water. I never did know if they saved that building.

Ludi, with Mavis on the springboard seat beside him and Teddy Blue and Lois in the back, pulled the buckboard a little way up the road away from the heat and smoke. Ludi reined in his nervous horse. I rode my roan up beside the Wilson horse and it seemed to settle both. We all sat a moment watching the townspeople scrambling to keep the fire from spreading. Mavis suddenly seemed to sense something in the air besides fire and smoke. She turned to Ludi.

"Did ye say ye come to git me?"

Ludi wrapped a big arm around her shoulders and hugged her to him. I suddenly felt weak all over, like the weight of the world suddenly lifted off my shoulders. My daddy was hugging my momma. Aunt Lois held Uncle Teddy Blue in the back.

Grandpa and Grandma Wilson waited at home. I suddenly had all this family and me thinking I was an orphan child. Ludi slapped the reins.

"Thet's right Mavis. Ah come to git ye, to take ye home."

"Home, Ludi?"

"Thet's right Mavis--home."

THE END

Mavis Abbott

Made in the USA
Charleston, SC
01 February 2012